PRAISE FOR

A FAMILIAR STRANGER

"A whiplash suspenser that's a model of its kind."

—*Kirkus Reviews*

"The author skillfully reveals the characters' many lies and secrets. Torre knows how to keep the reader guessing."

—*Publishers Weekly*

THE GOOD LIE

"Ambitious and twisty . . . Great bedtime reading for insomniacs and people willing to act like insomniacs just this once."

—*Kirkus Reviews*

"This kinky tale is compulsively readable."

—*Publishers Weekly*

"A blend of serial killer story, court cases, and even romance, this is a tricky story that will keep readers going."

—*The Parkersburg News and Sentinel*

EVERY LAST SECRET

"Deliciously, sublimely nasty: *Mean Girls* for grown-ups."

—*Kirkus Reviews*

"Torre keeps the suspense high . . . Readers will be riveted from page one."

—*Publishers Weekly*

A
FATAL
AFFAIR

OTHER TITLES BY A. R. TORRE

A Familiar Stranger

The Good Lie

Every Last Secret

The Ghostwriter

The Girl in 6E

Do Not Disturb

If You Dare

A

FATAL

AFFAIR

A. R. TORRE

THOMAS & MERCER

Published by Thomas & Mercer, Seattle

www.apub.com

Amazon, the Amazon logo, and Thomas & Mercer are trademarks of Amazon.com, Inc., or its affiliates.

ISBN-13: 9781542039901 (paperback)
ISBN-13: 9781542039918 (digital)

Cover design by James Iacobelli
Cover images: © KK.KICKIN / Shutterstock; © Image Source / Getty Images

Printed in the United States of America

To Jen Webster. Thank you for your friendship and support.

The oldest love affair in Hollywood is that of an actor with themself. It's not so much that they love who they are—but they fall for that image on the screen. They fall for the way that the public looks at them. They fall for the story that they're telling. But the problem is, that story is a lie. The affair is a farce.

Eventually, they realize that, and that is when things typically seem to fall apart.

—Mayim Place, *The Hollywood Report*

CHAPTER 1

9-1-1, what's your emergency?

I'm calling from the Iverson residence in Beverly Hills—1224 Canary Drive. There's been a murder.

What's your name?

Brenda McIntyre. I'm the house manager.

And you said there was a murder? Do you need an ambulance?

No. No. They're both dead.

Is anyone in any danger at this moment?

No. I mean, I don't think so.

1224 Canary Drive. Can you confirm that this is Hugh Iverson's residence?

Yes. We'll need discretion, if you can—

We understand, Miss McIntyre. Just a moment, let me connect you to the chief's office.

CHAPTER 2
THE DETECTIVE

"Well, this will be interesting." Farah smoothed down the front of her blouse, hoping the bit of strawberry yogurt on the right breast wasn't too apparent. The bright-blue, long-sleeved button-up was her favorite—it refused to wrinkle, no matter what she put it through—but she hadn't expected to meet celebrities in it, or to have needed one of the Shout Wipes she typically kept in her car. She glanced at Kevin, who yawned, clearly unconcerned by the address or his rumpled appearance.

They were on their second call of the day, the first one—a gas station robbery—having come in at 8:00 a.m. This was just two miles east but a different world from the dingy 7-Eleven. This wasn't just rich people—this was Hugh Iverson and Nora Kemp, Hollywood's golden couple. There hadn't been a bigger "it" couple since Brad and Angelina, and Farah's mind was ticking through the potential ways that two dead bodies had ended up behind their private gates.

Kevin rapped the knocker on the copper double front door and smoothed a hand over his thinning salt-and-pepper hair. The doors had probably cost more than Farah's Grand Cherokee and were a glistening standout on the modern white adobe mansion, which was accented with dark woods, more copper, and rich foliage. "Nice place."

"Are you surprised?" she asked dryly, glancing back as two crime scene vans pulled through the gates and parked behind their unmarked SUV.

"Nah. You know, me and Trish looked at a place just two doors down last week. Didn't pull the trigger on it. No tennis court, so . . ." He tucked his hands in the pockets of his light-gray pants and shrugged. "You know Trish and her tennis."

Farah smiled at the mention of his wife, who would rather eat a tennis racket than swing one at a ball. "Well, you'll find something else. I hear Bel Air has some nice places."

The irony was, even if Kevin won the lottery, he wouldn't move out of his trailer, which sat on three acres an hour outside the city. Farah and her husband had gone over there a few times for dinner and "enjoyed" delicacies like fried squirrel and fresh goose while seated at a splintered picnic bench in their screened-in porch. Kevin's wife favored a decorating motif of florals and lace curtains and had welcomed Farah with a warm hospitality she hadn't expected. Not that she'd thought the woman would be jealous or suspicious of their relationship. Farah, with her stubborn New Jersey accent, and Kevin, who swapped out his detective suit and shield for an adult softball league T-shirt and camouflage pants, were an unlikely match. No, her trepidation about Trish (and initially Kevin) had been based on her opinion of people who kept hunting guns on display and watched NASCAR on the weekends. She was happy to admit that concern had been unfounded.

The door swung open, and a petite woman wearing a dark-green pantsuit nodded at them with a strained smile. "Please come in. Miss Kemp is waiting for you."

Past a dramatic entranceway and water feature, Nora Kemp stood in the modern version of a formal living room, one with thirty-foot-tall windows and a wall of bloodred roses. She was in a cream camisole and legging set that appeared to be cashmere, her feet bare, toenails painted a fire-engine red that matched her hair. Farah reached her first and gave a short nod. "Miss Kemp, I'm Detective Farah Anderson. This is Detective Kevin Mathis. We're with Beverly Hills PD."

The actress nodded and attempted to smile, her lips trembling on the edges. Dabbing the corner of one eye, she made a visible attempt to square her shoulders and keep her composure. Farah watched closely, aware that the appearance could be an act. This was the woman who had brought audiences to tears with her role in *Collapse*, when she had nursed her cheating husband back from AIDS, only for him to die in the end.

"Hugh is upstairs. He'll join us in a bit. I'm sorry, he just—" Nora inhaled a shuddering breath. "This is very hard for him. He and Trent were extremely close."

Trent? Kevin's and Farah's eyes met, and she fought to hide a reaction. If Trent Iverson—Hugh's twin brother and Hollywood's resident train wreck—was one of the two dead bodies, their investigation was about to take a huge turn. It would be the biggest case of their careers. One that would require a task force, press conferences, a media liaison, and a mountain of oversight. They'd have to do everything perfectly, while not ruffling any feathers.

"You're saying that Trent Iverson is one of the deceased individuals found?" Kevin asked the question calmly, as if the outcome wouldn't change the trajectory of their careers.

"Yes. I thought you knew." She glanced between the two of them, probably wondering what idiots had been sent to investigate the case.

"Your house manager didn't share any details. I'm so sorry for your loss," Farah said.

"Well, thank you." She pulled another tissue from a holder on the table. "Hugh's really in pieces right now . . . I'm not sure if you know what it's like for twins, especially identical ones. There's a bond there."

"I have a good idea," Farah said. "My sister had identical twins."

4

Nora's bright-blue eyes warmed for a moment, and if anything, she was even more beautiful in person than she was on the screen. "Boys or girls?"

"Girls." *Nine-year-old hellions* would be a better descriptor.

"Mind if we see the scene?" Kevin interrupted.

Nora gave a quick nod. "Yes. I'm sorry. They're in the west guest-house. Follow me."

CHAPTER 3

THE HUSBAND

Kyle Pepper was slowly realizing that he was a slob. The living room, which had been tidy and clean when Kerry and Miles had left for California, was now littered with beer cans, dirty glasses, half-eaten bags of chips, and a few used Q-tips. Typically, Kerry would move along behind him, cleaning up as she went, and now, with her and Miles away, everything was starting to stack up.

It had been just one day, twenty-four hours, and he'd already lost the remote and grown tired of cooking for himself. Kerry would be back in three days, and he had decided the first meal he wanted to eat. Her cream of mushroom hot dish, topped with French's fried onions, and her double chocolate chip brownies for dessert.

He opened the bifold door to his side of the closet and pulled a fresh work shirt off a hanger. Stepping over his towel, he put on the gray button-up shirt with the plumbing company logo on its left pocket. The top drawer of the dresser had his underwear in neat rolls—like sushi—and he grabbed a pair of black Hanes boxer briefs and stepped into them, then pulled open the heavy bottom drawer for a pair of Carhartt khakis.

At least he didn't have to worry about laundry. Before Kerry had left, she'd stocked his work shirts and pants, plus emptied the dryer and left a stack of fresh towels right by the shower, so he wouldn't have to yell for her to get one when he was soaking wet.

Once he laced up his work boots and tucked in his shirt and buckled his belt, he moved through the narrow hall and into the kitchen. The dark-green counter was already crowded with leftover pizza, plastic cups, and his tool belt.

Taking a seat at the round table where they normally ate breakfast, he moved a bowl of soggy Frosted Flakes remnants to one side and called Kerry again. It rang through to voice mail, just as his earlier call had, and his irritation grew.

For a woman who liked to get in his ear the minute she rolled out of bed, she could have called him by now. It was past ten in California. Miles would still be on Wisconsin time, so he had probably been up for hours—Kyle wasn't asking for a blow-by-blow account of their time, just a quick call. Let him talk to his son and give Kerry some safety instructions so he could head to work and not worry about them.

He tried to remember what she had said last night, when they were getting ready for bed, about what time they'd be leaving in the morning. Had it been eight? Nine? He hadn't been listening, his attention focused on popping open a brewski without her hearing and calculating if it was too late to make it to the Kwik Trip on the corner before it closed.

Whatever the pickup time had been, she and Miles were definitely at the park by now, probably decked out in Disney hats and T-shirts and on some VIP tour. Miles would be bouncing in his seat with excitement, and Kerry would be taking pictures of it all and posting them with some annoying hashtag.

Two brain cells connected with the realization that social media would be the easiest way to see her activity. Kyle ended the call without leaving a voice mail and tapped on the Facebook app, ignoring the bright-red flag of notifications with new friend requests and updates that had occurred since the last time he'd logged in, at least a year ago. Unlike his wife, Kyle put the idea of reconnecting and communicating with people online right in line with getting a colonoscopy. Unfortunately, Kerry was the queen of documenting everything about their life—even Miles's cancer—and would have definitely posted something about their day and schedule, if not three or four posts, by now.

Kyle pulled up her page and was surprised to see that Kerry had changed her profile photo from one with her and Miles to a solo image—just her, giving a bland smile into the camera. It was a selfie, taken in their bathroom, based on the blue-and-white wallpaper behind her. Something about the picture was off, and he stared at it, trying to figure out what it was.

It was her smile. It was so stiff, so forced—but also so weak. Like she wanted to smile but at the same time wanted to cry.

He scrolled down to see her last post. Something was wrong and he moved farther down the page, then back up. He checked the dates on the posts, certain he had made a mistake.

This couldn't be right.

CHAPTER 4

THE DETECTIVE

Farah, Kevin, and Nora cut through the house, which was a quick tour in how the upper echelons of society lived. Farah had forgotten, in the eight years since she had worked private security in Bel Air, what this life was like. The memories hit her in the gut—the familiar twist of both envy and frustration. Her awe of the environment that was always followed by the painful recognition that it would forever belong to someone else.

Nora strode in front of them, her bare feet silent against the black wood, and the house had a hush—like a museum, or a mausoleum. Though a museum was a better fit, at least in terms of decor. Based on Farah's untrained eye, that was a Picasso they had just passed, framed in gold and lit by a spotlight pendant. And as they stepped down a geometric metal-and-glass staircase, a collection of Andy Warhols graced the wall beside them. The walls, furniture, and curtains were all white, which set off the expensive art dramatically. The only thing more distracting to the eye was Nora Kemp herself, and if God had set out to design the perfect woman, he'd done an annoyingly good job with her.

Even Kevin, who typically didn't notice a woman unless she was dead or guilty, had straightened up at the sight of her and checked the tuck of his shirt in his pants.

The movie star moved lightly down the stairs, her red hair bouncing and streaming behind her, like a tiki-torch flame caught in the wind. "I've put the staff in the pool cabana. You can talk to them there, though everyone was off last night, which is when it must have happened." She faltered, then took the last step.

"What makes you think that?" Kevin beat Farah to the question. "You hear anything?"

She twisted to face them, and the smooth skin between her eyebrows wrinkled as she thought. "Not that caught my attention. I guess we should have heard the gunshot, but we probably assumed it was the fireworks starting up, or we were already asleep by then."

Gunshot. Trent Iverson dead. Another body. This was like putting together a puzzle backward, and they were now passing through a dining hall with a chef's kitchen, a table big enough for twenty, and wide windows and doors that gave a view of palm trees and a pool. "What time were the fireworks?"

"Around ten is when they normally go off. The hotel just over the hill does them every weekend. In the backyard they can be pretty loud, but inside we barely hear them."

The dining table was set for three, each setting holding a variety of quiche, poached eggs, fruit smoothies, and a rainbow selection of mango, pineapple, strawberries, and melons. Three people. She glanced at Kevin, who nodded in understanding. The food appeared to be untouched and had sat out for at least a half hour, if the melted ice in the waters was an indication.

Nora ignored the food and slid open the door to a balcony. "We can take these stairs down to the pool deck. The west guesthouse is just through the gardens. This morning, Brenda went to see if Trent wanted to join us for breakfast. That's when she found them."

Farah's steps quickened, her excitement rising in anticipation of the upcoming crime scene. "I'm sorry, who is *them*? Trent and who?" She followed the actress down the stairs.

"I don't know who the woman is. Trent doesn't typically bring guests. If he does, he entertains them privately or when we're out of town." Nora paused at the bottom of the staircase and pointed to a stone path that went through a manicured row of cypress trees to the left. To the right was a large rectangular pool, with a cabana at the far end. Under its metal roof, eight or nine uniformed staff huddled in conversation.

Nora headed down the path, still barefoot. "We didn't even know he'd brought a guest—neither Hugh nor I saw her last night. Granted, Trent doesn't use the front gate. There's a service entrance in the back that he uses to come and go."

As the path curved, a miniature version of the house appeared—one that was still bigger than Farah's two-bedroom Bell Gardens bungalow. And this was only the west guesthouse. There were north and east ones as well. Welcome to Beverly Hills.

"How often is Trent here?" Kevin asked.

"It's hard to say." Nora paused a dozen feet from the modern cottage. "It's important to Hugh that Trent has privacy, so we don't touch the west guesthouse, unless he requests it, which he does directly with the staff. There are times, especially after rehab, when he'll stay for a while, sometimes for months. Other times, it's just a night, if he doesn't want to make the drive back home, or if he's been drinking with Hugh." Something crossed her features, just a brief hint of emotion, and Farah tried to catalog it but failed.

"So your house manager came to get Trent for breakfast, and what happened?"

"She told me that she knocked, then glanced in the window. Once she saw—" She inhaled and pointed to the thin strip of windows that crisscrossed the black front door. "Just. There. You can look for yourself."

CHAPTER 5

THE KID

It was a good thing that Mr. Frog had a glowing belly, because this room didn't have any light in it at all. Not even a window, or a clock with lighted numbers, or a night-light. There wasn't even some coming under the door. It was dark dark. Maybe the darkest place he'd ever been. When he'd first woken up, he had been confused because he had opened his eyes and it had been like they were still closed. He couldn't see anything. He had cried, screamed for Mommy, but no one had come, even when he had done it for hours, maybe days—so long that his throat was sore and his eyes had run out of tears.

Finally, he had stopped because crying and screaming were a lot of work and he could see a little better in the dark, enough to see that there wasn't anything too scary in here. It was small, about the size of his bedroom, and by the door was his backpack. He got excited by that because his backpack had all his good stuff in it, including Mr. Frog, and when he crawled over and unzipped the top, there Mr. Frog was, staring up at him with his big googly eyes, as if he had been waiting for him.

Now he sat against the wall and held Mr. Frog against his tummy, the glow from the frog's belly making the whole room red with light. It was like being inside a strawberry. A big adult strawberry, with boxes and pipes and a big machine that hummed on and off, like a monster breathing. It was the type of room that his daddy would have said he needed to stay out of, but now he was stuck in here, all alone.

He hugged the stuffed frog tighter, and his breathing got faster and faster. He tried to call out again for his mommy, but all that came out was a whisper.

CHAPTER 6

THE DETECTIVE

Through the thin strips of glass, Farah could see a man lying on the floor, his head out of sight. She leaned farther to the right and spotted a woman tied to a chair, her chest a mess of blood. And just like that, the case grew more complicated. Farah pulled on a pair of blue latex gloves as Kevin did the same. "Who's been in there?"

"Just me, Hugh, and Brenda. Brenda didn't actually go in, I don't think. She saw Trent and thought at first that he was just passed out." Nora flushed. "Finding him passed out is common—at least it used to be. He's been clean for a while now."

A while was an interesting way to put it. The Los Angeles Police Department was very familiar with Trent Iverson and the chaos that accompanied his intimate relationship with cocaine, alcohol, and pharmaceuticals. Trent's last rehab stint had been within the year, but maybe you celebrated small milestones while you could claim them.

"So Brenda came and got you or Hugh?" Kevin asked.

"She found me first. I went and got Hugh."

"Where was he?"

"Asleep in the theater." At Farah's look, she hastened to explain. "There's one on the lower level. We were watching a movie down there last night, but I moved upstairs when he fell asleep. I have back problems."

She pulled back her narrow shoulders as if suddenly remembering her posture. "I'm like a pretzel the next day if I don't sleep in bed."

Kevin tilted his head toward the house. "We're gonna need to bring the techs in. Can you have someone show them back here?"

"Sure." Nora gestured to the guesthouse. "Will you need me in there?" A shudder passed through her thin frame, and Farah wouldn't have been surprised if she never set foot in it ever again.

"Oh, no." Kevin gave her a comforting smile—and it was funny that, out of the two of them, he had somehow assumed the role of nice guy in their duo. The guy liked to sit in a tree stand and shoot delicate forest animals, yet he was the one all the suspects cozied up to. Maybe it was the magnetism of one type of killer to another—a theory Kevin always scoffed at but Farah thought held water. Kevin continued, "We'll take it from here. Once we finish, we'll talk to Mr. Iverson, then the staff."

"Sure." Nora pinched her cherry-red lips together, and for a moment, it looked like she was about to cry. "I'll go and show your techs in. If you need anything, just let me know."

"Will do," he said. "Please make sure Mr. Iverson stays around so we can talk to him."

Kevin's solicitous tone grated on Farah's nerves. Why were they letting Hugh Iverson grieve in solitude? He should be right here beside Nora, getting peppered with questions while they analyzed his reactions. Being related to a victim didn't eliminate him as a suspect—far from it.

Farah watched as Nora disappeared around the bend in the bamboo-lined path and wondered how many other allowances they would be making—and how much that would risk the outcome of justice.

Movement in one of the upper windows caught her attention as a curtain was pulled aside. She stilled, curious at who was inside the home. A man moved into view, and there was no need to guess his identity. Everyone in America knew those handsome features, easily recognizable even at thimble size. A lock of dark hair hung over his forehead, and he pressed a strong forearm against the glass and leaned forward, peering down at the guesthouse. Without thinking, Farah lifted a hand in greeting and gave a small wave. Even though the Iversons were fifteen years her junior, she wasn't immune to the twins' staggering good looks. Trent had given them a bad-boy vibe, while Hugh rocked those same classic good looks with a Prince Charming perfection.

Hugh didn't wave back, and after a moment, Farah dropped her hand, feeling stupid.

"You coming?" Kevin held the door open for her, and past him, she could see the dead woman's knees.

"Yeah," she managed and moved into the guesthouse, the scent of death and blood already clogging the air.

CHAPTER 7

THE LEADING LADY

After dropping the crime scene techs off with the detectives, Nora returned to and moved quickly through the house. The modern museum-like feel, which had once seemed so cold and impersonal when she'd first moved in, now felt normal. She'd grown to appreciate the lack of clutter and the clean, stark decor. Hugh was a minimalist, and this home had been a nice change from the overflowing duplex she had grown up in—one where there hadn't been enough space to breathe, every foot crowded with cheap crap. Now she walked down the wide hall and wondered how much of it—if any—would change in the next few months. Hugh's stiff regime of no clutter, animals, or children . . . She placed her hand on her stomach, the muscles still tight and flat, despite the fact that she was almost two months pregnant. That conversation would have to wait until the dust settled.

She pushed open one of the black mahogany doors to the bedroom and faltered at the sight of her fiancé standing by the window and looking down at the guesthouse. There was a clear view from that vantage point, and she wondered how much Hugh had seen of the activity that had happened there.

"Hey." She paused by the end of the bed and gripped the polished stone footer. Like everything in the room, it was black. Their designer had told Nora that a room required at least seven textures, and this one had a dozen, all variations of black. Black leather in the chair by the window. A black-dyed mink throw on the bed. Black pebbled stone on the fireplace, black onyx marble in the bathroom. Even the floral arrangements, which were replaced every other day, were black blooms. Black tulips, hellebore, and roses. "How you holding up?"

He turned from the tall window, and she was reassured by the sight—he looked calm and in control, his dark-green irises studying her from under furrowed brows. His shock of short jet-black hair was wet from a shower and pushed away from his strong features. The twins had an Italian and Swiss heritage and had inherited their parents' glowing olive skin and stunning bone structure, along with their fame. He cleared his throat. "Do they know who the woman is?"

"No. They asked, but I told them I didn't know."

"The security system was off last night." It wasn't a question, but it sounded like one.

Nora nodded. "It was."

"So no camera footage, and the front gates were unsecured."

"Yes."

"The police will want to know why."

She waited, curious whether he would provide a reason. When he didn't, she offered one. "Well, you know, the security system kept alerting us with false positives. It was so annoying we finally just shut it off."

He stayed silent, his mouth tightening into a hard, flat line. It was difficult to know what he must be thinking, and she fought the urge to walk over and wrap her arms around his torso and bury her face into his neck. Whether he knew it or not, he needed her right now, but the energy bristling off him was one that screamed *stay away* in bright-red letters.

"They want to talk to you," she managed.

"Don't worry. I'm good at tap-dancing." He flashed a smile, and it was like turning on a blinding floodlight. That megawatt grin, the one full of straight, perfect teeth, both confident and tempting, the one that screamed *trust me, love me, obsess over me*. It was the smile that Trent never used, but one that'd made Hugh into the highest paid name in Hollywood.

"Or is it the distraught brother you want?" Just as quickly, he dropped all traces of the smile, and the haunted look returned, his posture weary as he crossed his arms tightly over his chest and both of his eyes moistened, as if he'd turned on a faucet behind them.

She had seen him fall into character before, but this was wrong, and her tension and unease grew as she watched him straighten back to his full height and lock the emotion away.

"Just tell me what they want," he ordered. "Tell me who to be."

"Just be yourself, Hugh," she said tightly. "You can be real. You can be upset. This isn't"—she spread her arms in frustration—"this isn't a handbook I know either."

"Yeah," he said slowly, studying her with an intensity she didn't like. "Are you the grieving friend? The future sister? The lover? I'm curious what you plan on saying to the detective, my future wife."

She ignored the dig. "I already told them the truth. That you fell asleep in the theater room, and I went to bed, and neither of us knows anything about what happened out there."

CHAPTER 8

THE HUSBAND

Kyle studied his wife's most recent Facebook post, which she'd made more than a year ago. It didn't make sense. Kerry obsessed over social media and never missed an opportunity to update her small following with every detail of their boring life.

Though . . . he tried to remember the last time she had smiled for a selfie or had him take dozens of photos of her at different angles. It'd been a while. Maybe even a year. But why would she have stopped posting and not mentioned it to him? Kerry shared every detail of her day with him—yet this was a development she'd been completely silent on. Why?

In the living room, the television blared as a discussion over sports-conference rivalries heated up. Kyle picked up his phone and tried her again. Voice mail. For the first time, his annoyance turned into concern.

Miles and Kerry had been staying at the Radisson in Los Angeles. She'd video-chatted with him last night, giving him a tour of their suite, which had a separate living room, where Miles was going to sleep. Kyle looked up the hotel's website on his phone, then called their number.

At the crisp greeting, he asked to be connected to her room. As it rang, he glanced at his watch, a high-tech rubber piece that Kerry had gotten him for Christmas. Indestructible, she had said. So far, it was true, though the only action it had seen was an occasional brush against a wall or pipe.

His shift started in a half hour, at one. It was two hours earlier in California, and Kerry and Miles had probably already left for the theme park. After a dozen rings, he ended the call.

It was stupid to worry. He and Kerry had gone longer than this without talking. Hell, when he'd gone on that "fishing trip" to the lake with Nicole, he'd gone an entire weekend without talking to Kerry. And when he'd returned home, hiding a hickey under the neck of his hoodie, everything had been just fine.

Kyle could try the charity—the one that the Make-A-Wish prize had been granted through. He'd sent in the application in secret, an idea from his mom, and a gesture that he had been really proud of, especially when he had been able to surprise Kerry and Miles with the award letter. That letter was still stuck on the fridge, underneath a dinosaur magnet, and had a number they had called to make the arrangements.

He glanced again at his watch, and he'd be late if he didn't leave in the next few minutes. Dwayne was a prick about being on time and was the only plumber in Wisconsin who actually wrote his guys up, like they were a big company with an HR department and not a three-truck operation running on duct tape and word of mouth.

Standing up, he pulled the letter off the fridge and folded it into thirds, then tucked it into the front pocket of his shirt. He'd call the charity on the way in or after his first job.

There wasn't a rush. Kerry knew how to take care of herself and Miles and was probably halfway through a Mickey Mouse Popsicle right now.

CHAPTER 9
THE DETECTIVE

You could see the pain on the dead woman's face. Her eyes were open, her mouth agape, the agony etched into her features. The grimace of the murdered was one of the reasons Farah had once turned in her badge and moved into private security. She had started dreaming of Ty's and Anaïca's faces, contorted into frozen grimaces, and had woken up in full-body sweats, turning first to him, then hurrying down the hall to check on her daughter. It had taken Anaïca's decision to enter the police academy to bring Farah back to the force—and to faces like this. She moved her gaze from the woman's vacant stare and focused on other elements of the crime scene.

Both bodies were to the left of the guesthouse foyer in a large living room with a hallway exiting to the left. One victim was definitely the gorgeously troubled Trent Iverson. Past him, a sleek, modern kitchen with red cabinets and another hall. She returned her attention to the woman, who had her hands knotted behind her back, an ankle tied to each leg of the chair.

Farah crouched. The female was in black workout pants and a striped Mickey Mouse tank top, her auburn hair pulled back into a low ponytail. The end of the ponytail hung over her shoulder and was stiff with blood. So was the front of her top, which was ruined by four stab wounds and soaked in dried black blood.

Kevin whistled. "Not a good way to go." He bent forward and lifted the end of her ponytail with his pen, surveying the details. "Looks like she bled out." He tilted his head, looking at the back of the chair. "Lots of abrasions on the wrists. A hobble knot. She fought to get out of this chair."

Fought and failed. Farah stood, her knees cracking in protest, and turned her attention to the second body. While the tortured woman was forensically more exciting, this was the death that would affect America. Trent Iverson was on his back, his legs folded beneath him at the knees, his green eyes open and still. Unlike the woman, he looked at peace, and even in death, he was gorgeous. She bent at the waist and peered at him. "Gunshot wound to the right temple." She looked around, then spotted the muzzle of the gun by his right hand. "We've got a"—she tilted her head—".38 revolver."

"I gotta say, this was not what I was expecting to walk into." Kevin glanced out the open door, where the crime scene technicians waited. "We're gonna have to keep a lid on this as best we can. This is going to be a media shitstorm." He lowered his voice. "Anyone out there you think will be a problem?"

Farah studied the group on the porch. "You've worked with most of them longer than I have. I don't know . . . Tupperfield likes to gossip. But honestly, if a tabloid throws a hundred grand in any of their directions, it's a risk."

"Two dead bodies on the Iversons' property, one of whom is Trent?" Kevin shook his head. "We're talking seven figures, easy. Hell, I might jump sides for that."

"Funny." But he was right: the temptation would be too strong for a lot of uniforms. Hell, on a weak day, she might consider the perks of a million-dollar bribe. "What's your first gut? Murder-suicide? Or do you think these are both victims?"

He looked from one to the other. "I don't know. Murder-suicide would make sense as to why the deaths are so different. What are the chances someone else would come in, torture her, then just shoot him?"

She shook her head. "He would have to have been shot first, in that case. Get him out of the way so they could focus on and take their time with her. Even though Trent is more interesting to us, he might not be the main focus here."

"I'm not up to date on Hollywood, not unless they've done something wrong." Kevin gestured to the woman. "She look familiar to you? Maybe an actress? His latest fling?"

"No, and she's wearing the same brand of flip-flops I've got in my closet at home," Farah said dryly. "I bought mine at Target. If I was betting, I'd say she's middle class, at best. And look." She crouched and pointed to the woman's hands. "Wedding ring. Tiny diamond. Cheap band."

Kevin glanced around. "I'll see if I can find a purse, something to identify her."

The female victim wasn't beautiful.

Wasn't rich.

Wasn't single.

So how did she end up in a Beverly Hills mansion with Trent Iverson? And why was she dead?

CHAPTER 10
THE LEADING MAN

"Hugh, I just spoke to the publicist." Nora joined him at the window.

Below them, four men in crime scene jumpsuits entered the guesthouse. These assholes would be going over the space with fine-tooth combs, and there was a lot in that guesthouse to find. Some of it would probably make the tabloids, for reasons that had nothing to do with murder.

"Caitlyn thinks we have six hours at most before this leaks. She's worried about the optics," Nora said.

The optics. At what point in his life would he escape those? He glanced at Nora, and despite the stress lining her face, she was still the most beautiful woman in the world. Even this close-up, you couldn't see the scars, couldn't tell the fact from the fiction, and whenever he did . . . it only made her beauty more interesting.

She shook her head, and a lock of that thick, fiery hair fell in front of her face. "We've obviously dealt with a lot of press with Trent before, but this . . . well. You saw the scene. This is murder."

"And you think Trent is capable of that?"

Her gaze flipped from the window to his face. "It doesn't matter what I think. It matters what it looks like, and what the press will report. You'll need to make a statement."

"Not happening." He turned away from the window. "Fuck the press."

It was rare for Hugh to curse, and Nora recoiled at the statement. He knew what she was thinking. That they couldn't dismiss the press, not when it was responsible for their career trajectories, not when it was their lifeline to the audience, not when it would be their judge, jury, and executioner, depending on how they decided to spin this news. The next twenty-four hours might, quite literally, determine their next twenty-four years.

And he didn't give a damn. His brother was dead, and he wanted to lock himself away and never come up, not until he wrecked his mind and body in a hundred different ways.

Fuck the press.

Fuck the cops.

Fuck Nora.

As if sensing his rising emotions, she jumped to a new topic. "If they haven't already, the police will go to Trent's house." She adjusted her watch, then smoothed her sleeve back over it. She always said he was the best actor she'd ever seen—but Nora had nailed her part to perfection. It was the details that she had mastered, the costume and effortless air of a wealthy woman, even though she had spent decades as poor white trash. "You knew him best," she said. "Is there anything there we need to get rid of?"

He pinched his eyes closed and let out a frustrated breath at the thought of uniforms going through that monstrosity of a house. Hugh and Trent had grown up there, dubbed it the House of God—the mansion purchased with the wealth from their parents' religious empire. Trent had lived there for the past five or six years, and more than a couple of things inside would raise some eyebrows, including the charred clinic in the south wing. "Shit."

The clinic's walls peppered with spatters of blood. His brother, his face tight. The mess all around him.

More than a year ago, the room had been doused in gasoline and lit on fire, in the hope it would burn the entire house down with it. It hadn't, but at least any evidence of what had happened there—past or present—was long gone in the blaze.

"I mean, I'm sure there's drug stuff there, but anything like this?" She tilted her head toward the guesthouse.

"You mean like a dead woman tied to a chair?" he asked dryly. "No. I mean . . ." He scraped his nails through his hair and thought about the horrors that had occurred on every floor of the home. "I'll go there."

"It's going to look bad if you show up and clean it out."

She wasn't wrong, but her tone of authority pissed him off. He couldn't deal with all this. Cleaning up the mess, the death, the emotions with her—Nora moved closer and he stiffened as she leaned in, her needy lips seeking his.

He turned his head and stepped back, his elbow bumping the wall. "We can't ruin Trent's name," he said tightly. "I won't allow it."

"Hugh," she pleaded. "You have to think about the future. You can't go down with Trent's ship. Right now, you have everything. The adoration of a nation. Incredible wealth. The power to pick any role you want." She placed her hand on the center of her chest. "A woman who needs you. Don't fall on the sword for him. Please."

She acted like it was easy, but she had no idea how many women had died.

CHAPTER 11

THE HUSBAND

After unclogging a shower and a garbage disposal backup, Kyle pulled onto the side of a residential road and parked. He pulled the charity letter out of his pocket and watched as a bright-orange leaf landed on the windshield, followed by a small yellow one. Fall had hit Appleton last week, and Kerry had whined over the timing as they'd driven to the Green Bay airport yesterday, hating that she would miss a few days of the changing leaves.

Such a stupid thing to pout over. They were leaves. If she loved them so much, she could rake their yard up when she got back.

He unfolded the letter on his steering wheel. It had arrived via Priority Mail three weeks ago. The embossed letterhead was now stained in a few places, but no less impressive. Kyle had been proud of the award of an all-expenses-paid trip to California, but Kerry's face had gone white. She hadn't even seemed grateful for him going to all the trouble to apply and submit the paperwork. He had been puffed up, expecting gushing thanks and, later, a non-date-night sex session, but she had seemed panicked by the letter. Her hands had trembled as she read the page twice, then shook her head and announced that they couldn't accept the trip.

It had been a strange reaction, but around a year ago, Kerry had gone through some sort of midlife crisis or menopause—something that caused her to act weird. She had started changing everything—from what she fixed for breakfast to what they did on the weekends to how she handled Miles's treatments. It was like being married to a different woman, and he would have complained, but the new Kerry was actually nicer to be around and seemed to be more focused on family and less on what the nosy neighbors thought. In fact . . . the timing of her metamorphosis likely synced with her stopping on social media.

A car pulled around his truck, and Kyle refocused on the letter, scanning it quickly and finding the contact information in the final paragraph. Propping his elbow on the open truck window, he dialed the number and held the cell phone to his ear, watching out the windshield as a leggy brunette in a matching red windbreaker and leggings jogged by, her breath frosting in the crisp air.

"This is Nolan Price," a chipper male voice said.

"Hey, Nolan. This is Kyle Pepper. My wife, Kerry—"

"Mr. Pepper, I'm glad you called. We've been worried about Kerry. I didn't have your number, or else I would have called earlier." The upbeat tone was gone, replaced by a serious tone that immediately increased Kyle's concern.

"Why? What happened?"

"Well, we were supposed to meet her and Miles in the hotel lobby this morning at nine thirty, but they weren't there. We haven't been able to reach her on the hotel phone or her cell."

"So she's not with you all? She's not at Disney?" That didn't make any sense, and he put a hand on his chest, feeling that familiar ache that precipitated heartburn. He pulled open the glove compartment and withdrew his antacid medication, twisting off the lid and shaking a few pills into his palm.

"No, we haven't heard from her since we dropped her off at the hotel last night. When's the last time you spoke to her?"

"Uh, last night. Around nine. She was putting Miles to bed."

"Is it common for her to disappear like this?"

"No. Something's wrong." Even with Kerry's 180-degree flip in personality, her reliability had never been in question, especially not with Miles. He thought of the way she had flatly told him that they couldn't go to California, the fear—yeah, looking back, it had been fear—that she'd had over the trip. He should have asked more questions, listened when she'd said that she didn't want to go. But Miles had been there when Kyle read out the letter, and he was already cheering and jumping and beaming at the two of them with that big ear-to-ear grin.

No one with a sick kid could say no when they smiled like that. You just couldn't, because you didn't know how many more smiles you were gonna get—how many more trips Miles might get to take. So Kyle had run over Kerry's excuses and concerns and practically pushed them out the door and into the airport.

Kyle pinched his eyes closed and rubbed at his forehead, trying to remember why Kerry hadn't wanted to go. All the reasons she had given were dumb, even looking back at it now. She'd said that Miles might get sick on the plane—but Miles had flown to visit his grandparents several times and never had any issue. She'd said she had too much to do at home, but Kerry's to-do list was cooking and laundry, nothing time sensitive or unavoidable. She'd said the parks would be crowded, but they were going to be getting VIP tours with the charity. They weren't going to be waiting in lines or walking miles on foot. All her concerns had been cleared away easier than standing water in a drain.

"What do you think we should do?" The man's voice trembled, and it was scary that this was the guy he'd trusted with his wife's safety and travel plans.

Kyle tapped his fingers on the top of the steering wheel and looked at the clipboard on the seat beside him. Next up, he was headed to an Arby's to check on a bathroom leak. Maybe Kerry was okay. Maybe she'd lost her cell phone, maybe they were at Disney with some other charity employee, or maybe—worst case for him but okay for her— she'd run off with his son to start a new life, sans husband.

But in his gut, he knew something was wrong. Kerry was a lot of things, but she wouldn't go MIA, not with Miles.

"Call the police," he said. "I'll look into getting a flight."

CHAPTER 12
THE ACCOMPLICE

At the Protect the Children headquarters, Nolan Price ended the call with Kyle Pepper. He was sweating through the collar of his seersucker suit and loosened the white tie in an attempt to get in more air. Pulling back the mint-and-white striped sleeve, he checked the time on his watch, then crossed his ankles primly beneath his desk chair and moved his mouse blindly across the screen, just so it would look to anyone watching as if he were working.

He picked up the phone and tried Kerry Pepper's cell again, listening to the ring. *Come on . . . Come on . . .*

He shouldn't worry. No need to worry. He repeated what his boyfriend always said, over and over, hoping the concept would stick, but it slid off his chest like oil. If now wasn't the time to worry, when would it be?

Uppers—that's what they called the parents—were *never* not at a pickup. This morning, he had waited outside the Radisson for an hour, then gone up and knocked on the hotel room door, but no one had answered. Today was a big day, with Disney expecting Kerry and Miles at ten fifteen for a VIP park tour and meet and greet with all the big stars. If anything, the families were normally early, never missing.

Call the police. That's what Kyle Pepper had told Nolan to do, and he was right: that was a logical step—though didn't people have to be missing for twenty-four hours for the police to do anything? It had been only three hours. Still, he had to do what the husband said; otherwise it would look suspicious. And he should tell Ian. The Protect the Children director would flip if Nolan called the police without first clueing him in.

Nolan had always told himself that Monica Kitle had been a horrible coincidence. Her dying—that horrible, painful death—couldn't have been related to Protect the Children or what Nolan had done. It had been two coincidences that just happened to stroll by each other in the hall one day and high-five Nolan as they passed. With Monica, he had told himself that his connection would never be found, and he had been right. It had been almost two years, and no one had ever even called about her. They hadn't thought twice about her original application to Make-A-Wish, and really . . . why would they?

But this was different. Kerry Pepper was *in* Los Angeles, literally *on* a Protect the Children–sanctioned trip. Nolan had been one of the last people to see her, had given her and Miles a ride from the airport to the hotel last night, and now she was gone.

Maybe dead.

Feeling faint, he pulled open his metal desk drawer, withdrew a pack of cinnamon gum, and unfolded a piece with trembling fingers. Maybe Kerry had run off. Left that sick little boy and all his problems behind and hopped a bus to Mexico. Right now she was probably perched on a stool at a bar and tilting back a giant blue margarita with sugar on the rim.

It was definitely possible. Women abandoned their families all the time, didn't they? He was sure they did. Men couldn't be the only ones who ran off in search of an easier life. Hell, maybe Nolan could do that now. Just push away from the desk, take the back stairs down to his car, and never come back. Leave Josie and Pumpkin and go somewhere where none of this had ever happened.

If something did happen to Kerry, the police would probably investigate him. They'd look into his life—shit, his finances. The pool renovation, the new steam shower, the payoff of his credit cards. They would track the money, and soon Nolan would be in jail and they'd ask who was behind it and he'd have to tell them or he'd be locked up forever.

Men with his dark ebony skin and delicate bone structure didn't do well in prison. He was too pretty, as Josie said. Too pretty and too spoiled.

Spots appeared in his vision as the stress took over, and he moved his braids to one side and lowered his head to the desk. Breathing deeply, he counted to six, then exhaled. Okay, the to-do list wasn't long.

Tell Ian. Call the police. Feign innocence and confusion.

He could do all that. But what about the boy? Monica had been alone at her house, her kid in day care. If Kerry had fallen into the same situation as Monica . . . where was the kid?

Was Miles still in the hotel room?

Nolan closed his eyes and sent a fervent prayer up to God to keep the little boy, wherever he was, safe.

CHAPTER 13
THE DETECTIVE

Farah and Kevin met the medical examiner on his way out of the guest-house, both bodies already tagged and bagged. "What can you tell us so far, Harry? Got a time of death?" Farah asked.

Dr. Harry Martin tucked a pen into the pocket of his striped jacket. The doctor was as short as Farah, with a thick silver mustache, matching bushy brows, and a shiny bald head. "I'd guess between midnight and 2:00 a.m., for both of them. I'll confirm that once I get them on the slab."

"Know anything that'll help us out?"

"Not much. There's gunshot residue on the male's hands. I feel good about suicide, but an attorney could punch a few holes in that if they wanted to—"

"What about the woman?" Kevin interrupted.

"Oh, she was murdered," the medical examiner deadpanned. "I'd say that for certain."

"Funny." Farah didn't give him the satisfaction of a smile. Dr. Martin would start a full-out comedy routine if given an ounce of encouragement. The running joke was that he practiced his routines on the dead, though there were rumors he hit the open-mic clubs too.

"I didn't see any prior trauma on the woman. Clothing looks undisturbed, so I don't think there was sexual activity. And unless she likes to have affairs in grandma panties, this wasn't a planned romantic encounter. I'm guessing that she was drugged and woke up tied to that chair. I'll verify that with her stomach contents and blood work, but that'll take some time. As you could see, there were four deep points of impact—looks like she bled out."

"Any hesitation to the knife wounds?"

"None." Harry's mouth flattened in a grim line. "He knew what he was doing. The wounds were all strategic locations. They would have hurt like hell but been slow to kill. The techs have the knife and the ropes, but I can tell you from looking at the knots, he must have been a Boy Scout."

"Did you ever watch the show?" Kevin asked. "Both twins were Eagle Scouts."

"Their characters were," Farah interjected. "Doesn't mean they knew anything in real life."

"I'm lost," the medical examiner said. "What show?"

"*Story Farm*," Kevin explained. "It was a religious kids' show, popular about twenty years ago. It's how Hugh and Trent Iverson became famous."

Harry's blank expression remained, and Farah had to remind herself that if someone didn't have kids or if they weren't young enough, it was possible they hadn't heard of *Story Farm*—though it had dominated youth pop culture for more than a decade. Trent and Hugh had been adolescent heartthrobs who'd grown into megastars, and Farah's daughter had been in love with the twins, even though they were ten years older than her.

"Any other questions?" the doctor asked.

Kevin turned to Farah, who shook her head. "No, but put a rush on everything," he said. "The chief wants this prioritized."

"Oh yeah, I get it." The doctor bobbed his head. "And I'll run the tests myself. I know how things seem to walk away or leak in these situations."

"Appreciate that." Kevin glanced at Farah. "You ready to talk to the big man?"

"Let's do it." She glanced up, but Hugh's window was now empty, and it was disarming, not knowing where the actor was. "I'm dying to see what light he sheds on this."

"Yeah. Me too."

CHAPTER 14

THE DETECTIVE

On their way back to the house, Farah and Kevin took the path by the pool. The white limestone deck surrounded an indigo-blue lagoon-shaped pool that glowed in the late-morning sun. Four teak chaise lounges framed the water, each with its own white umbrella and red pillows on white cushions, creating a resort-like oasis surrounded by towering palm trees and lush tropical plants. A massive cabana framed the far end and was the current location of the Iverson staff.

The employees were scattered throughout the covered space, and it looked like they were segregated by uniform type, with the maids reclining back on the white sectional, the kitchen staff perched at the bar's island, and the maintenance workers standing by the right row of columns. They were all in dark-green attire, but each with a distinct style for their position. As they neared the cabana, Farah made a quick appraisal of the group, who all seemed to be impeccably put together with ironed uniforms, bright-white sneakers, and professional hair and makeup. "I don't see a single cell phone," she murmured to Kevin.

The conversations quieted as they passed, and a tall dark-haired woman stepped away from the columns and approached, introducing herself as Xiying Lee, a landscaper. "May I speak to you in private?" she asked. "There are some concerns among the staff."

Well, that had been quick. Farah wondered at her need for privacy, but Kevin nodded as if it were common practice. "Sure," he said easily. "Let's move into the shade." He gestured to the side, where there was a small alcove under a clump of banana trees.

Once they were alone, the woman tucked her short hair behind her ear, exposing a pearl earring. "We haven't had access to a phone, but we'd like to call an attorney and understand what we can and can't talk about."

We. A union, already formed and united. Farah's patience took a nosedive. "We aren't arresting any of you," she said. "We just need some information to aid in—"

Kevin held up his hand, halting her explanation. "What do you think you can't talk about?"

"Well, we all signed confidentiality agreements. Very strict confidentiality agreements."

He shook his head. "Those are void in the case of a crime."

"Only if the information is related to the crime," Xiying argued. "We don't know what you're going to ask us, and—no offense—you aren't going to know what you should be asking us without fishing in a lot of empty waters first."

"Do you know where we should be fishing?" Farah interrupted.

The woman ignored her, and for a landscaper, she sure seemed to have a strong handle on the law. "We'd like to speak to an attorney and will want them to be present during our questioning."

Shit, this was going to take forever. "Does everyone feel this way?" Farah asked.

"Yes, and we're all under the same contract." The woman met her gaze squarely, and if this was how tough she was with law enforcement, Farah would have hated to see her against a hydrangea.

"What does the contract specifically forbid?" Kevin asked.

"Discussing anything that occurs on this property or that we are exposed to at any point in our employ, including off property.

39

Sometimes we travel with the primaries or go with them on location. Not me, of course." She shrugged, and Farah tried to place her age. She looked twenty-five but carried herself with the quiet maturity of a woman twice that. "But the other staff does."

Kevin looked at Farah with a scowl, and she could match his frustration tenfold. If the employees were all forbidden from talking about anything on this property, they would be dealing with a houseful of mutes. They'd eventually get them to talk, but it would require a judge's stamp of approval, and in Hollywood, who knew which judge they'd get.

Kevin pointed toward the house. "If Hugh Iverson tells us you can talk, will you?"

She glanced toward the cabana, where her fellow employees were lined up along the edge as if waiting for a firing squad. "I can't speak for them, but personally, I won't."

CHAPTER 15

THE KID

When things get tough, you get tougher! That's what Big Billy on his favorite cartoon always said. It was time to get tougher. Being tougher sounded exciting, which was good because he was bored. He had tried to practice his numbers by counting the boxes in the room, but he couldn't remember what came after thirteen.

Then he tried pretending that the cord coming out of a big white box thing was a snake. That was pretty fun for a while but then got old. Getting tough sounded fun; the only problem was . . . he didn't know how to do it. Whenever Billy got tough, he just made a fist and punched it into the air and then had a great idea that solved whatever the problem was. Billy had never been locked in a room in the dark, but he did once fall down a hole. He had torn his shirt into thin pieces and tied them together and made a rope and somehow used it to climb out.

That was a cool idea, but he wasn't in a hole. He was in a room, one without any windows and with just one door. The handle was locked, and he'd tried to take off his shirt, but that didn't seem to help with anything.

Get tougher.

He took a deep breath, but a sharp pain shot through his head and he couldn't remember when he'd last had his medicine. What if he had a seizure, right here? Who would help him? He was starting to feel scared, and to distract his tears from coming, he pulled Mommy's notebook out from his book bag. Almost all the pages were filled with her squiggly cursive writing, but the backs of the pages were empty, and he pulled off the cap of the pen and started to draw Big Billy being tough, his hand resting on the lines of text on the opposite side of the page.

CHAPTER 16
THE MOM

Dear Kyle,

If you're reading this letter, I'm probably already dead. If I'm not dead, please close this journal right now, stick it back where you found it, and just call and ask me about it.

Are you still here? I'm serious—don't read any further if I'm alive and well. I'll never have sex with you again if you keep reading on.

I mean it.

Stop reading and respect my privacy or I swear to God I'll tell your parents that we had to file bankruptcy because of your online poker addiction.

Okay. You're still reading, so I guess I am dead.

There are two things you need to know, from the start.

I'm not the first dead one. At the time that I'm writing this, there have been at least four of us killed.

And second, I'm sorry. I'm so sorry. Please don't show this notebook to anyone or tell anyone about what's in it, not until you have a chance to read it all.

After that, once you know everything—it's up to you.

I love you, and I always have.

Kerry

CHAPTER 17

THE DETECTIVE

"The staff seems scared." Farah stood in the middle of the Iverson living room, her voice soft.

"Yeah, I got that too. But of what? Getting sued, or something else?" Kevin placed his palms on his butt and leaned back, earning a pop somewhere in his lower back.

Farah glanced up, listening for sounds from the second floor, but this house was built like a bunker. Supposedly Hugh was coming down, but it had been—she glanced at her watch again—twelve minutes since Nora had gone to get him, and this was getting ridiculous. Screw the kid gloves and the confidentiality agreements. Two dead people deserved justice, and someone needed to start answering some damn questions. She was about to say that when Hugh Iverson rounded the corner and strode into the living room.

The cameras, as it turned out, didn't do the man justice. Farah forgot her irritation, her line of questioning, and her marriage vows at the entrance of Hugh, who met her gaze head-on, with eyes that were slightly red. "You must be Detective Anderson." He shook her hand— nice strong clasp—and then turned to Kevin, who seemed oblivious to the stunning specimen before them. "Detective Mathis?"

"Should we take a seat?" Kevin asked, looking around the pristine room.

"Sure, anywhere you like. And blame Nora's designer for the chairs. They're hell to sit in."

He wasn't wrong. Farah chose a white number with wooden arms and a backward tilt that forced her to do a crunch just to stay upright. Kevin looked equally miserable on a square armchair, while Hugh looked like a model, one ankle resting on the opposite knee, an arm slung over the back. He was in a cream cashmere sweater that clung to his athletic build and dark-wash jeans. His feet were bare, and it felt strangely intimate to have a glimpse of Hugh Iverson's feet.

"I'm sorry I didn't come down earlier. This is—ah—hard." He swallowed, and the line of his jaw grew more pronounced. Farah forced herself to look away before she could be accused of gawking. "Especially given the situation and the fact that another person is involved."

"You're referring to the woman?" Kevin asked, and rearranged his position, trying to find a more comfortable one.

"Yes. Who is she?"

"We haven't made an ID yet. Your fiancée wasn't familiar with her, but do you know anything about her? Did you meet her last night?"

He frowned and shook his head. "I saw my brother out by the pool, but he didn't have anyone with him, at least not that I saw. One of the employees mentioned his car was still here this morning, so Nora had someone go down and invite him to breakfast."

Given that he'd been asleep during those events, Nora must have given him a play-by-play of the morning. Farah frowned, not happy, but also not surprised, that they had discussed and probably collaborated on their stories.

"You talked to him out by the pool?" Kevin asked, and now the little notepad from his breast pocket was out, and his pen was moving. From Farah's viewpoint, it looked like a doodle of squiggly boxes.

"We shot the shit a little. Talked about the USC game. Maybe five minutes' worth. I invited him to watch a movie with us, but he declined."

"How did he seem? Nervous? On edge? In a hurry? Anything suspicious?"

"If I had to guess, Trent was high last night." He shrugged. "Though whatever blood tests you run might say differently. But he seemed a little hyperfocused. Tense. Not any way I haven't seen him before."

"From the appearances of the scene, it looks like your brother tortured this woman, then killed himself. Does that seem to fit with his character?" Kevin asked.

Hugh sighed. "I don't think anyone wants to think that someone they love would do something like that. But to answer your question, my brother was always a big fan of the Old Testament. Isaiah 1:17 and all that."

"I'm afraid I'm not familiar with that verse," Kevin said. "Enlighten us."

"It's about delivering justice. Believe it or not, my brother had a very strict moral code. He didn't get his kicks off hurting people. If you're saying he tortured that woman, then she must have deserved it—at least in his mind. And maybe then he couldn't handle what he'd done."

It was a lot to absorb, and Farah tried to stay ahead of the information. "So you think she might have been guilty of something? This woman?"

He grimaced. "I don't know. I hate to cast suspicion on some woman I have no idea about. All I can speak on is my brother and what I know about him. You asked if a murder and suicide fit with his character, and I'm telling you the only scenario I can come up with for how and why he would have tied someone up and stabbed them to death."

Kevin had stopped with the doodling. Farah could see only half his pad, but it looked like he had written down the Bible verse and the word *GUILTY* followed by a question mark.

"What time did you talk to Trent by the pool?" Kevin asked.

"It was late. Maybe eleven."

"And after that you went down to the theater?" Farah asked.

"Yeah. Nora and I watched the movie, had a few glasses of wine, and I fell asleep in the theater."

"What movie?" she asked.

He gave her a long look before answering. "*Brothers of Sam.*"

It was a Western, one that was still in theaters. Her husband had been wanting to see it, but between their work schedules and the guest bathroom retile project that seemed to be stretching into next summer, they'd never make it. "What'd you think?"

He shrugged. "Entertainingly mediocre."

She stowed away the answer for future personal use. She would never be able to share the origins of it but would always, for the rest of her life, tie that phrase in with this moment, when she sat in Hugh Iverson's living room and talked about movies and his dead twin brother.

"So you slept until Nora woke you up. Did you wake up at all during the night? Hear anything?"

"The theater is pitch dark. It's easy to get disoriented without the sunlight coming in the windows. I think I woke around six or seven, then rolled over and went back to sleep."

"And is it normal for you to sleep so late?" She glanced at her notes. "It was, what? Around nine thirty when Nora woke you up?"

"It's not, actually." He met her eyes, and his direct gaze was like a warm spotlight of attention, one she didn't look away from. "I'm normally up by six thirty or seven during the week. But I do tend to sleep later on the weekends, and like I said, the theater is dark."

Nothing too suspicious about that. Still, Kevin made the notation. He cleared his throat and jumped back into the fray. "Prior to last night, when's the last time you spoke to Trent?"

Hugh's dark brow pinched in concentration. "Tuesday—no, it was Wednesday. He came by to get something from Nora. We talked in the driveway for a bit."

"What did he need from Nora?" Farah leaned forward, and the strain on her lower back eased.

"I don't know." Hugh shrugged. "You'd have to ask her."

"Were you and Trent close?" Kevin asked.

The question seemed to sadden Hugh, and he took a moment to collect himself, studying his ankle before turning his head and staring out the window. By the time he spoke, his face was composed, but a tremor of emotion existed in his voice. "My brother is—was—a very complicated man. There are traits that we have in common and many things that we differ in. I chose to handle the difficult things in my life one way; he took a different path. We disagree over those paths, frequently. But there is always—has always been—love and support there. I don't understand why he does certain things, but I'll help him however I can. No, we weren't close." He cleared his throat. "We were more than that. We were one. I've lost a part of me, and I have to learn how to function without that part. To be frank? Right now, I want to die, and that woman upstairs is the only thing that is keeping me living."

A weaker woman would have swooned, but Farah was too cynical for that. The monologue was flawless, and she critically analyzed the tone, the energy, the man before her, whose perfect edges were fraying and cracking before their eyes.

If he was acting, he was the best actor in the world.

But that right there was the problem. He was.

CHAPTER 18
THE LEADING LADY

Nora Kemp stood in the house's two-story library, her cell phone pressed to her ear, and listened to their attorney drone on about legal processes. As soon as he took a breath, she cut in. "I just want to know if we can keep them quiet."

"Well, it depends. About what?" Jeff Bourdin had an infuriating way of speaking as if he had all the time in the world and his clients were whiny babies waving their pacifiers in the air.

"About everything!" she snapped. "Does it matter? I don't want our personal staff blabbing things about our lives. If they didn't see Trent, and they weren't here when the murder happened, I don't understand why they're even being questioned."

"In the police's defense, Nora—they don't know what the staff did or didn't see, or who was working when."

"Then can we restrict their questions to just that?"

"Well, now, I don't want to get into your personal business, Nora, but what—"

"Then don't, Jeff," she said sharply. "I asked you a question. Answer it."

He hesitated. "Let's bring Hugh in on this conversation."

"Answer the damn question."

There was a long pause, and Nora straightened to her full height, reminding herself that she was Nora Kemp. Even Jeff didn't know her past, or about the blood, money, and heartbreak that had led to this throne.

If he thought he could push her around, he was wrong. Everyone who pushed her around learned that lesson at some point.

When the attorney finally spoke, his aw-shucks tone had turned to steel. "No offense, Nora, but I don't respond well to orders. You wanted the best and I'm it. How about treating me with some respect?"

A first-edition hardcover fell victim as she ripped it from the bookshelf and threw it against the wall. "You're evading the question, and I want to know the answer to it. *Please.*" She gritted out the final word, hating the taste of it on her tongue.

"If we play hardball, we risk the cops going to a judge and getting the confidentiality agreements thrown out completely, in terms of the investigation. The agreements will still be in force against speaking to the paparazzi or their kid's soccer coach, but in terms of the police or the court, they'd have to answer questions on *any* aspect of their job or experience with your household that's deemed relevant, and that can be a wide-ass net. Want my opinion? Let the staff talk to them, but have me present. I'll squash any questions that aren't material and keep your butt covered. That work?"

Fear rippled through her, and while she hadn't had a panic attack in years, this time felt close. "Okay. Stop any questions that aren't directly related to Trent's activities in the last forty-eight hours. Hell, any of our activities in the last forty-eight hours."

"And what about the dead woman?" he asked.

The dead woman. Talk about a clusterfuck of a situation. She stepped over the book, its dark-green spine flexed open, pages splayed, then thought better of it and crouched to pick up the item. Guilt rippled through her at the damage to the expensive book, one that could have paid a year of her rent at one point in time. "What about her?"

"Are you good with them asking questions about her?"

She held the phone against her shoulder with her cheek as she carefully slid the book back into place. "I don't give a damn about that. I guarantee you—no one in this house, including me, knows who that woman is."

CHAPTER 19
THE HUSBAND

Kyle stared at his phone. Same-day flights were insanely spendy, and their finances, which had been tight for a while, were about to get worse—especially if he had to take time off to go to California. Kyle scrolled farther down the travel site to the cheaper options. There was an economy seat available tomorrow afternoon, which would give Kerry a day to turn up and him a chance to work one more shift.

Officer Sam Meeko with the Los Angeles Police Department had called him on their way to Kerry's hotel. Kyle could tell from the man's voice that he saw Kerry as a runaway wife leaving a loveless or abusive marriage and taking the kid with her. But that wasn't Kerry and that wasn't him, and no matter what he said, he hadn't seemed to convince the officer of that.

He stared at the price of tonight's late flight, and his concern over Kerry warred with the financial repercussions of the trip. Maybe she was just being flighty. Maybe she'd lost her phone and overslept her alarm. Maybe she was an hour or two from popping up, full of apologies, with Miles hugging her leg.

He looked out the truck's window at the brick, two-story house beside him, one with a leak that had flooded the laundry room. It would take at least an hour, maybe two or three, depending on whether the leak was in the wall and how much of the brick he would have to chip into. Sighing, he locked his phone and stepped from the cab.

As he walked up to the house, his tool bag heavy on one shoulder, his phone rang, the cop's California number on the display.

"Hello?" He paused in the shade of a bright-orange sugar maple tree, halfway to the home's porch.

Officer Meeko didn't mince words. "No one's in the hotel room. There are some dirty kids' clothes on the floor. Suitcases are here, toiletries. Medicines. No cell phone or purse."

"I tried to look up her cell phone," Kyle managed. "It's not showing up."

The pale-blue front door to the house opened, and a short woman with glasses and a Packers sweatshirt appeared in the doorway. She waved and Kyle held up a finger, hoping she would turn around and go away.

The officer continued. "If she doesn't show up, we can track her phone on our end. She might have turned 'Location Services' off, but we can get around that."

"But what do you think after seeing the hotel room?" Kyle scratched the back of his head, tugging on the thinning strands there, not sure whether to be relieved or worried over the fact that their luggage was in the room.

"Well, it looks like she's coming back. There's a lot of medicine here. A breathing machine. A—"

"Our son is sick," he said tightly. "Cancer."

The statement, one that normally evoked a reaction, was ignored. "The hotel is pulling the room-key activity report. They'll be able to tell us what time she left this morning. I gotta say, I think this is all premature. It's been, what, a few hours that no one's heard from her? We'll dig, but ninety percent of the time, the person just shows up. There's no sign of disturbance or foul play in the room. She's probably out shopping."

"So you don't think I need to come there?" Kyle's heartbeat slowed to an almost-normal speed. On the porch, the woman stepped onto the front mat and crossed her arms.

"It's up to you. I'd give it a few more hours to see what happens. Text me a photo of them and let me take a look at the key record, and then maybe we can pull security footage of the lobby. Get a glimpse at them leaving and how it looks."

"That would be great." Kyle exhaled. "Thank you for all of this. Really. I don't—Miles needs pretty strict medical care. I just—"

"Yeah, I got two kids. I get it." But Meeko didn't. He didn't know how desperate a parent became when he had a ticking clock on experiences with his child. This guy would see his kids graduate. Dance at their weddings. Bounce his grandchildren on his knee. Kyle and Kerry couldn't expect that; they could only pray for a miracle. Miracles did happen. The doctor kept telling them that. Miles wasn't terminal yet, just high risk. As long as they kept working hard with his care, there was a chance. A chance for another five years. Maybe ten. Maybe even a full lifetime.

"Please call as soon as you know something," he rasped, and took another step toward the front porch. The woman hadn't budged, and he could feel her staring at him.

"Will do. In the meantime, look through your wife's stuff. See if you can tell what she packed, if something is off, if she took a lot of cash or sentimental items, something that would make you think that this wasn't a normal vacation. I know we don't want to think it, but she could have planned this. We don't always know everything about our spouses. Trust me on that."

CHAPTER 20

THE DETECTIVE

"Finally." Farah balled up the foil wrapper of a blueberry energy bar and stuffed it into the pocket of her black blazer. "Maybe we can solve this murder before next month."

It was almost eleven, and the questioning of the staff had already been delayed a half hour as they'd waited for Jeff Bourdin, the Iverson attorney, to arrive. Now, he stepped out of a chauffeured SUV in a tuxedo T-shirt, red capri pants, a pair of designer sunglasses, and leather flip-flops.

Kevin gave Farah a bemused smile, but she wasn't entertained by the carnival this was turning into. "This is Hollywood," he reminded her as Jeff ambled up the front steps. "Everyone's a character."

Yeah, especially the slow-paced peacock who was currently pumping Kevin's hand as if he were running for mayor. She knew about Jeff Bourdin. They all knew about Jeff. Behind his caricature-worthy exterior, he was ruthless, connected, and smart. There was a reason that Trent Iverson had never been arrested or put in cuffs, despite the mountain of incidents that had occurred during his love affair with drugs and alcohol.

He introduced himself to Farah with a wide-toothed smile and a grip that seemed to claw into her skin. She swallowed a reaction and nodded toward the back. "Let's head out to the pool deck. Nora set up a place for us to conduct the interviews."

At the far end of the cabana, in a private alcove out from under the roofline, they sat—Farah and Kevin on one end of a round table, Jeff and the staff member on the other. Farah moved a tall glass of lilies that was interrupting their view across the table and flipped to a fresh page in her notepad.

First up was Brenda McIntyre, the house manager. Farah wrote down a brief description of the witness, who was in her midforties, extremely professional in both looks and appearance, and literally tight-lipped. Sitting stick straight in the tall-backed rattan chair, she pressed her dark-pink lips together so hard that they cracked like dry mud.

"Miss McIntyre, how long have you been employed with Hugh Iverson?" Kevin asked.

Brenda glanced at the attorney, who nodded his approval. It had been decided (Farah wasn't sure by whom) that he would be present during all the staff questioning, unless the staff member preferred to be alone. Farah was betting the second energy bar in her pocket that no one would.

Brenda still hadn't answered the question, and Jeff gave her a gentle nudge. "Don't worry. I'll step in with any questions I'm concerned about. Just remember what I told you all."

Oh yes. While Farah and Kevin had stood by, waiting as their interview area was set up by Nora and a housekeeper, the attorney had told the staff to provide only direct answers to their questions and *nothing* else. "Be succinct," he had preached. "Succinct and accurate." Farah was certain the accuracy part of his instruction was purely for their benefit.

"I've been here nine years." The lips immediately repursed.

"What are your duties?"

After another glance at the attorney and a nod of approval, she cleared her throat and spoke. "I run the house. I manage the staff, work with Miss Kemp to plan the menus, keep inventories, and oversee the arrangements for on-location furloughs."

"On-location furloughs?" Farah asked, and made a mental note to call her daughter on the next break. If anyone had an ear to Hollywood goings-on, it'd be Anaïca.

"That's when Mr. Iverson is on location," she explained. "He's away for two to three months, so we move a portion of the house and staff with him, so that we can set up a home away from home. It requires quite a bit of coordination and effort."

Farah wondered if they did the same for Nora, but took a different approach. "How long has Miss Kemp lived in the house?"

"Just over a year. She moved in after the engagement."

The proposal had been something that even Farah, with her limited awareness of celebrity news, had heard about. The ring was insured for $10 million and had a stone that once belonged to an Egyptian princess.

"Can you walk us through this morning? What time did you arrive?" Kevin asked.

"Around six thirty. I'm here in time to open up the property, make sure that the kitchen staff arrive and have everything they need. I also like to be on hand in case Mr. Iverson or Miss Kemp have any requests, though they normally keep to themselves until eight or nine."

"Did anything seem out of place this morning when you arrived?" Farah asked.

"Well, Mr. Iverson—Trent, I mean—his car was in the back. That was the first thing I noticed. So I knew that he'd stayed the night."

"How frequently did that happen?" Farah asked.

"Oh, every other week or so. I mean, sometimes I won't see him for months. Sometimes he's here for a few weeks at a time. It just depends on . . . well." She hesitated and knotted her brown hands together tightly. "On things."

The verbal stutter caught their attention, and the detectives shared a look; then Kevin spoke. "What kind of things?"

"Whether Mr. Iverson is in town, how the brothers are getting along, and—to be frank—whether Mr. Iverson—Trent—is using or drinking. He often stays away when he's on a bender or if he's out of town filming."

"For ease, can you just refer to them as Hugh and Trent? I don't want to get confused." Kevin gave a sheepish grin, and the house manager's posture relaxed a little.

"Sure, I'll try."

"Does Trent only stay here if Hugh's in town?" Kevin asked.

"No, he comes and goes as he wants." Brenda glanced at the attorney, and there was something there, something she was afraid to say.

Farah watched her closely, curious at what was there. "How does he get in? He has a key?"

Brenda nodded. "The doors are mostly on fingerprint locks, and Trent is fully authorized, with free rein of the property."

Kevin tapped his pen on the pad. "Let's go back to when you arrived this morning. Do you pass the guesthouse on your way in?"

"No, we all come along the side of the house and up the staff stairwell, which opens into the east hall, or past the house and to the maintenance shed or garage. The backyard is off limits until ten in the morning, and the guesthouses are always off limits, unless we receive specific instruction to the contrary."

The attorney cleared his throat, and Brenda repinched her lips, then gave an apologetic smile.

"The guesthouses are always off limits?" Farah pressed. "Don't they need to be cleaned? Maintained?"

"There are call buttons in the houses where the guests can alert us if they need service, same with Hugh or Miss Kemp. We try to respect their private spaces. This is, after all, a home."

"Are any places in the home off limits?" Farah asked.

Jeff Bourdin stepped in. "Let's focus on the topic. You were asking her about this morning. Brenda, just let them know if anything else was out of place or noteworthy."

She considered the question for a moment, then shook her head. "Not really. I did a quick walk-through of the home and ran into Miss Kemp on the upper level. She let me know that Hugh was still sleeping in the theater room so I wouldn't disturb him. She was dressed, so I had MaryBeth go ahead and do a turn of her bedroom and Mr. Iverson's—Hugh's."

So they had separate bedrooms. Farah made the note, then underlined it. It didn't necessarily mean anything but was an interesting factoid, especially for a couple as high profile as they were.

"What's done in a turn?" It wasn't exactly pertinent, but the attorney let Farah's question slide.

"Fresh linens, floors, surfaces, windows. We replace the flowers every other day. Take any laundry, dishware. Refill the fridges, restock the firewood, and clean the hearth if it was used. Check levels in all of the toiletry and hygiene products and refill if low."

"You do all of that every day?" Farah clarified. She had always thought that she wouldn't like in-home help, no matter how wealthy she was, but that sounded glorious.

"Yes, unless they request otherwise."

"Fresh sheets every day?" she pressed. Kevin shot her a look, but she ignored him. The man didn't understand, had probably never changed pillowcases or a duvet cover in his life.

"Yes."

"Did you actually see Hugh in the theater?" Kevin asked.

"No, but it was common for him—for any of them—to fall asleep in there. To be honest, all of us, at one point or another, have taken a nap in the room. It's dark, soundproof, and the couches and chairs are like butter." She gave a guilty smile, and Farah decided that she liked the woman, despite her reluctance to share information.

"What happened next?" Kevin glanced at his watch, and as if on cue, Farah's stomach growled. At the rate this first interview was going, it would take five or six hours to move through the rest of the staff. After this, they still had to hit Trent's house. Between that, paperwork, and a visit to the morgue, it'd be midnight before she got home to Ty.

"Breakfast preparations began. I told Maria that Trent was here, so she prepared for three. We didn't know at that moment, of course, that he had a guest." She winced. "Not that the guest ended up eating."

"How often does he bring guests over?"

"Never. I mean, he did all the time, before."

A long moment stretched as Kevin and Farah waited for her to continue. When she stayed silent, Kevin prodded. "Before what?"

"Oh." Nervous, Brenda looked at the attorney for help. Why? Farah leaned forward, and her Spidey-sense flared to life.

"We've moved outside the scope of the criminal investigation," Jeff Bourdin drawled. "She answered the question. Trent doesn't bring people by."

How often does Trent bring guests over?

Never. He did all the time, before.

Before she forgot, Farah wrote down the question and the answer. Before what? What would have caused Trent to stop bringing guests over? A fight?

"Now wait a minute." Kevin held up a hand. "Let me rephrase the question. Prior to this, when's the last time Trent brought a guest to the house?"

Brenda sighed, unhappy with herself. "Two years ago. Maybe longer."

Farah wrote down the answer, along with a note to look into Trent's life, to see if there were any major events in that time frame.

Kevin continued. "Now, where was Miss Kemp while breakfast was being prepared?"

"I think she was in her office or the studio. She's been preparing for a film, so she works with her dialect coach in the mornings. Actually, she was in the studio, because she called the kitchen for a latte and some frittata muffins to be brought up to her."

"What time was that?" Farah asked.

"Maria could give you an idea of the time. I would guess eight thirty. She typically likes her coffee around then."

"Wait." Kevin interrupted. "I should have asked this earlier—but when you arrived this morning, were you the first employee to arrive?"

"Yes. My fingerprint access begins at 6:15 a.m. The rest of the staff can't access the property or open any locks until 6:45 a.m. So I'm always the first to arrive, unless there are extenuating circumstances."

"There's no overnight staff or security?"

"No. There's no need for overnight staff, and Mr. Iverson has never had security, as long as I've worked for him."

"That's interesting." Kevin rested his beefy elbow on the table. "Not even security cameras?"

"Not that I'm aware of."

"Wow." Kevin looked at Farah with surprise. "Do you know that he might be the *first* celebrity I've ever encountered who didn't have security?" He held up his pointer finger to emphasize the number. "Certainly the first of his magnitude."

Brenda said nothing, but Farah agreed with Kevin's point. It was strange. Hugh Iverson was one of the biggest celebrities in Hollywood, if not *the* biggest, and Nora Kemp was on track to equal his stardom. The idea that they were both here, unprotected except for gates that could easily be scaled, was insane.

"Well now," the attorney objected. "We're in the most hoity-toity gated neighborhood in Beverly Hills. The entire subdivision has a camera-monitored wall that Houdini couldn't slip past. It took me ten minutes to get through that security, and I'm on Hugh's preapproved list, with a background check on file. You're making this into something it's not."

Farah returned to her list of questions. "Let's fast-forward to finding the bodies. If the guesthouses are off limits, why'd you go down to get Trent for breakfast?"

"Miss Kemp asked me to. She came down to eat and was surprised Hugh hadn't shown up yet. She was going to go get him, and she asked me to ring the guesthouse. I did, there wasn't an answer, so she told me to knock on the door and see if he wanted to join us for breakfast."

"Is that sort of thing normal? You fetch everyone for a meal?"

"Yes and no. Sometimes they—Hugh and Nora, I mean—sometimes they want to eat in private; other times they want everyone around. It just depends. But it wasn't out of the ordinary, if that's what you're asking. I've gone and gotten Trent dozens of times for meal invites. Sometimes he answers the door; sometimes he doesn't."

"And this time he didn't," Kevin said.

"No. And the door—well, you've seen the door. I leaned closer and could see the woman in the chair. I moved a little to the side, and then I saw Trent." Her face crumpled with emotion, and she took a deep breath and visually composed herself. "I ran back upstairs and told Nora—Miss Kemp. She was still in the kitchen, in a conversation with Maria, and when I told her what I saw, she immediately went and got Hugh."

This was what Farah had waited for, and she leaned forward, trying not to appear too eager. "What was Nora's reaction?"

"She went pale, and she said something like, 'Are you sure? Trent's dead?' And I said, 'Well, I'm not *sure*, but I think so. And I think the woman is too.' I mean, that's not exactly my words, but something like that. She kind of sagged and grabbed the counter for support. I asked her if I should go tell Mr. Iverson—Hugh—but she shook her head and said she would do it."

"And when did you call 9-1-1?" Kevin asked.

"After Mr. Iverson went out to the guesthouse. He came back in and told me to call the police."

"Why didn't you call them immediately?" Farah asked.

To her credit, the woman didn't flinch or look to the attorney for approval. "I knew Hugh would handle it properly and be fully transparent with the police, but he deserved the opportunity to see his brother first."

It was interesting that she referred to Hugh's transparency and honesty, but not Nora's. Farah made the notation but wasn't sure if it really meant anything. "Were you there when Hugh went to the guesthouse?"

"No. I was in the kitchen. Nora went with him."

"When you saw Hugh afterward, how would you describe him?"

"He was very quiet. I would say that he was shaken. They both were. He told me to call the police, and then he went upstairs. I haven't seen him since."

CHAPTER 21

THE LEADING LADY

Hugh had insisted, from the very beginning, that they have separate bedrooms. While Nora had initially been opposed to the setup, she'd quickly seen the benefits of it.

Now she moved down the long second-floor hall and into her suite. After the wedding, she would push for a shared bedroom. Given the circumstances and her future baby bump, the wedding date should be moved up. The public always loved celebrity weddings, and if handled appropriately, theirs would be a good distraction from all this ugliness.

Shutting her bedroom door, she walked through the spacious room, past the California king bed with its three rows of pillows, and took a seat on one of the two soft chairs that faced the window and overlooked the backyard. Her suite had a balcony as well, one with a fireplace, wet bar, and seating area, but that balcony faced the gardens, and right now, she wanted a view of the pool deck. She tucked her bare feet underneath her and settled into the chair, resting her cheek on the cushion and looking down to the cabana. Most of it was hidden from view—she knew that better than anyone—but the private alcove on the far edge, where she had arranged for the interviews to be conducted, was out from under the roofline and shaded by palms, in easy view of her bedroom window.

It was also in earshot of a staff walkie, which Nora had hidden under the guise of helping the maid set up the space. Before tucking it into the bushes, she had flipped it to a permanent "talk" position, turned down the speaker, and set in on channel 9. Now she listened.

It was only the third interview, but so far there was a recurring theme, one not verbalized outright but still communicated. As it turned out, she was disliked by Hugh's staff.

Nora smiled in irony at the thought—she had spent the last seven years in fierce pursuit of the America's Sweetheart crown, a role that was exhausting, to say the least. Who had the energy to smile all the time, be sweet, funny, thoughtful, and generous? On set, when someone stepped on her cue, she laughed it off. When lighting made her look like she had a double chin, she blamed it on herself. When her driver had passed a stranger with a flat tire, she'd told them to stop and help the woman, then smiled for photos and hugs. Continually and constantly, she was onstage and playing that part.

So when Nora was in this protected cocoon of luxury, she relaxed. She enjoyed the perks that this life provided her. And maybe, apparently, she was a little demanding and bossy in doing so. Hey, it was better to discover it now, rather than in some anonymous tabloid tell-all.

She decided, while listening to the detectives question their sous chef, a woman who couldn't see past her own paring knife, to try her best to be nicer to the household employees. After all, she knew better than anyone what it was like to be treated like shit. She understood, more than they would ever know, the stresses they faced at home and how agonizing it must be to step into this house each day, knowing that this life was already earmarked for someone else.

It was how she'd felt the first time she'd gone into the House of God, back when Momma Beth, the twins' famous mother, had lived there. It had been everything she had ever wanted—a huge mansion with double staircases, gigantic rooms, fireplaces, multiple pools, even a ballroom—but all with an expiration date, a visitor's pass that could be revoked at any time if Nora said the wrong thing, looked the wrong way, irritated the wrong Iverson. And Momma Beth had been the exact opposite of Nora's mother. At their very first meeting, she had wrapped Nora into a hug without hesitation, without the stench of cigarette smoke and alcohol, without the sharp comments or hateful glare, without the questions followed by judgment over her responses.

She had loved that house. She had loved Momma Beth. She had craved that life and had initially been blind to the ugliness that lay beneath the finery.

She had learned so much from Momma Beth—mostly that outward appearances meant everything, and that the right facade could hide everything you held in your heart.

Their staff couldn't be blamed for jealousy and resentment. Hell, it was still ingrained in Nora, still pushing and fueling every action, reaction, and plan.

She closed her eyes, emotionally and physically exhausted. Experiencing all this was one thing—figuring out how to present herself to the outside world was another. What would the police, the staff, her future husband . . . what did they expect to see? What role did she need to perform?

What she wanted to do, more than anything, was just cry. Crawl under the sheets, hug one of those impossibly soft pillows to her body, and cry.

Eventually, the police were going to find out the truth.

CHAPTER 22
THE KID

He didn't know what time it was, but he was hungry. Really hungry. Like, hungrier than he had ever been in his entire life. Daddy once said that he had a little monster in his belly that ate up all his vegetables, and Miles had never believed that. Now he was wondering if the monster was real, and if it had eaten all the contents of his stomach, because he had never had so much hurt in his belly before. All he could think about was food. He'd even eat broccoli at this point. Even carrots. Everything sounded good, and the thought of food was so overwhelming that he wasn't even scared of the dark anymore.

He had already looked in his backpack and found the orange crackers. Those he ate right away, with some of the water in the silver bottle. He had looked in all the other places also, even the little zippered thing on the side, but there was nothing else to eat.

He lay flat on his back and stared up at the ceiling, wondering if he should pee again.

He had already gone once, over by one of the boxes. Peeing inside was a big no-no, but he hadn't known what else to do. And if Mommy showed up and yelled at him about it, he wouldn't even care because he just wanted to see her so bad. To see anyone.

Did anyone even know he was in here?

CHAPTER 23

THE DETECTIVE

"We need to get them out of the house." Farah fastened her seat belt as Kevin started up the SUV. After four hours of staff interviews, they had finally taken a break. The majority of the staff had been dismissed with only the groundskeeper and a few maids left to question.

Four hours and bubkes in terms of clues. Between the hippie lawyer's interference and the fact that no one was working during the crime, they had dozens of pages of notes but no helpful facts.

"Get who out of the house? Everyone?" As they waited for the line to clear at the neighborhood's exit gate, Kevin turned on the radio, and a country song twanged through the speakers.

"It's a crime scene. We can do the rest of the staff interviews in the station. We need a team to search the whole house. Dig deeper."

"Ain't gonna happen." He pushed out a piece of nicotine gum from a foil packet and popped it into his mouth. "Only the guesthouse is the crime scene. Think of it as a hotel. You got a stabbing in room 307, we aren't going anywhere else, except entry and exit corridors. You can't start digging through underwear drawers, and you know it."

Farah curled her lip in protest. "You're saying that because they're famous."

"I'm saying that because it's true, and I'm underlining it because they're famous. Speaking of which, the chief wants an update from both of us today. In person."

"Oh, wonderful." Farah stretched out her legs and closed her eyes. "I got four hours of sleep last night. You?"

"About five." He leaned forward and peered through the window at the approaching intersection. "Jack in the Box looks slammed. You good with Subway?"

"I'm good with whatever." She yawned and pulled her cell phone from her pocket. "I'm gonna call Anaïca and check in."

He grunted in disapproval. "The chief will have your ass if you talk shop about this."

"I'm not gonna say anything to her," she snapped, huffing in irritation.

When Anaïca answered, Farah immediately switched to Italian. "Come va?"

Kevin threw the gum packet at her in response, and she blocked it with her hand.

"What's up?" Anaïca asked, a clatter of keystrokes in the background.

"I'm on a double homicide. It's a movie star." Farah chose her Italian words carefully to disguise them from Kevin. "The one from the show you watched as a kid. The religious one."

Her daughter, who was brilliant by anyone's standards, immediately caught on. "No shit. Hugh or Trent?" She gasped. "Don't say both."

"The bad boy. I'll try to get you put on the case, but in the meantime, can you start to dig?"

"Of course. I'll jump in and get enough to give you a crash course in all things Iverson. Was it an overdose? Oh shit, wait. You said double homicide . . ."

"We're still figuring it out. Keep it quiet." Farah glanced at Kevin, who was glaring at her as if she were murdering kittens. She switched to English. "I say go for it and enjoy your date. You deserve it."

"Yeah, whatever. Addio." Anaïca ended the call without waiting for a response, and Farah smiled as she placed the cell phone in the empty cup holder.

"You told her everything, didn't you?" Kevin asked dryly.

"Oh please," Farah chided. "If I can't trust my own daughter, shoot me dead. She's a cop, she understands the rules."

"You know, we could request her from TID," he said slowly. TID—the department full of data nerds, including Anaïca—was focused on and utilized for cybercrimes, research, surveillance, and data dives. It was one of the safest places a rookie in the LAPD could work, but that wasn't why Anaïca had chosen that division. While Farah loved the boots-on-the-ground hunt, Anaïca loved the research. And mother's bias aside, she was great at it.

"Yeah, we could request her." Farah shrugged, as if she wasn't planning on pitching her involvement to the chief at tonight's meeting.

"A case of this caliber would have a TID assignment anyway," Kevin pointed out. And he was right. With a celebrity involved, budgets would find room, and scarce department resources would suddenly be plentiful.

Farah changed the subject. "We've got to move faster through the rest of the staff. If all they did was show up for work and then hear about what happened, we should be able to knock them each out within a few minutes."

"Says the woman who kept peppering Brenda with questions."

"Yeah, well . . ." Farah sighed as traffic backed up. "She's hiding something. Did you see the way she froze when she said Trent didn't bring guests by anymore?"

"Well, maybe they're all hiding something. And, maybe it's something unrelated to the murder. People hide things, Farah. Maybe Hugh and Nora have sex parties on the weekend. Maybe they just had a miscarriage that the paparazzi haven't caught wind of. Maybe they like to snort cocaine with their breakfast."

"So you think it's all innocent? The location of the deaths was just happenstance?"

He made the turn into the strip mall and parked a few spots down from the sandwich shop. "You're making my point. We have to take our time and cover our bases."

"Well, we have a lot of bases waiting for us. We haven't even gone to Trent's house or discovered who the mystery woman is. The chief is going to have our asses if we show up tonight with nothing but a bunch of footnotes on Hugh's and Nora's lives." Anxiety rose in her chest at the enormity of the work ahead of them. Normally, it wouldn't faze her, but they had a clock ticking above their heads.

It was only a matter of hours before the press would catch wind of this. When that happened, all hell would break loose.

CHAPTER 24
THE MOM

Remember when Miles was three? He was a good kid, but so stubborn. I remember when he was going through potty training and knew how to go to the bathroom on the toilet but preferred doing it in his diaper. And you were at work and he had to go but was refusing to do it until I put a diaper on him. He was screaming at me— SCREAMING—to put a diaper on him. I refused, and he told me to call you.

I told him fine, but that you were going to tell him the same thing—that he had to go in the toilet like a big boy. I called you on speakerphone and he used that voice he uses, like he's going to cry, and asked you if he could—just one time—use his diaper, and you folded immediately and told him yes.

When I hung up the phone, he was beaming at me with this big smug look that I wanted to smack off him— and that was Miles back then. He was bratty. I know, I'm not supposed to say that, but he was. He shoved the diaper in my face and ORDERED me to put it on him.

And I did, because I knew if I didn't, he would tell on me as soon as you got home. And even though I was the parent and he was three, you would have been annoyed at me, and you would have taken his side and asked why I was being such a bitch about "just one damn diaper" so I did it. I put the diaper on him and then had to watch as he sat on the couch and pooped, and then I had to change it and wipe his butt and deal with the smell, and at that point, I hated him. I hated him and I hated you and I felt all alone—like it was you both against me, and I knew I was going to lose that battle every single time.

And that day . . . it was like a breaking point for me. From that point on, every single thing I did for both of you—washing your clothes, cooking your food, picking up after you—it felt like I was your personal maid, and the resentment . . . I don't know how to explain it, but I almost left. Every morning when you left for work, I considered packing a suitcase and just driving away. You could both have just taken care of each other.

I should have. It would have been better for both of you—for all three of us—if I had.

CHAPTER 25
THE DETECTIVE

"Initial autopsy report is complete." Farah read out the text from Dr. Martin, then bit into a ham and provolone sandwich with extra banana peppers.

"Hell yeah." Kevin looked at his watch. "That was fast. Is that all it takes? A Grammy nomination and you get fast-tracked on Dr. Martin's slab?"

"Grammys are music, you doofus." She plucked a fallen pepper from the wrapper and popped it into her mouth, savoring the sweet flavor. "But yeah, a Grammy winner would probably also get their chest cracked within the hour."

Kevin winced and rubbed a hand protectively over his own wide chest. "We swinging by there before we head back?"

Farah nodded and half rose, taking a final bite of her sandwich before she surrendered it to the trash. "They're at the coroner's office at Beverly Hills. Technically, it's on the way."

"Let's do it." Kevin grinned, and he had a chunk of Doritos stuck to the front of his left incisor. She gestured to the spot, and he used the tip of his tongue to hunt down the morsel.

By the time they made it to the BH station and pulled on booties, hairnets, and gloves, Dr. Harry Martin was waiting for them, his clipboard in hand, the two bodies side by side in the largest autopsy room. Harry waited for the door to click shut behind them; then he pulled the privacy window over the door's window and started right in.

"First, let's talk about the woman. I have nothing yet on identification," he announced, walking over to the closest body. "Her fingerprints are on rush, but you know how long that takes. I tried the new facial-recognition tool, but a slack face has different structure points than a live, and closed eyes were another missing data point for the analysis. Still, I attempted it twice"—he held up two fingers in case they didn't speak English—"both with failed results."

With two bodies, the smell in the room was stifling. Farah tried to breathe through her mouth and mentally urged Harry to hurry up.

"She's an average middle-class mom." He pulled the sheet off, fully exposing her body. "Five two, a hundred and forty-five pounds. I would guess between thirty-one and thirty-four years old."

The same age range as Nora Kemp, but there was nothing similar between this woman and Nora, other than their skin color. This woman had a tattoo of a dolphin on her ankle, a half-closed belly button piercing, a brassy dye job, unpainted fingernails, and red toenails. Farah walked down the length of her, looking for signs that would point to her lot in life. Her legs had about two weeks of growth on them, her pubic area looked unmaintained, and she had pale legs. It was odd for California, for a town where everyone, even older women, wore shorts.

The woman wasn't fit but wasn't overweight and probably approached exercise with the same lack of enthusiasm that Farah had. She leaned closer, looking past the stab wounds, and noticed a series of stretch marks on the side of her closest breast. "She had children?"

The medical examiner nodded. "At least one. And no recent intercourse, in case that's pertinent to the investigation." He lifted her arm by the wrist and turned it upward. "You can see the damage from the binding. She struggled hard against it, and for a while. At least an hour, maybe two."

The wedding ring rubbed Farah the wrong way. It was a piece of the puzzle that didn't fit. Somewhere, she had a husband. Where was he? And what was Trent Iverson doing with a married mother?

"Anything else we should know?" Kevin asked, and she could tell from his stiff posture and constipated expression that the smell was getting to him too. An autopsy always carried the scents of decomposition, blood, and feces, and with two on the table, it was overpowering.

Harry didn't seem to notice it. "Not yet. Looks like your average woman, if you ignore the four stab wounds in her torso. But then again, maybe that's what makes her notable. Definitely not a druggie or prostitute."

Kevin turned to the second body. "What about him?"

"Well, identification should be easier. He is an identical twin, so that makes it fun." He smiled under his face mask, the corners of his cheeks lifting, and anyone who found anything *fun* about dead bodies was always suspect to Farah. He pulled back the sheet to the waist, and Farah was grateful that she was at the non–exit wound side of Trent's head.

"How do you verify one twin from another?" Kevin asked.

"In this case, I was able to get medical records for Trent. It's very interesting, I have to say."

Interesting was something that always caught Farah's attention, especially in an autopsy. "In what way?"

Harry waved them to the side, where a large light box displayed four X-ray images. "Trent hasn't been to the doctor in almost a decade, probably due to his affection for narcotics, but these are X-rays and an MRI from when he was younger." He pointed to each of the screens. "Dislocated shoulder. Snapped rib. Cracked jaw."

"Okay." Farah couldn't see what was interesting about this. "Does his body not match the damage?"

"Oh, it does. I took the liberty of running a full-body X-ray on him." His eyes twinkled. "Figured the department could afford it."

"And?" Kevin said impatiently. "We got things to do, Doc."

"Oh, don't spoil my fun. You'll like this, I promise." He swapped the jaw X-ray with a full-body image of a skeleton, presumably Trent's. "Lookee here." He used the tip of his pen to point to various parts of the X-ray. "Shoulder. Rib. Jaw. Match, match, match."

Farah stared at the screens and tried to understand what he was getting at. "Yeah? So? They match. It's Trent Iverson. What's your point?"

"Look at the other damage." He zoomed in on an arm, then a leg. A hip, then another rib. "It's like he's been in a car crash, but one that isn't on his medical record. There's damage all over, an excessive amount for any individual."

"Wasn't he . . ." Farah turned to Kevin and wished that Anaïca were here. She was an encyclopedia of celebrity events. "There was a car crash, wasn't there? Drunk driving, somewhere in the Hills?"

"Yeah, but he walked away from that one. Literally. Cops found him at a bar on Sunset, ordering drinks for the entire place."

"How old are these injuries?" Farah asked, staring at the screens.

"Hard to tell. Some are adolescent, some maybe from his teens. Some look treated, some aren't."

"But you can definitively say that it's Trent Iverson?"

"Other than the obvious visual identification—yes. We took fingerprints and DNA, just to cover all of our bases, but I think anyone with working vision could identify him."

Kevin swore. "I liked the guy, but I can't say I didn't see a short life span coming."

Dr. Martin paused. "You know him?"

"Not personally, but the LAPD has dealt with him a lot. He's a junkie of anything he could get his hands on. I don't know what kind of demons he was trying to outrun, but he wasn't happy with them."

The doctor gestured to the woman. "Maybe it was the demons that cause you to tie a woman to a chair and do that."

"Maybe so." He leaned forward and peered at Trent. "Handsome fuck, even dead."

"What about the connection between the two? Any information there?" Farah interrupted.

"So far . . . it looks like murder-suicide, at least from the bodies and what I saw at the scene. I'll let CSI confirm trajectory of the gun for suicide, but just eyeballing things—no red flags. He obviously had the strength to stab her, and the angle of his wound is consistent with a self-inflicted shot to the head." He raised his hand and pantomimed the action, pointing his finger to his temple and mimicked pulling on the trigger.

Kevin shook his head sadly. "What a waste."

"Eh. For the fans, yes. But look." Harry turned to the woman and pointed at the deepest of the stab wounds. "These are clean and decisive. The locations are designed for pain, not immediate death. She was dying, but that wasn't the goal. He wanted to torture her while keeping her alive, and he knew what he was doing."

"So, what, you're saying that he had beef with her? That's why he did this? This is a crime of passion?" Kevin asked.

No, that wasn't what he was saying. Farah caught on immediately, and knew what was coming as Harry shook his head and spoke gravely.

"I'm saying this isn't the first time he's done this. Trent Iverson has killed before."

CHAPTER 26
THE HUSBAND

Back home, Kyle took a shower and changed into workout shorts and a T-shirt, then stood in the middle of their bedroom and considered his next steps. Officer Meeko's instructions had been clear—figure out if Kerry packed anything strange—but it seemed odd to look through his wife's stuff.

Still, maybe she had left him a note, or there was something odd in her drawers, something that he wouldn't understand or think about until he saw it.

He started with her dresser, which was quick and easy, because she was a neat freak. Kerry used a board to fold their shirts, guaranteeing they were all the same width in the stack. Her socks were rolled and color coded. He did find a lace thong in her underwear that he hadn't seen her wear in years, and he put it on top of all her baggy cotton ones as a suggestion.

With that done, he moved to the double closet that they shared. Best he could tell, she'd taken their suitcase, plus the small plastic Transformers one that Miles used. Her makeup bag was gone, but all their shampoos and soaps and that really spendy hair straightener that he'd gotten her for Christmas two years ago—those were all here.

He looked under their bed, behind the dressers, in shoes, on the top shelf of the closet, and behind boxes. All the places that someone might hide things, but there wasn't anything, other than a few mothballs and dust.

We don't always know everything about our spouses. Trust me on that. The cop had sounded so confident, like there was no doubt that Kerry had some *big secret* that she was keeping from Kyle, but that wasn't what their relationship was like.

That wasn't what Kerry was like.

But there were two possibilities here. Either his wife was up to something or something bad had happened to her. To her and Miles.

He'd rather suspect Kerry of something than consider the latter.

He moved into the office and flipped on the light. The small square room held a pale-blue wooden desk, two file cabinets, a fabric sewing-board thingy, and some rolling storage organizers. The walls were covered in a floral wallpaper left over from the previous owners, and the carpet smelled faintly of dog piss from their old Chihuahua, who'd preferred this room over the yard when it came to using the bathroom.

He sat down in the rolling chair and looked through the papers on top of the desk, feeling a little guilty. Unlike her clothes drawers, which had been in their shared bedroom, this sort of snooping felt more personal, like he was spying on her. And maybe, in a sense, he was. But she *was* missing. Any digging that he was doing was only to see if he could help find and keep her safe.

The explanation didn't sound right, and he would need to practice it again before she got home. Kerry had a tendency to flip out over certain things, and he was pretty sure that this would be one of those triggers.

Her computer was his old one, passed down and still with the same operating system and password he had used: Warlock99$. He skipped over it for now, since the detective had said to focus on what she did or didn't bring with her. Opening the top two drawers of the desk, he saw both were filled with neatly organized office supplies, but the third drawer was different. At first glance, it was full of file folders, but when Kyle picked up the first one, he realized it was really just covering up what was beneath it.

Pill bottles, dozens of them. He sifted through the sea of orange bottles to see how deep the pile went, and his hand disappeared to the wrist. He closed his fist around a bottle and brought it up.

Kerry Ann Pepper
ENULOSE, 10MG
Use 1-2x daily, as needed for constipation

The prescription was almost two years old, and the bottle was pretty full. Which made sense, because Kerry didn't have any problem passing stools, at least none that he was aware of. And she wasn't the sort to go to the doctor for herself, except for her annual female exam.

He set the bottle on the desk and picked up another. This one had Miles's name on it and was also full. He set it to the side and pulled out another one, then another.

He began to divide them into two lines, one for Kerry and one for Miles. When he was finished, both lines stretched about twenty bottles long.

This didn't make sense. Why would she not give Miles his medicine? And why wasn't she taking her own?

Kerry didn't have any aversion to medicine. If anything, she was OCD about it. She set timers, carried pill organizers in her purse, and always had something on hand to manage Miles's unpredictable health.

His cell phone vibrated from behind the second row of bottles, and he reached for it, knocking one over in the process. It was the cop, and he answered the call right away.

"Hello?"

CHAPTER 27

THE DETECTIVE

As the final remnants of rush-hour traffic clogged Santa Monica Boulevard, Kevin's department-issued Tahoe rolled to a stop at the security gate of Hugh and Nora's Beverly Hills neighborhood. The wide-gated entrance was staffed by three uniformed officers who looked straight out of central casting, all ex-military and all with faces that only a mother could love.

They waited in the rightmost lane of the entrance as their IDs were checked and scanned. At the rear of the SUV, a guard raised the lift gate and checked their back seat.

"You do this every time?" Farah asked the man with the ID scanner.

"Every time, unless it's an emergency vehicle."

That would explain why they were waved through this morning with just a flash of their badges, after the 9-1-1 call. "You ID both passengers and drivers?" Farah asked.

"Yep, unless a homeowner is driving. It's quicker if you're on the approved list, which requires a background check."

"We'll need a list of everyone on the Iverson approved list," she said.

"Not unless Dottie authorizes it." He turned his head and called for a woman, who walked over in a monogrammed golf shirt and khaki pants. She came to Farah's side of the car and leaned toward the window with a warm smile that contradicted the security team's stern manner.

"Hi there."

The woman turned out to be viciousness wrapped in grace, and despite her steadfast refusal to turn over any information without a warrant, Farah found herself smiling back by the end of the exchange, the woman's manner infectious.

"Now, I can pull everything quickly," Dottie reassured them. "You get that warrant in hand, and I'll turn over tag numbers, vehicle photos, entry and exit logs, driver's license photos . . . anything that warrant says. But we just can't violate every visitor's—and the homeowners'— privacy, just because of an incident."

"Trent Iverson's not protected anymore," Kevin pushed back, leaning over the armrest so that he could see into Dottie's face. "Deceased, we have full right to his information."

The pep left her body, and Farah was suddenly reminded of the fact that this death was still somehow under wraps. "Oh," she said quietly. "We didn't know. I mean, we suspected that it might have been—" She huffed out a breath. "Well. In that case, I'll pull Mr. Trent's file, but you need a warrant for the rest, okay?"

Kevin raised his hands in surrender. "Whatever you say, boss."

"And that information is confidential," Farah added. "So please don't—"

The woman shook her head stiffly. "Won't leave my lips on my mother's soul." She patted the top of the doorframe and turned away, heading to the guard station.

They were instructed to pull to the side, and a silver Rolls-Royce moved past.

"Maybe it's not so odd that Hugh and Nora don't have private security or cameras," Farah remarked, watching as the next car was stopped. "This takes neighborhood security to a whole nother level."

"Yeah, I heard the entire eight-mile border of the neighborhood is fenced with infrared cameras and motion-activation alarms. No one can get in or out without being seen."

Farah thought of her own street in Bell Gardens. Last week, she had opened her front door to head to work and found a man sleeping on her front porch. Their house windows had bars, and they used one of the old-school Club steering-wheel locks on Ty's car. Compare that with the Iverson garage, where keys to the Ferrari and Bentley were in easy reach on hooks inside the four-thousand-square-foot, climate-controlled garage. She made the observation to Kevin, who chuckled.

"Yeah, but you aren't paying eighteen thousand dollars a month in HOA dues. So there's that."

Farah let out a low whistle. "So that's the price of all of this? I'll keep stepping over strangers on my front porch, thanks."

"Yeah." They watched as Dottie approached, a stapled set of papers in hand.

"I did the last three years. Not sure how far back you wanted me to go." She passed the pages through the window to Farah, who flipped through them quickly. "Those are just entry and exit logs, plus any call records from him."

"You keep records of any call to the gate?"

Dottie nodded. "Records and notes. They're organized by the phone number that originates the call. So these are only calls Trent made to us, not any call that mentions him, though we could pull those too, with the right warrant." She held out a second set of pages. "And this is the entry and exit logs for the entire neighborhood for the last twenty-four hours." She gave Farah a stern look. "You didn't get this from me, understand? They're sorted by homeowner address, but given that the Iverson property is unsecured, I thought it might be relevant to know everyone that was inside the neighborhood gates during the time of the incident."

Farah gave a solemn nod and tried to contain her reaction to the gift. Taking it from Dottie, she passed it to Kevin. In truth, there wasn't any reason a judge wouldn't grant a warrant for the info. But still, she appreciated the gesture. A warrant would take time, and their clock was tight.

Dottie paused. "We're included on any 9-1-1 calls from homeowners, so we *were* aware of what was said on the call. And no ambulances have come through, just the coroner's van. So I can only make assumptions, but . . . it sounds like Mr. Trent wasn't the only death. There was someone else?"

Kevin responded. "We can't verify that, but we *are* trying to identify a guest that Trent Iverson had with him yesterday evening. The activity log should help with that."

"Well, I was on shift until eleven. Trent came through right before I got off, but he was alone in the car."

"Do you search the vehicles when they come in?" Farah was thinking of their own entry, but Dottie's head was already shaking.

"Not if they're approved guests. Trent's been on the list for over a decade and has a gate fob on his car. We wave him right through, same as we would a homeowner. But his car—he was in his Shelby—it doesn't have tinted windows, so I got a pretty good look when he came through. There wasn't anyone in with him."

That was interesting. Farah and Kevin exchanged a glance. "She look familiar?" Kevin fiddled with his phone and pulled up a photo of the woman. It wasn't her best look. Her head was tilted to one side, her eyes open, her features pained. The photo was a tight crop and didn't show any blood, but it was still clear that the woman was dead.

Dottie peered closely at the screen and didn't flinch at the view. "Definitely not a resident or one of their friends. And I don't recognize her as one of their employees. This is the woman that was found with Trent?"

"No recollection of her coming through here?" Kevin pressed.

She gave it a final study, then looked up and shook her head. "She didn't come through here. Not unless she was hiding in someone's back seat or trunk."

"Yeah, hiding," Farah mumbled, as they waved to Dottie and pulled forward through the gate. "More likely tied up there."

CHAPTER 28

THE HUSBAND

"Mr. Pepper, we're not quite sure what your wife is up to," Officer Meeko said, his tone more serious than earlier.

Kyle closed the drawer on Kerry's desk before spinning the chair in the opposite direction and standing, needing to get some separation between him and the pills.

"We looked at the hotel lock record, then brought up the lobby cameras, just to see if we could make sense of things. On the upside, we know more. The bad news is, it isn't good."

Kyle sat back down. "Tell me."

"Your wife and Miles came through the lobby at seven forty last night and took the elevators up, then unlocked the door to their room. They left the room over two hours later, around ten, and went down to the lobby and out the front doors. We couldn't find any footage of them returning."

"Wait. So she's actually been missing since last night?" A sharp pain flared in Kyle's chest, and he pressed a hand to the muscle, willing himself not to have a heart attack, not right now, not when his family needed him more than ever. Needed him, and he had skipped over buying a flight because the prices were too high.

He looked at the clock on the wall—7:35. Too late for him to catch the 8:30 p.m. flight, even if he walked out the front door right now, ticket in hand. Maybe there was a red-eye, something with a connection. He sat back down and pressed the power button on the front of her computer, intent on checking the options as soon as they got off the phone.

"That's what it looks like according to the key report. We'll keep looking through the lobby video, but we're talking almost twenty hours of footage. Multiply that by several cameras and . . ." He sighed. "We just don't have a lot of manpower. Not for a missing person."

"*Two* missing people," he said tightly.

"It could still be something else. She was going somewhere for something. Maybe to meet someone. A boyfriend, maybe. I know you don't like the idea of it, but they could have just gotten in someone's car and gone to their house. Might not have needed all the stuff in their room."

"That's not what happened." Kyle's hands fisted into balls, and the urge to punch something was overwhelming.

"I'm not saying it is. I'm just saying that we have to look at it as a possibility. The fact is, people don't normally snatch a mother and child. It's . . . messy. And this was a safe area and not too late at night. I'd let my wife walk around on that street. It's just—it's odd. Something doesn't feel right."

Kyle set his elbows on the desk, knocking over another pill bottle in the process. He ignored it and rested his head in one hand. "Miles was definitely with her?"

"You said he was six years old, right?"

"Yes." Kyle's mouth felt dry and his chest cramped, and maybe this was what a panic attack felt like.

"From the photos you sent, it looks like them. He's wearing a backpack. I'll send you the footage and you can confirm it. They walk through the lobby and out the front doors. I got no idea where they go from there, but they don't come back in their room. Now, that doesn't mean that they didn't come back into the hotel. They could have returned and gone to a different room."

"What's she wearing in the video?"

"Looks like yoga pants and a tank top. Hair was in a ponytail. Flip-flops. Like I said, I'll send you the footage."

"It's . . . um . . ." Kyle tried to think of the right word. "Suspicious, right? I mean, she obviously isn't leaving me."

"It's worrisome, yes. There are a lot of possibilities right now, but foul play is definitely a concern. If you have the access, check your wife's banking—her credit and debit cards. See if she has any activity in the past twelve hours. And keep your phone on. I'll call you the minute we have any news, good or bad. Earlier, you asked me about coming here. Now that we know she didn't come back to her room last night and has been missing a lot longer than since this morning . . . I would get here as soon as you can."

CHAPTER 29

THE LEADING LADY

Nora lay naked on the teak bench in the middle of the steam room, her earbuds in, the sound of the interviews clear over the hiss of the hot and humid air.

The police shouldn't even be talking to the cleaning staff, but here was Jenny Cottle, rambling on about dirty dishes from last night.

Nora inhaled deeply, then let out a slow breath and tried to stay calm. Just one more staff interview after Jenny; then the detectives would leave them alone. She'd already told Brenda to send everyone away once they finished with the police, so soon they'd have the house to themselves for the rest of the evening.

Nora had made excuses to be alone so she could eavesdrop on the interviews in private, but she was anxious to get back to Hugh's bedroom and see how he was taking this—and what he had said to the detectives.

"I can always tell when Trent's been here."

The maid's know-it-all tone scraped up Nora's spine. The girl didn't understand her place, and frankly, Nora was surprised Brenda had hired her. Most of their staff was more mature, but this girl was barely twenty-five, and that worried Nora. Not for temptation's sake, but more for media leaks and sought-after tell-alls. It took time to learn to keep your mouth shut. Twenty-five-year-olds—especially ones like Jenny—hadn't yet learned that skill.

"In what way?" That was the male detective. Kevin. He was okay, but she didn't like the suspicious way the female cop looked at her. Nora hadn't dealt with that sort of look in years, not since she was back in Kansas and counting out change at the supermarket line.

"Well, Hugh's very neat. I don't need to do much of anything to pick up after him. He'll leave a drinking glass out, but it always has a coaster under it. He puts his dirty clothes into the hamper. His toothbrush back into the holder, that sort of thing. Trent is like a tornado. When he moves through a room, everything is topsy-turvy. When I got here this morning, I knew right away, even if I hadn't seen his car by the back gate, that he was here."

Sure she had. Probably spent extra time in the staff bathroom, plumping up her lips and putting on a second coat of mascara. Nora had noticed Jenny lingering around the kitchen, waiting for him to show up for breakfast. Nora had intentionally stayed in place when Brenda went to fetch him, giving Jenny a list of instructions that would have kept her busy and out of the main areas for the better part of the morning.

"What time did you get off yesterday?" The male detective continued the questioning.

"Around four."

"So you didn't see Trent yesterday?"

"Nope."

"But you saw his car when you arrived this morning?"

"Yes. That happens a lot. He comes over late and then stays over."

Shut up, Nora thought. *For the love of God, shut up.*

"And you said that you saw evidence of Trent in the house? So you think he came in the main house last night?"

Nora pinched her eyes shut. A bead of sweat rolled down her neck and into the gap between her breasts.

"Yeah. Definitely."

They needed to fire this one. Immediately, before she cleaned another room.

The woman stepped in. "What areas of the house did he go in last night, based on your best guess?"

The good news was, this would never hold up in court. What—a misplaced wineglass meant that he had come inside? This girl was an idiot. A joke. They were wasting their time with this. Jeff needed to step in and stop it. Why wasn't he? What were they paying him for?

"Well, I didn't have time to go through the whole house. I had just gotten there around the time that they found—that they went to the guesthouse. But the door to the cigar room was open, and I saw some mess in there. And the porch had some glasses left out."

"Does Trent always stay in the east guesthouse?"

Nora forced herself to breathe and waited to see what the girl would say. *Be smart, Jenny. Be smart.*

"Yeah, typically."

Nora winced and hoped they wouldn't pounce on the word.

"Typically?" God, that bitch detective. "Where else would he stay?"

"We're moving outside of the relevance of the crime." Jeff spoke for the first time in ages. "It doesn't matter where Mr. Iverson would stay on other visits. He was found in the guesthouse and has stayed there on frequent occasions in the past."

Easy, Jeff. Nora was torn between applauding and muzzling him. Curb the conversation, but don't protest too much and raise suspicion.

"How often did you meet Trent's guests?" the man asked.

"What do you mean?"

"Trent was found with a woman. How often did he bring people to the house?"

"Oh." She hummed a little in thought. "A lot of times. Brad Vincent came with him once. And Kevin Hersch. Oh, and that guy from the *America Vice* movies." She laughed. "Literally all the celebrities

I've ever seen in real life were people that were hanging out with Trent. Plus, of course, Nora and Hugh."

Oh, of course. Glad to know that she was an afterthought in Jenny's starstruck gush fest.

"What about women?" Farah asked. "Any female visitors?"

"No," Jenny said too quickly. "Never."

"Never until now," Farah pointed out.

"Yeah. I mean, I guess."

"Did his guests drive separately?" Kevin asked.

"Um, I don't really know. I mean, by the time everyone gets here, sometimes there's like ten cars in the back. I don't keep track—but I notice Trent's car. I mean, it kind of stands out."

Yeah, Trent's car did do that. The man didn't have a retirement plan, but he had a collector's-edition muscle car that could make your panties weep. That car was the thing that had first caught her eye. So impractical. So feral. So fucking sexy and powerful.

"Want to drive it?" Trent stopped beside her and crossed his arms over his chest, flashing her a grin that both challenged and enticed, all at once.

"Nah, I'm fine." Nora glanced up at the house, wondering what was taking Hugh so long. They should have left for the studio already, but Trent had unexpectedly shown up, and then Hugh had disappeared into the office with some paperwork he'd given him.

"Ah, come on. If I recall correctly, you're excellent at handling a stick."

She swallowed the smile that threatened to come, along with a memory of the two of them, in his father's truck, a dozen years earlier. Instead, she tossed her hair over one shoulder with a scoff. "Try your lines on the other girls, Trent."

He gave her a wounded look and took a step closer, his shoulder almost brushing against hers as they both regarded the car. "You know you want to," he whispered. "Come on. Put that sexy ass in her seat and open her up."

"In this neighborhood?" Nora asked dryly. "Great idea."

"*But you want to, right?*" *He leaned in and the question was soft, his voice almost guttural, and she stepped to the side, needing some space before she drowned in the intoxication of his presence.*

"*I'm good,*" *she snapped, and fought to remember why he was a hundred future mistakes rolled into one.*

Trent stayed in place, and when she glanced back at him, that smirk was on those famous lips, and it was amazing how two identical men could use the same features in such different, and equally devastating, ways. "Keep telling yourself that, princess." He chuckled and took the steps slowly, flipping the key chain around his finger as he approached the car at the curb. "And when you decide you aren't good, call me."

She had lasted four more months, and then she had done just that.

CHAPTER 30
THE MOM

When Miles's tumor first showed up on that MRI, I thought that our world was ending. I thought that you'd leave and that I'd have to take care of him on my own, and that we'd lose the house to bankruptcy and I'd break under the strain of it all.

I faced the idea that Miles would die, and suddenly all the annoying and infuriating things he did faded into the background, behind the overwhelming preciousness of his life.

You went through that roller coaster with me, Kyle, and instead of pushing us away, you brought us closer. You stopped going out with the guys, and texting strange women, and forgetting birthdays and anniversaries. You started to look at me as if I were a saint, and spent all your free time with Miles, and stopped spending money on crap and started saving it so that we could pay for whatever his treatment was going to cost.

We had no idea of the support that was going to come our way. It was amazing, when it hit. The online fundraiser, the food drop-offs, the Christmas shopping sprees, the scholarship, the spa coupons, and the Ronald McDonald grocery cards. Suddenly, we had everything. Money. Support. Sympathy. Attention.

It was really nice, Kyle. It felt like a big warm hug that I didn't want to end.

Months later, after the surgery, when the tumor was labeled as benign, everyone's concern dropped. Then Miles's scar healed and his hair started to grow back, and then everyone forgot that he was ever sick.

CHAPTER 31
THE LEADING MAN

The nice thing about Hugh's suite was that it was built for privacy. And now, in this moment, he needed the space. Needed the time to think.

Nora was hiding something. There were at least four different possibilities of what it could be, but he didn't have the mental fortitude to concentrate or decipher any of them. Right now, he just needed to get through today. Then tomorrow. Then the next day.

One day to a hundred.

One day to a thousand.

One day to forever.

The problem was, he wasn't sure he could make it through one day. Right now, he didn't want to make it through the next fifteen minutes, not without his twin.

Naked and dripping from the shower, he stood in front of the mirror that lined the massive primary bathroom. Placing his wet hands on the dark marble counter, he stared into his reflection.

Hugh Iverson. Academy Award winner. Hollywood's most beloved man. Future husband to Nora Kemp. Rich beyond measure. Respected without hesitation.

He had stared into that level of perfection for thirty-two years now. It was a part—a facade—that required precise strategy and diligent effort. While Trent had done whatever he wanted every day for decades, Hugh had followed a singular path. One where he played every hand in his deck flawlessly. A path destined for greatness, and he had achieved it. He had the perfect life.

The perfect woman.

The perfect reputation.

He stared into the mirror and wondered if it was too late to walk downstairs and confess everything. To give up this life. Squander all the hard work and the money and the fame behind it.

He needed his twin back. Needed the other half of his heart, needed the one person who didn't judge him, who loved him, despite the cracks in both of their souls. His brother was fucked up and damaged, but so was he. And now, without him, all he had was Nora.

Turning his head, he looked toward her suite, which took up the opposite end of the floor. Maybe he could tell her the truth. If anyone understood, she would. She'd had her own complicated relationship with both of them.

"Do you love him?" He'd asked her the question while they were naked, his body wrapped around hers, his leg over her hip.

She'd twisted in his grip, until she was facing him, her delicate breath huffing against his chin. "Of course I do."

"Like you love me?" He'd been both scared and desperate for the answer.

"I could never love anyone like I love you," she said softly.

"Then why are you with both of us?"

She had taken his hand and placed it between her legs. "Because right now, I need both chaos and stability. One day, I promise, I'll get over that and only be with you. He'll understand."

One day. He had never believed her. He'd wanted to, but never really had, until now.

Now, whether either of them wanted it or not, there was only one brother left.

One lost brother, a ship at sea that didn't know whether to moor to Nora or tie an anchor to her chest.

CHAPTER 32

THE DETECTIVE

"Next stop, Casa de la Trenta," Kevin intoned as they buckled into the SUV. He dangled the key chain they'd found in the ignition of Trent's Shelby. "It's on Loma Vista Drive. Fancy schmancy. Put it in the GPS?"

Farah took the set of keys, which were linked through a red carabiner. As Kevin pulled out of the Iverson gates, she tapped the address into the MDC computer mounted beside her seat. "Says seventeen minutes. Not too bad. Hopefully we can see most of it before dark."

"I already sent the address to Anaïca. She's meeting us there."

Farah swiveled in her seat to face him. "Don't tease me."

"I called the chief, asked him to assign her on."

"No you didn't."

He rolled to a stop at a four-way intersection and gestured for a vintage Mercedes to go ahead. "I did."

"And he agreed?"

He chuckled as he made the turn to the right. "You sound so surprised."

"I'm not," she defended, but she was. Anaïca was still green, with just three years on the force so far. With a case like this, Farah had assumed that—if a tech were assigned—it would be a senior officer, regardless of how strong her daughter's investigative skills might be.

"Well, good." She sat still for a moment, then let out a girlish shriek. "Oh my God, I'm so excited I could hug you. I won't, because you probably smell like Old Spice and body odor, but the idea of it, for once, is not cringeworthy."

"Well, that's very kind of you to say," Kevin said. "I should have Trish embroider that on a pillow."

"It's a little long for a pillow. I can come up with something snappier."

"Yeah, you do that."

"Thank you." She busied herself with the folder of interview notes and tried to contain her smile. This would be her first case with her daughter, at least in an official capacity. Kevin making the call would lessen the appearance of nepotism, though Anaïca would still bear some of the stigma. That was okay. Her daughter could overcome that hurdle. All she needed was the chance to prove herself, and this would be a shining opportunity.

"Don't mention it," Kevin said. "Besides, I'm not free. It'll cost you a breakfast croissant from Tasty's tomorrow."

"Deal," she said quickly. "I'll get you two. And here." She fished her second energy bar out of her pocket and held it out to him. "Consider this a bonus prize. Want to go over the neighborhood logs on the way?"

"Let's do it."

Farah flipped open the case folder and retrieved the printouts Dottie had shared. "Okay, let's see. Want to start with Trent's history or the exit/entrance logs for the last twenty-four hours?"

"Trent."

"All right, give me a second." Farah settled back against the leather seat. Scanning the report, she quickly understood its layout. The first few pages were one-liners showing when Trent had arrived and left the neighborhood. She studied the data, trying to see if there were any patterns there. He appeared to visit frequently during a period of time, and then there would be a gap, sometimes a month, sometimes three. That matched what Nora and the staff had said.

His visit times were all over the board. Sometimes two in the morning, sometimes one in the afternoon. A lot of late-night visits, some that crossed over to the next day, some that didn't. She glanced at Kevin. "You have a brother, right?"

"Yeah. A year older. Why?"

"How often do you see him?"

He shrugged. "Twice a month, give or take."

"There's a lot of activity here. In spurts, but still. Sometimes daily, but at least once a week, Trent comes to the house." Farah flipped to the beginning of the printout. The visits seemed to ramp up, with the first year being much lighter than the final. That being said, there were six-month stretches where the visits were rare, then frequent again. Did it mean anything? Probably not, but she still relayed the information to Kevin.

"Well, they are twins," Kevin pointed out. "Maybe they're closer than me and my idiot older brother."

That was a good point. Farah's nieces were only nine, but they were stuck to each other's sides on a constant basis, which was completely different from how Farah and the twins' mom had been when they were the same age.

She flipped to the call transcripts. There were only three, and each was in regard to a food-delivery authorization. Trent apparently liked pizza and Thai food. A man after her own heart.

She sat back and sighed, taking a moment to rest her eyes. "I think I need glasses."

"Welcome to old age. One day, it's like they just give up on you. Move the page farther away; it'll help."

She did, but it didn't. She put the reports to the side and returned to the computer, clicking on Trent's address and pulling up details of the home.

"Shit," she muttered. "Have you looked up this address?"

"No, just got it from Hugh and sent it to Anaïca. Why?"

She clicked on the property details and let out a low whistle. "We're gonna need a lot more uniforms."

CHAPTER 33

THE KID

Maybe he should have stayed where Mommy told him to.

Wait. That's what she had said. *Play with Mr. Frog and wait. I'll be right back.*

Normally he did wait. If you didn't do what Mommy said, bad things happened. Sometimes they were things like time-out, which really wasn't that bad, though he didn't want to tell Mommy that because she might trade it for a different punishment, and some of the punishments were really bad.

Like sentences. Wow, he hated sentences. It took *so* long, and if he didn't get every letter just like the one on the tracer, she made him start again.

And broccoli. Talk about gross. Jessica at school told him that her mom made her eat a broccoli birthday cake once. Apparently she had been so bad, all year long, that the cake and the icing and the layers inside—it was all broccoli.

Mommy wasn't that bad. And he hadn't been thinking about the possibility of a broccoli cake when he followed her. He had just wanted to ask her how long she would be gone. Because they had to get up early to go to Disneyland and it was already past their bedtime and if he didn't get a good night's sleep—this was what *she* always told him—he would be grouchy and tired the next day.

That was it—he was just going to ask that *one* question, which was why he'd followed Mommy.

And when she fell into the car like that, he just wanted to make sure she was okay. And when he called her name and the man she was talking to turned, he just wanted to make sure he wasn't a stranger, but then the man was pressing his head into a towel, one that tasted and smelled funny, and everything started to get dark and he thought that maybe this was what dying was.

And now he was here, and maybe this was Disneyland. Like, a waiting room at Disneyland.

But it didn't seem like Disneyland, unless Mommy was lying about what it was really like.

She did that sometimes.

CHAPTER 34
THE LEADING LADY

Nora couldn't find the attorney. With all nine staff interviews done, the cops had finally left, no one had been arrested, yet Jeff Bourdin was trying to duck out without talking to her.

She checked the cabana, then jogged around the exterior of the house, hoping to catch him in the driveway before he left. Moving down the side path, she spotted his ridiculous T-shirt over by his vehicle. He was talking to someone and she slowed her approach, then paused when she heard her name. Instinctively, she slipped into the shadows of a palm and crouched behind the hood of Hugh's Bentley. Carefully moving forward, she eased around the back of the car until she was just a few feet away.

It felt ridiculous to hide and eavesdrop, but the breeze was in her favor, and she needed all the information she could get right now.

"Hugh, you've got to relax. There are protections in place here. Just let the process do its thing."

"I need to know where in the house the police will have access to. What they can and can't search." His voice was thin and frantic, and she wondered what he was worried about the police finding.

"Depends on what they put in front of a judge and how that judge is feeling. Right now, they can search the guesthouse, his vehicle, and any portion of the home or property that he or the woman were in last night. The problem is that that location activity can be kind of hard to pinpoint, so technically, your whole house is at risk of search."

"Shit." There was the crunch of footsteps, and she tensed, afraid that her position would be seen. The sound receded, then increased. He must be pacing.

"Is there something you don't want the police to find?" Jeff asked.

"Doesn't everyone have something they don't want the police to find?"

"We have attorney-client privilege, Hugh," Jeff said. "Just tell me."

"There's some things in the basement I want to clean out. Nothing related to what happened last night—I just don't want the police to come across it."

"I can keep them out of the basement for now," Jeff assured him. "But I'd go ahead and do any housekeeping, just in case."

The two men said their goodbyes and Nora stayed in place, her question to Jeff abandoned as she heard the attorney's car door shut and the vehicle shift into gear.

There's some things in the basement I want to clean out.

Their home had two basements. The south one was used for storage, though Hugh also kept a secondary office and gym down there. The north one was more storage, mostly holiday decor and film paraphernalia and keepsakes.

Both were areas she ignored. Nora had her own fitness room on the third floor, an open, airy space with Pilates equipment, a bar, and weight machines for her butt, abs, and legs. She and Hugh didn't commingle their workouts, and if Nora could avoid the basements, she did.

Apparently, that needed to be rectified.

CHAPTER 35
THE MOM

Two years ago, in May, I joined a Facebook group for moms with sick kids. It was a support system—a way to talk to women who understood what I was going through.

It was also an enabler. A treasure chest of opportunities and insight into the possibilities that existed. There was a row on one of the threads one day. The conversation turned toxic, and several of us were kicked out of the group.

I tried to talk to you about it, but you were irritated about work, and then, a few months later, I was invited to join a different group. It was smaller, and it had a few of the moms who'd been kicked out of the other group.

Joining that group is why I'm going to die.

Of course, I didn't realize that in the beginning. At first, it was like I had found my people. Acceptance. And I loved it, ya know?

But clicking that button and accepting the invite— that was what started this hell.

CHAPTER 36

THE HUSBAND

Kyle purchased a one-way red-eye that was $468—an amount Kerry would lose her mind over, if only he could tell her. He printed out the receipt, checked into the flight, and sent his boarding pass to his phone.

There. And she always said he was useless on his own. He kept the browser open and went to Facebook, curious to see if Kerry had any messages from anyone, maybe a friend in California or an ex-boyfriend she was having an online affair with. Facebook, according to his softball teammates, was where all the hookups happened. Put up your profile on that or Instagram, and just start hitting on every woman you see, doubling down on your high school girlfriends.

Kyle knew his weaknesses, and it didn't take much more than a wink emoji to make him fall in love, so he'd stayed off everything, especially once Miles's tumor was found. Now, clicking past the log-in screen that remembered Kerry's details, he wondered if she had been the weak link in their marriage this whole time.

When the Facebook page loaded, he went straight to the messages, but they were all with other women, and at first glance, none of them seemed suspicious. They were mostly talking about other women, gossiping. His suspicions faded and he scrolled through her newsfeed.

Something was off, because the only posts in her feed were from a Facebook group. A quilting group, all full of women sharing photos of their families. Talk about boring. But also . . . had she changed a setting so that none of her friends' posts were showing? He clicked on her profile, then her friends list.

Another red flag flared. Kerry had once had over a thousand friends—ridiculous, because who actually knew that many people? But now she was down to zero. Zero friends. Cripes, she wasn't even friends with him.

He clicked on "Groups." Just the one quilting group.

He went back to messages. Glanced at the clock. He didn't have much time, not if he wanted to make sure that he made his flight. He clicked on the first message, scrolled down, boring boring boring . . .

Clicked on the next. Blah blah blah . . .

The third message was different, and he paused his scroll.

Kerry: Make-a-wish wants to send me and my son to Disneyland. All expenses paid.

Bonnie: Oh no. You aren't going, are you?

Kerry: My husband is making me. I can't get out of it.

Bonnie: You have to. Fake a sickness. Jump in front of a car. Do something.

Kerry: Maybe it'll be okay.

Bonnie: Don't risk it.

Kerry hadn't responded, and two days later, Bonnie had messaged again.

Bonnie: Kerry? Are you there?

The message had been delivered yesterday afternoon, probably when Kerry was midflight to California.

Kyle clicked on the woman's profile photo, bringing up her page. Kerry wasn't friends with her, and the profile was set to private, so there wasn't anything to see other than her background, which was a beach, and her profile photo, which showed a woman with platinum-blonde hair and a nose ring. She was in a hot-pink sports bra and matching leggings, straddling a bike and smiling, somewhere in a forest.

She wasn't Kerry's typical friend. This woman was at least five years younger than her and a lot hotter. She looked like a woman who enjoyed breaking a sweat and would bend into a pretzel while quoting Gandhi.

He typed a reply into the message box.

Can I call you? What's your number?

CHAPTER 37
THE DETECTIVE

The other uniforms had beaten them to the area, and Kevin slowed as they approached the six black-and-whites parked in a tight row along Trent's street. He flashed his lights as he passed, and they pulled out in neat order behind him.

"We're gonna look like a presidential convoy," Farah said.

"Or a funeral procession."

Farah studied the houses as they moved past. "Damn. I thought Hugh's neighborhood was nice, but this is *old* Hollywood money out here."

"You said this house belonged to their parents, and is now owned by a trust?"

"Yeah. I guess Trent won the coin flip to live in it." Farah glanced at the GPS screen. "Driveway should be coming up on the right."

"What happened to the parents? I remember the funeral but don't remember the cause."

"Yeah, I think everyone remembers that funeral. They died in a car accident, about ten years ago. Semi crossed the center line. Head-on collision." Farah had been in the morgue when their bodies had been brought in. Even in death, even mangled, Momma Beth had looked regal.

Farah pointed to an opening between two oak trees. "Here, this is it."

In Beverly Hills, parking spots went for six figures, so the size of the Iverson family estate was worthy of a long slow clap. The driveway was lengthy enough to be considered winding, and Farah glanced at Kevin as the SUV rolled along the paved entrance. "Nice, huh?"

"I didn't think this size of property still existed."

"Five and a half acres, based on the tax rolls. And forty-six thousand square feet. Almost double the size of Hugh's house."

"No wonder you called in the calvary."

Yeah, the extra bodies would be helpful in the search, but Farah hated to increase the pool of exposure. Between the crime scene techs, the famous body on a slab in the morgue, and now ten officers being brought in to search the old Iverson house—this would leak to a media outlet soon. Maybe it already had.

The massive house was almost hidden by heavy trees and hanging moss, and when the roof of it finally appeared, Farah inhaled with appreciation at what must have once been a masterpiece. Four stories tall, with Grecian arches and columns and framed by two enormous jacaranda trees, the white brick home had left and right wings that stretched out on either side.

A long algae-filled pool divided the entry and exit driveways, with overflowing gardens flanking each side. At one time, the beds had probably been neatly segmented by color and flower, but now they were heaping mounds of intermingled blooms that spilled out from their sections and journeyed along the pavered drive.

Anaïca's two-door Jeep was already parked to the side, behind a restored Bronco and a four-door late-model pickup truck. As they parked, her driver's door opened and she stepped out.

Anaïca was twenty-two years old and had inherited the dark coloring, wide hips, and generous proportions of her mother. She had not dressed to impress, and Farah's mouth tightened at the shirt-and-jeans combination that everyone on the TID team wore. As she always told her daughter, you never know what you might end up doing, or who you might end up meeting. Anaïca had selected a T-shirt of a cartoon baby with a football-shaped head, jeans, red Converse sneakers, and hoop earrings.

Granted, this was the same daughter who had shaved her head three months ago on a whim, so maybe Farah should give up on preaching about first impressions.

Kevin pulled her in for a hug, and Farah waited patiently for her turn. When she had her daughter tight to her chest, she put her mouth against her ear. "So glad you're officially assigned to this."

"Me too, Madre." Her daughter smacked a kiss on her cheek, then pulled back. "What's with all the backup?" She nodded to the cars, which were parking diagonally around the drive.

"They'll be assisting with the search. Ya know, big house. We don't want to be here all night."

"Right." She snapped her gum and gave a cheery wave to a ripped beat cop who was way too old for her.

Farah cleared her throat and held up Trent's key ring. "Ready?"

Anaïca rubbed her palms together. "Let's walk and talk. I need to catch you up on the history I've dug up so far."

As the other officers hung back, Farah and Kevin flanked Ana as they started up the wide steps of the massive front porch.

Anaïca kept her voice low, her eyes on the palatial mansion before them. "So, of course, Trent and Hugh are the only kids of Momma Beth and her husband, Royce. Royce and Momma Beth started the Church of Christians back in the eighties and made their fortunes on being the first nationally syndicated gospel service. If you turned on a television on a Sunday morning in the eighties and nineties, Momma Beth was who you saw on the pulpit."

Farah nodded as they stopped at the front door. "Your grandma loved that show. Remember?"

"She'd bite off your head if you considered changing the channel." Ana grinned.

Farah could remember the tiny television set in the living room and that faded image of Momma Beth, in her standard blue robe, smiling warmly into the camera as she delivered that week's sermon. Farah's mother had practiced her English, repeating after the pastor, but her pronunciation had always been hard and halting. Momma Beth's voice had been like a bowl of cinnamon oatmeal. Comforting, sweet, and filling.

It was hard to believe the cherubic woman who had captivated the nation and built a million-member church was Trent and Hugh's mother. They'd been born into looks, wealth, and the mother that all of America was in love with. Talk about winning the genetic lottery.

Kevin squinted in the fading light, trying to see enough to try the first key in the lock. "You said fortunes. How much money we talking about?"

"Tens of millions, just from the television rights. Add to that the donations, which were called in every Sunday, and the Church of Christians was worth, around the time of their deaths, about a hundred million dollars."

Kevin whistled as he gave up on that key and tried the next. "Not too shabby."

"Yeah, well, don't get too excited. When Momma Beth and Royce died, all their money went to the charity. The twins didn't get a dollar, except for this house, which is in a trust and can't be sold. The charity is, of course . . ." She paused and looked at them expectantly.

"Protect the Children?" Farah guessed. You couldn't live in Los Angeles without spotting a billboard or magazine with a photo of Trent or Hugh posing with a cancer-ridden kid or a group of underprivileged teens who had been awarded scholarships. Protect the Children had sponsored Anaïca's soccer team when they qualified for the state championship and had given college scholarships to two of her friends. The charity had a glowing reputation in the state and had been spearheaded by Momma Beth before the twins stepped in as spokesmodels.

Anaïca made a dinging sound of approval. "That's the one."

Farah glanced up. On one of the upper windows, a black shutter hung off one side, and birds had built nests in the eaves under the porch roof. The house would need an enormous amount of work, and money, to get it back into showplace condition.

"This key fits." Kevin wheezed upright. "Let's glove up."

Several minutes passed while they all donned gloves, disposable hairnets, and booties. Anaïca snapped her gloves on and jumped a little in place. "This is exciting. Shit like this never happens in the pen."

"Yes, how kind of innocent victims to die," Farah said dryly.

Anaïca ignored her and leaned against the white brick wall. "So, anyway. You've got these two rich parents who are Jesus freaks, and when Trent and Hugh become old enough to join the brand, they decided to expand their television contract with an additional show, one aimed at a younger viewership, and starring . . . big surprise . . . their twins." Anaïca rolled her eyes, like she hadn't been obsessed with the show.

"You're talking about *Story Farm*," Kevin said.

"Yep. Five seasons, sixty-five episodes. Trent and Hugh's fame is created, and by the time *Story Farm* is canceled, they already have a dozen other offers from studios. Surprisingly, they stop acting and enroll in a private high school, where they live like 'normal'"—Anaïca put the word in quotes—"teenagers until they graduate."

Kevin straightened, his booties in place, and pushed open the door. They all paused, expectantly, listening for an alarm to sound. When nothing happened, he stepped in the front door, and they followed suit.

"Alarm pad here," Anaïca announced, striding to a small white pad mounted on the wall. She pressed a series of buttons, then turned around with a shrug. "It's disabled. Guess Trent isn't worried about intruders."

Farah said nothing, just stared at the giant round room before them.

It was too big to be called a foyer—the size of a basketball half-court and just as tall. The ceiling was domed and had a mural of heaven, with a huge jeweled chandelier that extended from its center. With evening starting to fall around them, the room was dark. She reached out and flipped a series of switches beside the front doors.

Nothing happened.

"This place is creepy," Anaïca announced, peering into the left sitting room, which was empty except for an Aerosmith-themed pinball machine in the corner with a brown cord stretched from it to a plug in the wall. "Like, where's all the furniture?"

Farah wandered to the right, through another empty sitting room, and into a library, which had empty, dust-covered shelves and a mattress on the floor, a few pillows tossed on its pile of sheets. Beside the mattress was a collection of beer cans and some opened wine bottles. Classy. "Yeah. Maybe we don't need the search team after all. Won't take long to wander through an empty mansion, no matter how big it is."

"Come in here," Kevin called from another part of the house, and Farah retraced her steps to find him in a sunken living room. This area looked well used, with a red leather sectional facing a giant television, and a pool table off to one side, balls and sticks on its velvet surface. The television was on, the screen displaying a message that the pay-per-view event had ended. Kevin pointed at it. "That's probably the UFC fight that was on last night. Fight was at seven. So he was here at some point last night. Maybe the woman was too."

Farah glanced around the room. "We could have the team start in here."

"Yeah." Anaïca leaned over and examined a glass on the coffee table in front of the couch. "Probably *lots* of DNA to go through. Wouldn't want to blacklight this place."

Farah paused in the doorway of the kitchen, which had more bottles of beer and a stack of pizza boxes. "No wonder he'd stay at Hugh's. He probably needed fresh towels and toilet paper."

"Yeah, this isn't exactly fit for guests," Kevin said.

"Depends on the guest," Anaïca chimed in. "Ignoring the square footage, this is about on par for guys my age. I'd be down with it."

Great, Farah thought. *So much for raising a daughter with standards.*

"See any signs of a female? We're still missing her phone and any wallet or purse." Kevin moved some of the pillows on the couch and looked under the coffee table.

"I'm out of the loop. Who's the female?" Anaïca asked.

"There was a dead body with Trent. She's a Jane Doe so far. You haven't seen the file yet?" Farah glanced up to the second floor, wondering where Trent's bedroom was.

"No, but I'll log in to the database as soon as I get back to my desk and study the files."

Farah waved the uniforms in and directed a pair to the living room, then sent the rest up the grand staircase to the upper floors.

Closing the front door, she wandered down the left hall. The walls were bare, with picture lighting aimed down to empty plaster. The air smelled faintly of mothballs and marijuana. There was a thin layer of dust on the floor, with a clear path of shoe and footprints that trafficked down the center, then led to a door on the right. Farah glanced in the open doors on either side—all empty rooms—then nudged the popular door with the toe of her shoe, swinging it open.

Ding, ding, ding. At long last. The bedroom of one of Hollywood's most desired men.

Talk about disappointing.

The walls were pale blue, the windows uncovered, the dusk light gently revealing the space. She tried the switch on the wall and this one worked, wall sconces illuminating a king-size bed, the gray sheets and blankets in a tangled knot. There were more beers on the bedside table and the dresser. An overflowing hamper by the closet and a row of gym shoes along the wall. An open door to the left revealed a bathroom with avocado-green wall tile. Farah approached the bedside table and squatted, looking over the mess. One item in the midst of the amber bottles stood out.

"Well," she drawled. "Lookee here."

CHAPTER 38
THE LEADING LADY

It hadn't been fair, having two of them, mirrors that showed different reflections. When Nora stepped in front of Hugh, she was a project, a future star with unlimited potential, a career that he could engineer for success. When Nora stepped in front of Trent, she was a sexual goddess he craved with an addiction unmatched by drugs or alcohol.

It should have been enough, just having one of them. Any woman in the world would have been ecstatic with the attention and love of a single Iverson brother.

But not her. No, Nora had needed both the security of Hugh and the passion of Trent. She had tried to be with just one, had made her choice clear to both of them, and then reneged on that decision after just a few months of Trent's efforts.

The root problem was that she had given her heart to Trent years ago, and he had never, not in the decade that she was away, given it back.

"What are you doing in here?" One of the twins stood before her, looking down, his face twisted in confusion.

"I, um." Nora glanced around, trying to come up with a plausible explanation for why she was still at the studio, hours after filming had ceased. *"I don't know. Why are you here?"*

"Dad's up in the office." He jerked a thumb toward the staircase that led to the Story Farm *production offices*, and in the casual gesture, she identified him as Trent.

"Are you sleeping here?" He tilted his head to the right, trying to see what she was sitting on, and she pushed her jean jacket farther behind her, irritated that she hadn't heard him approach. She must have dozed off while leaning against the post. She had planned to wait here, in the shadows of the soundstage stairwell, until the night security began their sweep of the production offices. Then she'd sneak into the garage and sleep on one of the padded golf cart seats. The six seater was wide enough that she could lie on her side with her knees bent and be pretty comfortable—and hidden—until morning.

She snorted. "No," she said as haughtily as possible. "I'm just waiting on my dad. He's running late to pick me up."

It wasn't exactly a lie. He was late—about three days late—to pick her up, but no one had noticed so far. The show's wardrobe changes had supplied her with a fresh outfit each day, the craft services table had kept her fed, and she'd used the small shower in their dressing room to freshen up on lunch breaks.

It wasn't the first time, and wouldn't be the last, that her father had taken a short hiatus from parenting. As a daughter, she could never compete with a bar, or a woman, or a poker game, or even a hangover. She was, at least, an excellent payday, according to him. Ugly as hell, but profitable as heaven. That was his favorite line, one he'd deliver to anyone who would listen, and one he found knee-slappingly witty, given the religious connection of the show.

She didn't find it witty. She hated it, hated him, hated herself for hating her father, and hated her mother for leaving them both.

"You are sleeping here," Trent said, lowering his voice and crouching beside her, his eyes growing wide with the realization.

"Oh my God," she snapped. "I'm not. Go away. Please."

"It's okay, I won't tell anyone." He grinned at her. "It'll be our secret."

And it was. It was their secret when he stole her a key to the furniture trailer, and she started spending each night on a couch instead of a golf cart.

It was their secret when he winked at her and suggested they have a cast retreat at his house over the winter hiatus.

It was their secret when her dad showed back up, drunk and looking for her paycheck, and she had a bruise on her cheekbone the next day. Trent iced it and stole her some makeup from the set and told her that she should run away and that he would protect her.

She was thirteen and he was fourteen and she was in love and he was her protector.

Then the show was canceled, and she was sent back to Kansas.

CHAPTER 39
THE HUSBAND

Kyle threw a pair of jeans, a few T-shirts, and his shaving kit into a backpack. He checked Kerry's computer—still no response from Bonnie—then poured a few days' worth of food out for the cat and refilled her water. He checked the litter box, warred over changing it, then did.

He didn't have time for this shit, and there wasn't enough litter in the bag, so he had to go to the garage to get more, and he should have left five minutes ago but still checked the computer one last time.

Bonnie had responded, and he stared at the answer.

You know we can't do phone. Call me through messenger.

You know we can't do phone. Well, why the hell not? Kerry, who had always been a bit dull, was getting a lot more interesting. And dontcha know, turns out he liked a dull wife better.

Kyle hitched his backpack higher on his back and checked the clock. It was a thirty-minute drive to the Green Bay airport. He was already late and didn't even know how to call through—

A pop-up appeared, along with an incessantly loud ringing sound. Bonnie's face appeared in a bubble in the middle of it. There was a green

"Answer" button, and he clicked on it. "Hello?" he called out, not sure whether Kerry's computer had a microphone attached to it.

There was a bump on the line, like someone had knocked the phone over. "Who's this?" The woman's voice was sharp and suspicious.

Kyle spoke quickly, worried she would hang up. "My name is Kyle. I'm Kerry's husband. She's on a trip to California, but we're having trouble finding her. I know this is crazy, but maybe you know where she's at?"

The woman stayed silent. Kyle waited, then tried again: "Your messages with Kerry—why didn't you want her to go to California?"

"I can't talk about that," she said quietly, her voice strained.

"Please," he begged. "I don't know what's going on. Is she leaving me? Does she have Miles?"

"You're missing your kid too?" Alarm coated the question, and he wanted to reach through the computer and shake the answers out of this woman.

"Yes," he spat out. "Please. What do ya know?"

"I don't know anything," she said, her voice dropping to almost a whisper. "None of us do."

The call ended, and he clicked frantically on her name, trying to figure out how to reactivate the call. It wasn't working, nothing was working, and when he tried to send her another message, an error popped up.

This Person Is Unavailable

Kyle stood and grabbed his keys, out of time to try and figure out what the problem was.

I don't know anything, she had said. *None of us do.*

Who was *us*?

CHAPTER 40

THE ACCOMPLICE

Kerry Pepper had been swallowed up by Los Angeles and had left her kid behind. That was the theory the police were giving Protect the Children, and it was giving Nolan Price hives.

While a runaway mother was a possibility, there was a greater chance, at least in his mind, that the mother was dead. Probably in a gruesome manner. His mind had been running on horrible repeat through a variety of possibilities. Any minute, her body would turn up, likely with Nolan's business card gripped in her bloody fist.

So far, Nolan didn't seem to be under suspicion. When Officer Meeko had called earlier, Nolan had gone through a shocked "what could possibly have happened, I don't understand" routine, and the man seemed to have bought it. Thank God Nolan had gone up to the hotel room and knocked on the door. The Radisson's cameras, which he hadn't even thought about, would show his journey through the lobby and up the elevator, and what murderer could check on her and be killing her at the same time? Clearly, Nolan was innocent. Clearly.

Clearly.

Clearly.

Clearly.

"God, you're mopey," Josie complained from his perch on the kitchen counter. His boyfriend had a carrot stick in one hand, his phone in the other, and a big tub of ranch in his lap. As Nolan watched, he took a big swipe of dressing and stuck the end result into his mouth, munching happily away as he scrolled through his phone.

Nolan should have just ignored Kerry's name. When it came up in his search, he should have done the Christian thing and just kept scrolling. He should have learned his lesson with Monica, listened to his gut, and kept Kerry and Miles Pepper off the radar. *No Make-A-Wish trip for you, little kid—but hey, your mom gets to live.*

"I don't get why you're so down. Is this about your mother?" Josie rummaged in the bag on the counter for another stick, and they had an eat-at table for a reason. There was no need for him to sit on the counter in his pajamas and double-dip into the dressing.

Nolan was about to snap at him about it when the rail-thin man straightened, his eyes growing big at whatever was on his phone. "Oh my sweet Jesus."

Nolan's gut spoke first, warning him. This was bad, something bad—though how it had gotten to Josie before him was a mystery.

"Nolaaaannnn," Josie gasped out. "Have you seen TMZ?"

No, of course he hadn't seen TMZ. Nolan was in a dressing gown, sipping a glass of Merlot and reading a book about Cambodia's history of ethnic strife. "What is it?"

"It's Trent Iverson." Josie held out the phone and showed him the headline on his screen. "That sexy bitch is dead."

CHAPTER 41
THE DETECTIVE

As the news of Trent's death ricocheted around the internet, Farah bent forward, studying the item that was propped against the bedside table lamp.

It was a photo of Nora, beaming into the camera, wearing a men's shirt and standing beside a horse. Cutoff shorts were just visible under the hem of the blue shirt, and she was all long legs and white teeth. It was an innocent photo yet felt strangely intimate—a private moment. She yelled for Kevin and Anaïca and gingerly picked it up by the edges.

Kevin appeared in the doorway. "This his bedroom?"

"Looks like it." Farah extended the photo toward him. "This was on the bedside table. Seem strange to you?"

"Yeah, seems odd." Kevin bent forward, studying it.

"Maybe he was in love with her," Farah suggested.

"Or just sleeping with her."

She shook her head. "No, this is more personal. This is . . ." She turned to see Anaïca step into the room. "Ana, was Trent dating anyone?"

"Not right now. His last relationship was with Willow Black. They broke up two years ago, in July. She was a screenwriter. Heavy into partying. They dated for three and a half months."

"Why'd they break up?"

"Because of Nora."

Farah paused. "I'm sorry, what?"

"Willow and Nora hated each other. Word is that the fighting between the girlfriends got too bad, so Trent broke it off."

"So it wasn't because he was sleeping with Nora?" Farah asked.

"What?!" Her daughter let out a strangled laugh. "Not according to anything I've seen." She raised one pierced brow. "Wait, did Nora admit to that?"

"No." Farah held up the photo. "But does this seem suspicious to you? Trent had it on his bedside table."

She didn't touch the photo, just moved closer and peered at it. "Yeah. Super suspicious. Lucky bitch."

"What's Nora's background? Did she date around before Hugh?" Kevin leaned against the bedroom wall and crossed his legs at the ankle.

Anaïca hissed out a breath. "How far back do you want me to go?"

"How about when she arrived in LA?"

She cracked her knuckles. "Well, that's not easy to say. I mean, I've tracked her back six years. That was when Nora Kemp first appeared on the scene. And to answer your question, no—she didn't date around. She has a super-clean reputation in LA. But prior to that?" She shrugged. "I have no idea."

"What do you mean, you have no idea?" Farah drilled. Anaïca always had *some* idea.

"I mean that she's got a nice backstory that would satisfy ninety-nine percent of researchers, but I'm not buying it. It's well done, I'll give her that. She's got a paper trail that goes to Texas and is just specific enough to be legitimate but just vague enough to not be pinpointed. I think it's bullshit, but I'll need a full week to find leaks in it, if you even want me to."

It was a red flag, but one that Farah could ignore over the bigger, more glaring possibility that Nora had been boning both Iverson brothers.

"Okay. So let's go back six years and tell—"

All three of their phones chimed at once with a loud and incessant alarm, one that Farah ignored. "Tell me what you know. When did she meet—"

"Hold that." Kevin looked at his phone, reading the alert. "Amber Alert. Missing six-year-old, possibly with his mother."

"Yeah, so?" Farah fished out her phone and looked at the notification. There was a link to the report, and she clicked on it.

Her heart stilled at the photo, which was of an adorable little bald child and a woman with auburn hair. The dead woman from the Iverson house. She scrolled down to see her name. *Kerry Pepper.*

She met Kevin's distraught face. Six years old. She had barely thought about the woman or her family, outside the context of the investigation. Hadn't considered a child, not one who might be tied to the crime.

Six years old. She looked at the photo. The child looked sickly, and she couldn't think of any non-heartbreaking reason for a young child to be bald.

"I'll call the station now." Kevin lifted the phone to his ear.

Six years old. She stood and looked around Trent's bedroom with renewed purpose. Somehow this woman had ended up with him and dead. It was their job to find out how and why.

CHAPTER 42
THE HUSBAND

Kyle tried Officer Meeko on the drive to Green Bay. He left a message, then parked in the long-term lot, sprinted to the terminal, and sweated his way through security, letting out a sigh of relief when he made it through with fifteen minutes to spare before boarding.

He was buying a pack of sunflower seeds and a bottled water when the officer returned his call. Handing the attendant his debit card, he answered.

"I don't have good news, Kyle."

His information about the Facebook woman fell to the wayside at the man's tone. "What?"

"A woman matching Kerry's description was found this morning. She was unidentified until the Amber Alert went out for Miles and the detectives put two and two together. We're running prints, but I sent over the photo you provided and it looks like a match."

"Found?" The woman was holding out his card and he took it dumbly, along with the bag of items. "Where is she?" Someone behind him cleared their throat, and he moved to the side until he was back in the terminal and in front of an empty seat.

"I'm sorry, Kyle. She's dead."

His butt hit the hard seat. This couldn't be real. "Are you sure?"

"Did Kerry have a dolphin tattoo on her right ankle?"

He pinched his eyes closed, picturing the simple black drawing that she'd gotten done when they were on their honeymoon in Panama City Beach. She'd wanted it in color but fainted just before the outline was complete, so she had bailed on the rest, promising herself that she would have it done later, but never had. They'd said they would go back to Florida, but never had.

Now they never could.

"Yes." The word was too soft, and he cleared his throat and tried again. "Yes, she does." Even with the hours of worrying, of processing what might be happening with her—he hadn't arrived at this possibility. And if she was dead . . . Panic ripped through him. "What about Miles?"

"We don't know. There was no sign of him at the crime scene, but trust me, we're bringing in as many uniforms as we need to on this. We'll find him."

"Crime scene? What—what happened to Kerry?" So this was worse than a hit-and-run or an overdose in the bathroom. They announced the boarding for his flight, and he grabbed his backpack and stood.

The officer sighed. "It was a murder, in a private residence. I can't really tell you more until you get here."

"A private residence. So she was having an affair?" And she'd taken Miles to this lunatic's house.

"It's more complicated than that, but no, I don't think she was having an affair. When can you get here?"

"I'm at the airport, waiting on the red-eye now. I change planes in Houston, and I'll get to Los Angeles around 5:00 a.m., something like that."

"I'll text you the address to the police station. Call me when you arrive and we can meet there, unless you want to check into a hotel first."

"Okay." He would have to tell Kerry's parents. Was it too late? He looked at his watch, then realized that he wasn't wearing it. He'd also forgotten a phone charger. Cripes. He cleared his throat. "How did— how did she die?"

"We're trying to figure out the circumstances, but she has some knife wounds."

That didn't make any sense. Not Kerry—who made brownie-marshmallow squares and put them in his glove box, along with apple-scented hand sanitizers. "So you think the person who killed her has Miles?" Maybe this was all a nightmare, one of those where things started to twist into such strange and unnatural situations that his brain finally realized it was making all the shit up and he forced himself to wake up.

"Like I said, we're trying to figure out the circumstances. She was found almost twenty miles away from the hotel, in Beverly Hills."

Beverly Hills. A private residence. His confusion multiplied.

Stabbed. He couldn't wrap his head around that. He couldn't take care of Miles without her. She knew all his medicine, all his doctor's appointments, all the things to do when Miles had an issue.

The office drawer popped to mind and the long row of orange bottles on the desk. He pushed the image aside.

"I've got to go," the officer said. "But I do have one quick question."

"Yeah?" Kyle watched helplessly as a toddler ran past a baggage cart, chased by a haggard mom wearing an apologetic frown.

"Did Kerry know Trent Iverson?"

CHAPTER 43
THE MOM

What's great about a support group, you know, is that in that group, you aren't the weird one. You're the normal one, and when the first person doesn't gasp or react when something crazy is said, then the second person doesn't either, and before you know it, someone can post about food additives that can trigger vomiting or creams that cause hair loss, and no one blinks. Everyone accepts.

When Miles's surgery went well and our lives returned to normal, they were the only ones I could turn to with my disappointment. They were the only place, in a world where I had to have a happy face all the time, that I could mourn what I was losing.

And then, Kyle, you turned to Her. The fire alarm in our marriage had been muted, and things began to return to normal, and you went back to Life Before Miles's Tumor.

You started going out again.
Working late.
Drinking again.
Being on your phone.

Working out.

Ignoring me.

I followed you once. I strapped Miles into the booster seat and drove to the plumbing office and waited in the shade of a tree for you to come out. There you were, your phone to your ear, a shit-eating grin stretched across your face, your key ring flipping through your hand as you walked toward that giant extended-cab truck that we couldn't afford yet you still had to have. I watched as you drove to the honky-tonk bar right across the county line, the one that sells buckets of brewskis. I watched as you met that Trixie in the parking lot, and slung your arm around her neck, and kissed her on the top of the head and then on the lips.

I refused to let you go, Kyle. We were a family. We were married. You loved me, even if you didn't remember it in that moment in time.

I needed to get you back and knew how to do it. I knew how to put everything back together again.

CHAPTER 44
THE DETECTIVE

The massive house wasn't done sharing its secrets. In the opposite wing from Trent's bedroom were a laundry center, a chef's kitchen, and a room that had been burned almost to the ground.

Farah, Anaïca, and Kevin stood in the middle of the room and tried to decipher what the room had once been used for. The far exterior wall was burned past the Sheetrock, down to the concrete block and rebar. A portion of the roof was missing, and ceramic tiles and branches had fallen into the space, with a wedge of purple and pink sky visible.

A blowtorch backpack had been dropped in one corner beside a red plastic can of gas. Farah lifted the can. "Empty."

Anaïca sniffed the air. "If it was burned, it was a while ago. Just smells moldy in here."

"Walls over here are tile," Kevin remarked, knocking on the surface. "Kinda odd."

"There's some cabinets here." On the interior wall, Anaïca tugged on a handle, trying to get the door open. Kevin reached over, putting his meat hook of a hand into play. The door cracked, then broke open, and they all leaned in to see the contents.

Medical supplies. The packaging was dusty, the faces of the bottles and bandages covered in a strip of soot that had come through the cracked cabinet.

Farah twisted to look at the table, or what was left of it, that had been in the middle of the room. It had metal legs, and she had assumed it to be a work desk on wheels, but now she understood. It was an examination table. "It's a medical clinic."

"Odd addition to a house," Kevin drawled.

"Remember the autopsy?" Farah asked. "All of the damage that wasn't on Trent's medical record? Maybe it was fixed here."

Kevin looked to Anaïca. "Momma Beth or Royce have any medical training?"

"Not that I know of."

They fell silent. After a few minutes, Farah brushed the soot off her hands and headed back to the hall. "Let's keep moving. See if they've found anything upstairs."

As they climbed one side of the wide marble staircase, Farah ran her hand along the bronze railing. "I feel like I need a ball gown."

Anaïca let out a giggle that was almost musical in nature. "I'm not sure that is necessary. Rumors are that this place was an orgy fest when Trent threw parties. Someone probably screwed all over this staircase."

Farah pulled her hand off the rail. "Thank you, my dear child, for ruining my fun."

"Well, that's what I'm here for," she said cheerfully. "Oh hot damn, look." She pointed to a life-size portrait of four young teens, all leaning into each other on a log in the woods. It was a painting but just realistic enough to make you take a second look. The framed piece was at the top of the stairs, beside a similar painting of Momma Beth and Royce, dressed in finery and holding Bibles.

Someone had taken a can of spray paint and decorated both of the paintings. In the foursome of teens, two were clearly Trent and Hugh, but the other two—a chubby brunette and a Black boy with glasses—looked only vaguely familiar. "These are the kids from *Story Farm*, right?" Farah asked.

"Yep. Dennis and Margaret. Margaret was the girl from the wrong side of the tracks, and Dennis was the smart one." She tapped her finger on the yellow graffiti. "Wonder who did this."

The spray painter had drawn a halo on one of the twins' heads and devil horns on the other. They'd also drawn a heart on the girl's chest and left the boy untouched.

"I'm more curious about this one," Kevin said, pointing to the painting of the famous couple.

Momma Beth had angel wings added and Xs over both of her eyes. Her husband had a painted-on noose, coming from the top of the painting and cinched tight around his neck.

"Weird," Anaïca remarked.

Yeah, Farah thought. *Super weird.*

CHAPTER 45
THE DETECTIVE

Trent Iverson has died at the age of 32.

Multiple sources connected to the actor tell us that he passed away Friday night at his twin brother's home in Beverly Hills. Trent is most famous for his adolescent role as Paul Baker in "Story Farm" and his bad-boy behavior, which has often landed him in hot water with the public, movie studios, and the press. Trent has battled an addiction to drugs and alcohol since his adolescence. At this time, it is unknown if those substances played a role in his death.

The Los Angeles Police Department responded to a 9-1-1 call to the Iverson residence on Saturday morning around 10 a.m., after a staff member found Trent and an unidentified woman in a building on the property. Our sources report that he died during the night.

Trent's twin brother is Academy Award–winner Hugh Iverson, who is engaged to actress Nora Kemp. Hugh is known for his blockbuster roles in movies such as "Galaxy Force," "Roar of the Elephants," "Columbia," "For Fear of Dying," and "V Square." Hugh has not issued a statement at the time of press.

"Dammit." The chief slammed a palm on his desk. "This place leaks like a sieve."

Farah tried not to yawn, but she was running on fumes and it was almost midnight. "I'm actually impressed it took this long."

The chief ignored her and fixed his watery green stare on Kevin. "You know what this means. All eyes are on us. Both of you look like you're about to fall over, so go home and get some sleep."

"What do you know about the boy?" Farah linked her hands together on her stomach and spun her rolling chair slightly to the side.

"Miles Pepper? Almost nothing. He walked out of the hotel with his mom around ten o'clock last night. That's all we got."

"Where's his father?" Kevin asked.

"Getting a flight here. The family is from Wisconsin, so that's where he's coming from."

Farah frowned. "What were they doing here?"

"Kid was on a Make-A-Wish trip to Disneyland. He's got a brain tumor."

"Make-A-Wish," Kevin said slowly. "What organization is sponsoring the trip?"

As soon as he asked the question, Farah connected the dots. *Of course.*

The chief shrugged. "Don't know. Work with Sam Meeko—he's the one assigned."

On their way out, she caught up with Kevin. "You think Protect the Children brought the kid to Los Angeles?"

"It'd be the only possible connection I can see so far. Tomorrow morning, let's talk to the organization, see what we can find out."

He held out his fist, and she bumped it with her own. "Don't forget my croissants tomorrow morning."

"Wouldn't dream of it."

CHAPTER 46

THE LEADING MAN

Years ago, Hugh had renovated his home's south and north basements, which had been left unfinished by the original developer. Crews had worked for a solid two months to reinsulate and fortify the area, install fiber-optic cables for internet, and upgrade the wiring, plumbing, and HVAC. They'd built rooms in the large open spaces and added a vault-like door to a newly created office, which they'd secured with an electronic keypad that the staff was restricted from.

Now, as his future wife soaked in a tub upstairs, he entered the south basement and headed to the office. He pressed his finger to the pad, and the lock clicked open. Stepping into the private sanctuary that held Hugh's deepest secrets, he closed the door behind him.

The room looked like any other home office. A line of cabinets. A desk calendar, mounted vertically to the wall. A computer and chair. A printer, shredder, and trash can.

He was going to need a bigger trash can and a match.

Taking a seat at the desk, he pulled open the top file drawer and quickly flipped through the folders, each one labeled by name. It was the drawer of possibilities, and he pulled out the first folder and flipped it open.

The folder was labeled *Theresa Biggle*, and inside there was the printout of a woman's photo, clipped to pages of handwritten notes. She was older than most of them. In her fifties, with salt-and-pepper hair and a pear-shaped body.

He spun to the shredder and held the folder over the mouth of it, then hesitated, his gaze drifting to the drawer. There were years invested in these files, thousands of hours in this room, watching these individuals and recording their progress.

Destroying the files meant throwing all that away.

Maybe there wasn't any harm in leaving them here. He could shut the door, go upstairs to his bedroom, and ignore the files. He could continue on with his life and pretend there wasn't a bomb of horrors below the mansion, loudly ticking its way toward destruction.

He stared at the folder for a long moment, then forced its girth through the mouth of the shredder and let the razor-sharp teeth chop it into confetti-size pieces.

And just like that, Theresa Biggle's life was spared.

It took less than fifteen minutes, and then it was done. He bagged all of it up, including the calendar, and carried it upstairs, where he tossed the bag into his bedroom's fireplace, added a few logs, and lit the edge of the plastic bag. The computer still needed to be handled, but he could do that after he saw every bit of this evidence turn to ash.

Sitting on the chair by the fireplace, he uncorked a bottle of wine, skipped a glass, and tilted it back to his mouth.

As the alcohol filled his belly, he watched it all burn.

CHAPTER 47
THE LEADING LADY

Nora silently moved past Hugh's bedroom. The door was shut, the room quiet. He was probably asleep. She had reheated plates of leftovers—lobster risotto and caramelized brussels sprouts—and he had barely spoken during the meal, which was fine with her. She had her own things to think about, and the grief was warring with the horrible things that seemed to be coming from every direction.

She needed to check the basement, needed to see what could possibly be down there that he was worried about the police finding. She was surprised that Jeff hadn't pushed harder with his questions, but that was Jeff for you. Nosy when she needed him to mind his own business and quiet when she didn't.

Once she'd finished eating dinner, she had excused herself to take a bath and killed an hour soaking in the giant tub as she'd kept an ear out for his movements in the house. Finally, almost an hour after she'd gone upstairs, she heard his steps on the stairs and the click of his bedroom door. She'd waited another fifteen minutes and now was at the staircase, her socked feet quiet on the steps, her body stiff for any sounds from behind her.

This was ridiculous, her sneaking around. She could just ask him, but there was the risk of him lying or, worse, covering his tracks.

No, her figuring out the truth was better. She moved through the first floor, skipping the elevator and taking the rear stairs, off the guest-bedroom wing. Normally, at the basement landing, she would have turned right, but this time she pressed on the door to the left—the one that opened to the south basement stairs. The door was locked and she paused, surprised. She used her fingerprint to open so many other locations in the house that she didn't think twice about it, but now she held her breath as she placed her index finger on the pad.

It glowed green, and the door clicked open. She passed through with a relieved sigh, then checked the first room to the right.

Every door seemed to be locked, and this level of security was ridiculous. There was no need for this stuff to be secured. She flipped on the light switch, revealing neat stacks of bankers boxes. Walking down the rows, she examined the labels. Tax returns, corporate documents, and personal files. *Okay,* she admitted grudgingly. *Maybe these should be locked up.*

Returning to the hall, she turned off the light and shut the door, moving to the next. There were two more rooms of miscellaneous items; then she reached Hugh's gym. He used this room frequently, and she walked slowly through the cavernous space, studying the weight benches, boxing bag, ice baths, and sauna without finding anything he'd care about hiding.

Moving to the opposite side of the hall, she unlocked and swung open the first door, then flipped on the light.

Stepping in, she let out an unexpected scream at the sight of a bald kid sitting cross-legged on the floor, who stared up at her in surprise.

CHAPTER 48
THE LEADING LADY

"Who the fuck are you?" Nora hissed out, and the kid's eyes widened at the curse word.

"I'm Miles." His face glistened with dried tears, and he held a green stuffed animal to his chest.

Nora immediately crouched and winced at her behavior. "I'm so sorry, Miles. I—how did you get here? How long have you been in here?"

She must have done something wrong, because her tone seemed to deliver the signal that freaking out was okay, and he hiccuped once, then began to cry. She looked around for something that would help, someone who knew something, because her only experience with kids was on movie sets, and those had all been forty-year-olds somehow birthed into little-kid bodies.

Nora patted the boy gently on the shoulder, and he launched himself toward her chest, scaring the crap out of her. He wrapped his hands around her neck, and she awkwardly patted his back, the same way that she once did to a cat, and it seemed to calm him because his sniffling quieted.

Detangling herself, she tried again. "Miles, sweetie. How did you get here?"

"I don't know," he sniffed. "I woke up here."

Well, that was unhelpful. She looked around and spotted an open backpack by the door, its contents splayed across the floor. A terrible thought occurred to her—that this child might have been put here before the murders and forgotten or lost in the events of last night. "Are you hungry, Miles? Thirsty?"

He nodded, and he didn't look good. He was shaking and looked almost gray. She tried to gauge his age, but she had no frame of reference. Three years old? Seven? She had no idea. "Stay here." She rose to standing. "I'll be right back."

Returning to the hall, she closed the door and jogged back to the gym and grabbed a few bottles of water from the minifridge there, then looked at the small pantry. There was protein powder, energy bars, and nuts. Nothing a kid would like, but she grabbed a few bars and some bags of cashews and almonds, just in case. Returning to the room, she dumped them into a pile on the floor in front of him.

The kid immediately twisted off the lid of a water and drank it greedily, his eyes on her the whole time. When he came up for air, he wiped his mouth with the back of his hand. "Thanks."

She looked away from his eye contact and pulled her hair loose and in front of her face. She didn't know where this boy had come from or why he was in their basement, but she had to be careful that he didn't recognize her. Thankfully, little kids weren't her target audience. She stepped back. "I'm going to get some things for you, then we'll figure out where your parents are and how to get you back home, okay? I may be gone for a little bit, but I'll be back."

His face twisted in alarm. "You promise?"

"I promise." She reached for the door, which had closed behind her. It was locked, and she felt a moment of panic, then saw the fingerprint sensor mounted on the wall. Pressing her finger to the reader, she pulled the door open, then gave a small wave to the boy, who was already tearing open the energy bar and stuffing the chocolate-covered granola into his mouth.

Easing into the hall, she carefully pulled it shut behind her and double-checked that it was locked.

Shit. Shit, shit, shit, shit, shit.

CHAPTER 49
THE LEADING LADY

Nora had planned, after discovering whatever her darling fiancé was hiding in the basement, to sit on the information and assess the potential risks before approaching him—if she ever did. That plan had to go out the window. There was no way to sit on a child, and she was furious that he had allowed that little boy to sit down there, in the dark, without food or water, while they sat at the fucking dinner table and ate lobster risotto.

For God's sake, she was *pregnant*. He was going to be a father. A father who apparently stuck kids off to one side and forgot about them.

Charging up the basement stairs, she tore through the lower level, then up the grand staircase and onto the second floor. Reaching Hugh's bedroom door, she tried the handle—locked—then pounded on the door with her fist. His bedroom was one of the few doors in the house that her print wouldn't unlock.

"What?" he called out from the other side.

"Open the door," she demanded.

He did, but just a crack. "What?" he repeated.

She shoved her way in, and her fury was distracted by the sight of the fireplace, which was ablaze. He'd closed the glass front doors, but the heat was still radiating from the area. It was September. Why in the hell was he running a fire? She pulled her attention away from the hearth and turned to face him.

He looked pissed. She didn't care.

"We need to talk about the basement," she spat out.

He stilled, and she could see the split second when he considered feigning innocence. She glared at him, and he let out a growl of frustration. "Dammit, I'm handling that."

"Well, you're doing a shitty job of it."

He held up his hand. "How did you even get in the office? Your print isn't authorized for it."

"He's not in the office. Is that where you put him?" She tried to think if there was an air vent or some way for the kid to tunnel through. Maybe he had set up the kid with a bed and food and drinks, and he had squirreled his way out. She hadn't made it to the office yet, but it must have been one of the remaining doors in the hall.

"Who?" He looked at her blankly.

"The kid," she snapped. "Who the fuck else?"

"What kid?" He jerked back his head in confusion, and her eyes narrowed as she watched his face and tried to decipher if the emotion was real.

"The little bald kid who is locked downstairs in the basement," she said slowly, enunciating each word.

"Right now? There's a kid in our basement right now?" He was a great actor—the best in the world—but this act, this harsh tone, his bewildered eyes . . . it was throwing her off, confusing her fury.

"Right now."

"Take me to him," he demanded.

CHAPTER 50
THE LEADING LADY

Nora decided, halfway down the stairs to the basement, that he really didn't know about the kid. Just before they reached the room, she stopped him, then backed them both up a few steps, so they were out of hearing range of the room. "Wait."

"What?"

"He's going to recognize you."

"So?"

She stared at him. "So? You don't realize the issues with a little boy who has been locked in our basement telling everyone that Hugh Iverson—Captain Voil—is the one who kept him there?"

Hugh sighed at the mention of the character, which he had played in four Galaxy Force movies, all of which were mammoth blockbusters. "Or Captain Voil is the one who saves him."

"If you didn't lock him up to begin with—"

"I didn't. I didn't even know he was here!" His face grew hard, and she reminded herself to tread carefully, that this was a man with a very short fuse.

"So if you didn't put him in there, who do you think did it?" She waited for him to connect the dots. "Maybe someone who looks *identical* to Captain Voil?"

"He wouldn't have." He shook his head tightly.

"Face the facts," she spat. "He tied up a woman and stabbed her to death. He was fucking crazy. You think he would draw the line at—"

"Watch it," he warned her, and his face turned cold and angry. "You're suggesting that he kidnapped a kid. *Hurt* a kid. No," he snapped. "One thousand percent he didn't do that."

"Well then, who did?" Nora spread her arms out. "Who else would have put him down here? Who else has fingerprint access? Brenda? And look at the timing. This is probably that dead woman's kid."

He clenched his fists and looked to the left and right, studying the walls as if gauging whether he should punch them. Letting out a hard breath, he looked toward the door. "You're serious? There's definitely a kid in there?"

She leaned against the hall wall and knotted her arms tightly over her chest, hoping that the worst was over. "Yes. There's a little boy in there, eating some energy bars and drinking bottled water. Let's ignore how he got there for a minute and figure out what to do with him."

"Okay." He rested his hands on his hips and looked at the floor for a long moment, thinking. "Why don't we call the police?"

"Well, first off, what are you hiding down here? You told Jeff you had something in the basement. If it wasn't this kid, what is it?"

"Oh." He dismissed the question with a wave of his hand. "Some files in the office. I already burned them."

Files. What a stupid thing to worry about, but one that explained the fire on a warm September night. She considered his simple solution. Call the police. Turn this kid over and let them deal with it. Easy peasy on one hand. A deeper level of involvement on the other. "Let's talk this through," she said slowly. "Looking at this from a cop's perspective."

"Okay." He matched her pose, leaning against the wall and folding his arms over his chest. "Let's go."

"This kid has to be connected to the dead woman, do we agree?"

He gave a reluctant nod. "Highly likely."

"So Trent picks up this woman—and her kid—from who knows where and brings them to our house. Manages to sneak the kid into the basement and the woman into the guesthouse, without either of us seeing it. They're going to ask what we were doing."

He paused. Weighed the question. "We could say we were fucking."

She considered the option. It wasn't a bad one. It would be a plausible excuse that would have kept the two of them sequestered together and not paying attention to anything that Trent was doing. "Okay. We were having sex. Where?"

"Your bedroom."

She let out a long breath and stared up at the ceiling. "The problem is, this is going to make the whole house a crime scene. Right now, they're limited to the guesthouse."

His mouth twisted. "I don't want them to go through the whole house. I'm going to be honest, I don't even know what's here. There might be incriminating items."

"Agreed. He might have put things anywhere in the house," she pointed out. "We don't know. The police could find something that somehow implicates one of us. We can't risk the Hugh Iverson reputation. We have to protect that."

"And *your* reputation," he said evenly. "Let's not forget about that."

"Well, yeah." She dug her fingers into her hair, pulling it back, away from her face. "The problem is, this kid is going to make us look suspicious. I mean, before, Trent takes a woman into our guesthouse and kills her. They'll wonder why here, instead of his house, but whatever. It's his crime, and he delivered his own punishment. But now, there's a kid here, inside the bowels of our house. It brings us into it. It makes us look like we were accomplices. Plus—what? He kills himself and leaves a kid behind, one no one knows about? Something's off there, and the cops are going to pounce on it."

He swore. "We don't need them looking at us. My relationship with him was messy. Your relationship with him—with both of us—was messy. When they find out that you were sleeping with Trent—"

"They're not going to find that out," she snapped.

"Nora." He gave her an exasperated look. "They're going to find out. And my hands aren't completely clean if they look closer at me."

She pinched her eyes closed and tried not to read too much into that statement. She needed to play out the chess game in front of them. Her career and his, their future marriage, the life of security and respect and adoration that she'd worked so hard for . . . all of it was tied to the strategic completion of this navigation. They were all on the board; now she had to figure out how to protect all the pieces and keep them in play.

This boy was a rook, a piece that should be sacrificial for the protection of the queen. She opened her eyes.

"Okay. Then we need to get rid of him. Tonight."

CHAPTER 51
THE ACCOMPLICE

Nolan Price slowly rubbed lotion into his hands, over and over, as he stared into the long, framed mirror that hung over the sink. This bathroom was the first remodel they had done, and was thanks to the Iverson money, which had discreetly arrived on his back porch, bundles of hundred-dollar bills tucked among the packaging of a box of wine. He hadn't yet moved in with Josie and had enjoyed a night alone where he had lined up the bundles, side by side, and just stared at them, unsure of what to do with his newfound wealth. A hundred thousand dollars, and no one, including the IRS, had known anything about it.

He'd never even told Josie where the money had come from, though his boyfriend was full of questions about Nolan's new, carefree attitude toward spending.

Nolan hadn't found out about Monica Kitle's death until three months after it happened, when he looked up her name on a lark and discovered the news articles around her murder. Still unsolved, though they suspected her ex-husband. He had spent dozens of nights staring up at the ceiling, wondering what he would do if the man was arrested and put on trial for the murder. Would Nolan call the police or keep his mouth closed?

When Kerry Pepper's name had appeared in the database, he thought about Monica, but just for a moment. Then he thought about the money. Another box. More wine. More cash. Future financial problems that would just go away.

And now she was dead and this blood was on his hands.

It wouldn't take too much for an intelligent cop to put the pieces together. With Protect the Children being responsible for bringing Kerry to Los Angeles, and Trent Iverson supposedly killing her—they'd assume that there was a tie, given the Iverson connection to the organization. They'd look for a link between the two. And there, with his shiny red bow tie on, would be Nolan.

Nolan, we see two large cash deposits into your bank account. Where did those come from?

Nolan, what made you select Miles Pepper, even though he was much farther down on the list, compared to the other applicants?

Nolan, we're going to need to see your phone records.

Nolan, your emails.

They would work backward from the date of the first deposit and look for other potential victims on the Protect the Children database.

He would be branded a criminal. A deadly errand boy. A serial killer's pawn.

Josie would leave him. The charity would fire him. He would be outed to the press and handcuffed and locked away.

He stepped quickly to the toilet and raised the porcelain lid and knelt in front of the bowl, then vomited until his stomach ached and his throat burned.

CHAPTER 52
THE KID

The candy bars the woman gave him tasted horrible, like someone had dipped them in medicine. After one bite Miles stuck the rest underneath his backpack, where the lady wouldn't see it, and then tried to open the nuts. The bag was hard to rip, and he tugged at both ends hard, hoping to tear it open, but nothing happened. He put the corner of the plastic into his mouth and began to chew the edge of it. Little bits came off, and he spit them onto the floor until he had a hole big enough to shake some nuts out. Pushing them into his mouth like a squirrel, he filled up one side of his cheeks, then started to chew.

Somebody was talking. Their voices were muffled, like how Mommy and Daddy sounded when they were in their bedroom with the door closed. Wait until they heard about this. Him, alone all day, and he didn't get into any trouble. Mommy might be mad that he had drawn on her papers, but he had lots of new drawings to show her. He had even done one of hearts and flowers, even though he wasn't into that stuff, just for her, to make her smile. And he would tell Daddy about when Mr. Frog's tummy light went out and he was in the dark all alone—he didn't even cry. Not a single tear. Which wasn't all the way true, but it would make Daddy proud.

The voices outside the door got louder, like they were fighting. He hoped the lady didn't get too angry and forget that he was in here.

He took another sip of the water but didn't want to drink too much, in case he had to go again. At least now the lights were on. He looked over in the corner with the boxes, and you could see the mark on the cardboard where his pee had hit. Hopefully the lady wouldn't yell at him. Maybe she wouldn't notice; she'd be too busy getting his stuff together and taking him to his mommy.

He needed his mommy. He'd never gone this long in his whole life without seeing her, and his stomach felt hard and painful. Mommy could fix it. She could always fix everything.

CHAPTER 53
THE MOM

It's so much easier dealing with a fake diagnosis over a real one. I just picked my favorite symptoms and threw the rest away. Brain tumors are convenient, in that no one understands them, so I was able to color-by-numbers the perfect sick child.

Bald head—I'd liked that. With a bald head, his scar showed, big and ugly, and a Nair cream application once a week kept the hair from growing back and immediately brought on the attention and sympathy I needed.

Seizures were easily invented, and I made sure that they "happened" only when I or made-up observers were around to see them. Miles was too young to dispute me, and I occasionally knocked his face into something or pushed him into a sharp edge to create injuries consistent with one.

Confusion and instability were also easy. I pretended I had my own health issues and went to the doctors, getting enough prescriptions that I could trigger just about any symptom that I wanted, all courtesy of this pill or that.

The changes in Miles were immediate, and you got real worried. I made an appointment for his doctor, and that night, you didn't go out or get snockered.

The next week, after Miles's appointment, one where the doctor assured me that he was fine and that his tumor hadn't grown . . . I told you it was growing in size and you held me when I cried, and Miles crawled up in my lap, and then we went to the living room and watched a movie together, with him tight against my side and your arm around me, and I could feel your guilt and regret.

It made your love more desperate, and it wasn't me against you and Miles anymore. We were united, and it was like it was before—only this time, I was the one who made Miles feel better because I was the only one who knew why and what was making him sick.

It was a superpower, ya know.

I tried to fight the enjoyment, to remind myself of the good reasons why I was doing it, but it was hard because honestly? I loved the results.

But then Andi died. Andi, then Blanche. They were the first two dominoes to fall.

CHAPTER 54
THE HUSBAND

Kyle sat in a window seat, his long legs cramped into place, his backpack under the seat in front of him, and tried to understand what in all of hell was going on.

Kerry's Facebook friend's voice was playing on repeat in his head. *I don't know anything. None of us do.*

Us? Who the hell was *us*? What had Kerry gotten into? Why hadn't she just told him, whatever it was, and let him help her solve it? Why hadn't she gone to the police? She could have done anything other than take their kid clear across to California and get herself killed.

Killed. A wave of emotion hit, and he let out a gasp and bit his fist, trying to contain the sob. Turning to the window, his upper body shook with silent grief. Beside him, he felt the man shift away in discomfort, and he was grateful for the extra space, for the privacy. He couldn't handle pity. When he'd handed his phone to the boarding agent, she'd taken one look at his face and asked if he was all right, and it was like puncturing a dam. He hadn't been able to speak, had taken back the phone and walked quickly past her, his breath shortening until he was practically gasping as he had climbed the ramp up to the plane.

He was not an emotional man, but this—this shouldn't have happened. Couldn't have happened. If Miles was dead also, if whoever did this to Kerry had him, hurt him, killed him—Kyle wouldn't make it. He'd live long enough to kill those responsible, but to be honest, he wasn't even sure he'd be able to do that. Wasn't sure he'd be able to function enough to walk to a car, much less go on a vindictive spree.

Already he wanted to die, and Miles . . . Miles was the only thing keeping him alive.

CHAPTER 55
THE KID

Miles was beginning to wonder if he was being kidnapped.

Scottie in kindergarten had told him about kidnapping. Apparently, some kids are so bad that their parents hire strangers to take them away and cut out all their insides and feed them to fish. He hadn't believed Scottie, but later that night, in the tub, he'd asked Mommy whether kidnapping was real.

She had stopped washing out his fire truck bucket and turned to him. "Yes, it's real. Why?"

He had asked if he was going to get kidnapped one day, and she had laughed and kissed the top of his head and told him that he wouldn't, not if he stayed close to Mommy and always listened to her.

So maybe that's what this was. He didn't listen, and now maybe he was being taken to be killed.

The idea, which had terrified him on the playground, didn't seem so scary now because in the movies, someone always saved the kid in danger, and maybe the Mustache Man was his rescuer, though he wasn't a very good one. Even now, inside the air-conditioned car, Miles felt like he was going to fall over and die.

He wished that he had stayed with the lady, even if her candy bars did taste like medicine, because at least she was a girl. The girls in comic books and movies were always good, and with her, he felt like she could hug him if he got sad or lonely, but he couldn't get a hug from Mustache Man. Mustache Man looked like Uncle Tito, who once got in a fistfight with Daddy over a hockey game with money.

The lady had eventually come back and packed him a bag with yummy food—grapes and white cake and some little sandwiches that were baby size. She'd also given him a small round clock and told him that by the time the short hand pointed to the twelve, he would be back with his family. Right now, the short hand was on the one, and it was moving *really* slowly, but it glowed in the dark car, and that was cool.

She had lifted him into the way-back part of a big black SUV and then sat back there and held his hand in the dark and sang him songs. They had gone for a short ride, and then she had kissed him on the top of the head and given him to the man with the mustache and told him that she would kill him if he hurt Miles.

Mustache Man had been real nice and smiley in front of her, but when he had bent forward the seat and put Miles in the back seat of his car, he'd given him three rules in a really mean tone:

1. Lie down in the back seat.
2. Shut up.
3. Don't move.

Miles had followed all those rules, but he was starting to feel sick. He wanted to ask about his medicine, which he hadn't had in days, but when he raised his hand to ask a question, the man just ignored him.

After a while, his arm got tired, and he dropped it. Maybe Miles just needed to spit out the question. That's what his dad always said, whenever Miles hesitated: *Just spit it out, Miles. What is it?*

It always seemed an odd thing to say, because no spit ever came out when he asked a question.

But spitting out the question would be breaking the second rule—*Shut up*—which seemed like an important one, but he had a feeling that if he vomited or died on Mustache Man's back seat, the man might also not like that.

So instead, Miles rolled to one side and brought his knees to his chest. Closing his eyes, he thought about cool racing cars and T. rexes running through the streets. By the time the car stopped, he was sound asleep, his thumb stuck in his mouth.

CHAPTER 56

THE HUSBAND

Kyle Pepper arrived at LAX at 5:22 a.m. and got in a taxi, which took him straight to the Beverly Hills police substation, where he waited in a hard plastic chair. Two and a half hours later, Officer Sam Meeko walked in the front door, a coffee carrier in one hand, and met his gaze across the white-tiled room.

As they shook hands, Kyle caught their reflection in the large mirror that divided the room. Meeko was probably six feet tall but still dwarfed by Kyle, who was in a blue hoodie, faded jeans, and steel-toe construction boots. Kyle looked exactly like he felt—like someone who hadn't slept in a day, hadn't shaved in a month—and when he took the coffee from Sam, it was with hands capable of crushing the skull of whoever had taken his child. "Thanks," he said. "Where's Kerry's body?"

"You want to start there?" Meeko hesitated.

Kyle gave a tight nod. "I need to see her."

There had been, prior to this, two horrible moments in Kyle Pepper's life. One when he got the news that his son might have cancer. The second when the cancer's presence was confirmed. With both, Kerry had been at his side, her hand gripped in his, and all he had needed to do was look into her eyes. She had been so strong, so confident. She had taken charge and handled everything, and now she would never ever be there to do that, ever again.

It didn't seem possible, and if he focused on it for more than a moment, he lost control and fell apart. It had happened in the airport in Houston. He'd locked himself in a bathroom stall and sobbed like a child, his chest breaking apart as he had gasped out her name and pounded the side of his fist into the tiled wall until it was bruised and swollen. He had gotten it out, but now he had to be strong. For Miles, if not for himself.

They rode the elevator down two floors, then walked through a maze of gray halls, until they reached an area that smelled like chemicals and disinfectant, and Kyle had to don gloves and a paper bonnet and a mask, and then the sheet was being pulled back, and she was there but she wasn't, and he could barely recognize her in this stiff, pale woman, but it was her.

It was her.

CHAPTER 57
THE DETECTIVE

Protect the Children might have an annual budget of $6 million, but they didn't spend any of it on their office. Farah leaned against a grimy window and surveyed the conference room, which looked like a hodge-podge of office surplus finds. There weren't two chairs that matched, and all of them were crammed around the edge of a long black table. At the head of the table was Ian McGomery, who was in a blue suit and tie, his long hair tied into a high man bun, the ensemble set off by a pair of purple plastic eyeglasses with matching tinted lenses.

Despite the fact that it was a Sunday, he had called in all their employees, a group that barely fit in the long skinny room. Farah fanned herself with her notepad and wondered if the air-conditioning was broken or just off.

"We're just waiting on Nolan, one of our social-needs leaders," Ian called out from his seat. "Do you want to go ahead and start, or should we wait for him?"

Kevin glanced at his watch. "Let's go ahead. Hopefully this won't take long. Could we have a quick introduction of each of you and your role and tasks in the organization?"

This was likely a waste of time, Farah thought as the group settled into the seats. Still, if the organization was how Trent and Kerry connected, this quick shakedown should kill a half dozen birds with one shot.

It was an interesting mix of people. Ian was a stark contrast to Momma Beth, who had favored creams and whites and was often found in muumuus and linen, the only spot of color her emerald jewelry that matched the brilliant green of her eyes.

To Ian's left, a pencil-thin woman with horn-rimmed glasses introduced herself as Becky in PR. Next, a dark-skinned man with silver hair: fundraising. The introductions quickened as they moved around the table. Accounting. Admin. Community Outreach. The last two were both in Social Needs, and then they reached an empty seat. The detectives looked to Ian.

"Nolan is in social needs also. Those are the team members that identify opportunities for us to help and arrange fulfillment of those opportunities."

Farah glanced at their report, finding the notes about Kerry's Make-A-Wish trip. The name of Kerry's contact jumped out. *Nolan Price.* Of course, the lone absentee. She flipped over to the next page, seeing a few emails between Kerry and him. "And Nolan was the one who identified and reached out to Miles Pepper's family?"

"Yes." Ian nodded, and everyone in the room looked at something other than the detectives.

"Walk us through the selection process. Does Make-A-Wish assign them to you?" Kevin asked.

"No, any application to Make-A-Wish goes into their database. We are one of hundreds of charities and organizations that have access to the database. Our social-needs workers review the pending applicants to see if any fit our specialties. Nolan would have selected Miles Pepper and probably did so because of the Disneyland request," Ian supplied.

"Where's Nolan at? Is he often late?" Kevin asked.

"No." Ian looked nervous, as if he might be to blame for Nolan's tardiness. "He's always on time. He's been here for four years. A great employee. But it is a Sunday, and this was a last-minute—"

"Get us his phone number," Kevin snapped. "Any numbers you have for him." He glanced at Farah, and they had been in this business long enough to know this wasn't a coincidence. Nolan wasn't coming.

"Take us to his desk," she instructed the man. "Anyone else here have anything to do with Kerry or Miles Pepper, in any way?"

The room was silent, and she waited another beat, then nodded at Ian, who was rising from his seat. "Let's go."

"Wait."

Farah turned to find the source of the voice and zeroed in on a woman in a blue T-shirt dress. "Yes?"

"I mean, I'm sure you already know this, but . . ." She flushed at the impatient look Farah gave her. "Well, um . . . just in case—I mean, I saw online that Trent Iverson had died and—"

"She wants to make sure you know about Nolan and *Story Farm*," the woman beside her cut in.

Farah's impatience dissolved at the awareness that a puzzle piece, somewhere, was about to connect. "We don't, so please fill us in."

CHAPTER 58
THE ACCOMPLICE

Nolan Price was dry heaving on the side of the Pomona Freeway when his cell phone rang, followed by another text from his Protect the Children boss, telling him that he was needed "urgently" at the office for the team's meeting with the LAPD. He read the text while a passing bus blew a thick braid of hair away from his face.

Sorry, Ian. Don't think I'm going to make it in.

Placing his hands on the roof of his Honda Civic, he turned his face into the morning sun and took a moment to just enjoy being alive, being free, being unknown and without stigma.

Two miles away, the Protect the Children offices occupied the fourth floor of an ugly brick building in Mission Viejo. Nolan was one of eight full-time staff members who raised, budgeted, and dispersed more than $6 million each year. Through the organization they had housed orphans; sent underprivileged kids to college; and rescued and supported battered women, drug addicts, and financially strapped families. They fed the unhoused twice a week, provided Christmas miracles for hundreds of families each December, and facilitated dream vacations for dying children. It had been a dream job for Nolan, except for the small administrative task that occasionally ended up killing someone.

Every job had a thing—that was what Nolan told himself when he got up in the mornings and stared at his reflection in the mirror. Something that marred the good. Maybe a bad coworker. Bitchy customers. A long commute. Shit pay. A secret that ate them apart from the inside.

It had been a good life. A good relationship, a nice job, a mended bond with his mother. He would be thought of fondly, by those who mattered. Be a failed Hollywood story to those who didn't.

Smoothing his suit down—he had worn the cheap one, just in case this was needed—he looked left, then right, gauging the traffic and waiting for a good opening.

When it came, between a red sedan and a FedEx truck, he took five steps forward and stopped in the middle of the lane, waiting for impact.

CHAPTER 59

THE KID

This motel room was super cool. Miles ran from one side of it to the other, then crawled onto the bed and jumped off.

"Hey!" Mustache Man yelled at him, and pointed at the floor. "Sit!"

Miles giggled, because it was exactly the same way that Daddy told Nana's dog to sit. He sat in the spot, like Nana's dog did, his hands flat on the floor between his feet. Sticking out his tongue, he panted.

The man eyed him like he was a little afraid of him. "You gotta calm down, kid. You're going to give yourself a heart attack. Just . . . lay down for a minute."

"Are we going to Disneyland?" Miles stayed where he was, because suddenly the idea of getting up to go to the bed, or to go anywhere, didn't sound so good.

"I don't know, kid. We're waiting right here for another"—the man looked at his watch—"two hours, and then I'm taking you to the park, where you can find your parent, okay? So we just need to—oh shit." The man stood up and stared at him, his eyes growing big.

He shouldn't *saybadwords* in front of a kid, but Miles wasn't able to tell him that because his jaw was *chatteringsohard* that he couldn't speak and he was *onhisside*, his shoulder shaking against the floor. This was gonna be a bad one, he could tell, and he needed *hismommywherewasMommy* and his head was rattling inside . . . rattling, rattling, like a rattlesnake's tail, and the pain was so sharp, like knives were inside his skull. The man crouched beside him, yelling at him and trying to pull him into his arms, and Miles *neededtoSCREAM* at him that that wasn't what he was supposed to do but he couldn't move his jaw wide enough or get his tongue out of the way to make any noise.

His head slammed backward, into the edge of the bed, and maybe this was his punishment for not listening to Mommy.

CHAPTER 60
THE DETECTIVE

Farah fanned herself as the elevator took her and Kevin down to the building's lobby. The car was slow and paused between the second and third floor, which was just long enough for her to shoot Kevin a look of concern.

"Don't worry," he said, leaning against the wall. "I'm the perfect person to get stuck in an elevator with. I've been called highly entertaining by at least two people."

"Being able to say the alphabet in fish species is not entertaining," she said dryly.

"Well, it is highly informative," he pointed out. "And do you know how many people can name a fish that starts with *X*?"

"You are, indeed, a marvel. Future civilizations will worship at statues of your image." The door opened and he gestured her to go first. "And manners also. Still my swooning heart."

As they stepped out of the lobby and into the glaring California sun, Kevin hitched his navy suit pants up and glanced back, making sure that no one was in earshot. "So Nolan Price was the Black kid on the show. Who saw that coming?"

"Not us," Farah said, weaving around a handicapped parking sign. "Then again, we didn't know about a Nolan Price or Protect the

Children connection to this crime until this morning, so I think we can be forgiven for that oversight." They had parked on the far side of the parking lot, in one of the few shaded parts, and she glanced at him as they walked in between two cars. "I'm thinking about that spray-painted picture from Trent's house, the one of the four *Story Farm* kids. Nolan was the only one of them that wasn't defaced somehow."

"The girl had a heart on her," Kevin pointed out. "Not really defacing."

"Yeah, I know, but it's still interesting."

"You think he's the one who did the graffiti?"

"I don't know." A pigeon bobbed ahead of them, then flew off when Farah got too close. "I'd be curious to find out how close Nolan and Trent were. If he went to parties at Trent's house—what kind of crowd he hangs with. Let's do an arrest check for Nolan on the way to Hugh's."

"Sure, but five bucks says it'll come up clean."

"I'll take that bet." Farah held out her fist and bumped Kevin's with it as they approached the SUV.

A few minutes later, she cursed and handed over a crumpled five-dollar bill. Nolan Price was clean as a church mouse, but still MIA. There was a backup of traffic on Pomona, so they zigzagged across to the 101 and took it north to Beverly Hills.

It was time to put Hugh Iverson's feet to the fire.

CHAPTER 61
THE HUSBAND

Kyle Pepper would give the LAPD one thing—they didn't mess around. It was a Sunday morning, just one night after he'd gotten the call from Meeko with the news of Kerry's murder, and already there was a tip line, press coverage, and a gigantic conference room full of people who were being managed with ruthless efficiency by a gray-haired woman in Crocs and a button-up fishing shirt.

"That's Gertie." Meeko nodded toward the woman, who was studying a clipboard, a pair of reading glasses perched on her wide nose. "She drove in this morning from Las Vegas. She's a bit of an expert in missing children and comes in when we need her."

"You the father?" Gertie stuck out her hand toward Kyle. "I'm Gertie Silver. Lost my own little girl in '03. Since then I've led sixteen privately funded missing-children searches. I understand how to coordinate with law enforcement, press, and the public, and how to get the most out of all of their lazy asses." She glanced at Meeko as she shook Kyle's bruised hand with a vise grip. "Including you, Minko."

"It's Meeko," he corrected.

"On my watch, thirteen of the children were recovered safely, and I'm committed to making sure that Miles Pepper is my fourteenth." She glared at Kyle as if he might stand in her way. Thirteen. Thirteen out of sixteen. He didn't like the odds.

Kyle cleared his throat. "He's sick. He has a brain tumor."

"That could work in our favor." She nodded in approval, like there was anything positive about a life-threatening growth on Miles's brain.

"You said 'privately funded,'" Kyle said. "We can't—" He stopped. Not *we*. There was no *we* anymore. The thought almost dropped him to his knees.

Gertie waved off the concern. "Protect the Children has put up a fifty-thousand-dollar reward and provided two dozen volunteers. We'll use them to man the tip line phones and the website. They've also taken responsibility for any administrative costs of the search."

Kyle nodded tightly and tried to contain his emotion. "That's really . . . that's great."

"Come with me." She turned and hustled by a long table, where a line of yellow-shirted individuals were already seated, phones at their ears, pens in their hands, taking notes on some clipboards. "We've got around a hundred tips coming in each hour," she called over one shoulder. "And most of those will be junk, so the key is precise organization and cataloging of commonalities."

She picked up one of the phone operators' clipboards and tapped her red pen against a questionnaire pinned to it. "Every field on this is gotten from every caller, every time. They'll then hand this off to the computer inputters, so it'll show up here." She walked over to a huge touch screen, which showed a map of Los Angeles County. The streets and suburbs were covered in dots, each one corresponding to a potential sighting. "Ninety-eight percent of the tips we receive will be garbage. The only way we can determine their accuracy is through tracking the time, location, and commonalities of the elements. That means, if someone saw little Miles on the 710, you need to know at exactly what time and exactly where on the road. If they can't remember, we press harder. Have them look at their phone logs, their text messages, the last time they remember seeing a clock anywhere. We need at least a window of time, and it needs to be the tightest window possible."

She pressed a button, and the screen changed to a list of descriptions that had come in so far. "When I say 'commonalities of the elements,' I'm talking about descriptions of the car, the person or persons with Miles, what he's wearing, what they're wearing, activities they are doing, what they're eating—anything. We will use these to find duplicates among the tips and identify the valid from the invalid."

She waved her hand and gestured for him to follow her toward the adjacent room. It was comforting, her no-nonsense manner and her explanation of the process that had worked so many times in the past. Finally, after two days of feeling helpless, things were happening. This giant city was shrinking. A hundred calls an hour? Any one of them might lead to Miles. She placed a hand on the doorknob. "In this next room are Minko's band of brothers."

Meeko gave an amused smile at what must be an intentional dig. "I'll take the tour from here, Gertie." He stepped into the room and held open the door for them. Kyle waited to see if Gertie would follow, but someone called her name from a desk by the front of the room, and she headed off before Kyle could extend his thanks.

The next room was crammed with monitors and nerds. While the conference room had been a sea of efficient yellow shirts, this room was a hodgepodge of glasses, graphic tees, and dyed hair. Most of the people were young, younger than Kyle and Kerry, and they all had cups of coffee in hand and their faces turned to a screen. "Here's the HQ of Miles's task force." Meeko stopped in front of an empty desk. "When an area of the city becomes hot—meaning that Gertie's team has received enough valid tips to confirm a high likelihood of an appearance, then this team pulls every security camera in the area, and they work to confirm the sighting and get additional information, like license plates and facial recognition."

"So these are all police officers?" Kyle asked as a kid in a Farrah Fawcett T-shirt and a shell necklace walked by, his attention glued to his phone.

"Believe it or not. We call them the Whiz Kids, though Joel over there is pushing forty."

Kyle counted eight officers at individual banks of screens, all their eyes scanning, mouses moving as they zoomed in, out, and changed views. "All of them are following up on tips?"

"Except for a couple who are focused on just the elevator and lobby footage from the hotel. We're double-checking to see if Miles might have been brought back in, or if anyone was following them."

"What's outside of the hotel? Any cameras there?"

Meeko scowled. "When I say that they couldn't have stayed at a worse hotel, I mean it. No cameras on the street, and about four different side streets, all with bars and coffee shops that stay open late. She could have gone into any of them. And most opened to back alleys, so we're talking about a really easy way for someone to get her into a car and out of there, if they wanted to."

"Is the hotel in a dangerous area?" Kyle asked.

"It's in a safe area, but hey—it's LA. Crime's gotten worse, and people are opportunistic. They see a woman alone, they have an opening, they take it."

"And my son?"

"It's possible she left him behind and someone else took him. Sort of a 'wait here, I'll be right back,' but then she couldn't."

Kyle looked around the room wearily, and the feeling of utter helplessness returned. "Okay. What about the woman on Facebook?"

Meeko made a face. "I'm not sold on that. I'm not doubting what she said to you, but Kerry not wanting to come on this trip could have been for a variety of personal reasons. A strange woman telling you that she doesn't know anything . . ." He shrugged. "What good is that?"

"She said, 'None of us do.'" Kyle stared at the cop. "Who is this 'us' that she's referring to?"

"I don't know, but you gotta worry about that mystery later, after we have Miles back to you, safe and sound." He clapped a hand on Kyle's shoulder and squeezed. "Trust us, Kyle. We're doing everything we can."

Kyle knew that. He could see that. But it still, somehow, wasn't enough.

CHAPTER 62
THE MOM

Before her death, Andi was kind of the ringleader of our group. Maybe that's why she was killed first.

She stayed the ringleader even after death, but in a much different sense.

On the morning after she died, a post was made from her profile with a set of rules for all group members. At first, I rolled my eyes—rules for the group? But then I scrolled down farther. Put on my glasses. Read them again.

They were simple and written in a way that left no room for interpretation.

The gist was that we were no longer "allowed"— and that was the terminology used—to do anything that might harm our family, spouses, or kids. But not just that. We also couldn't exploit them in any way, and it took us some time to figure out what that meant. Basically, I couldn't post pictures of Miles online to try and get attention. Not pictures of him being sick or even pictures of him being well. Nothing.

And apparently, if we broke those rules, we'd be killed.

KILLED.

I literally laughed when I read that. What was Andi talking about? It was so extreme that most of us didn't really believe it, especially not coming from her. And the other women agreed. We thought Andi was alive, giggling over a chai latte as she typed out a set of demands.

But Blanche knew. Blanche was the only one of us who took the threat seriously.

Blanche read Andi's post, walked out on the balcony of her downtown high-rise, looked over the view of the Seattle harbor, then hoisted her flat stomach onto the railing, swung one LuLaRoe pumpkin legging–clad leg over the side, then the other, and pushed off.

In the news article about her death, it said that a window washer on the fourteenth floor caught movement out of the corner of his eye and turned to see Blanche fall past him, her hair trailing like a flag.

He said she was silent, like a stone.

A stone that cracked upon impact with the pool deck below.

Andi's Facebook post took only a few minutes to kill her. That was the scary thing for me. That Blanche would rather die than stop what she was doing to her child.

Tonya left the group, saying things had "gotten too weird."

Rule #3 said we couldn't leave the group, and two weeks later, Andi's account posted a photo of her. Tonya was on the ground, and half of her face was missing.

I quickly decided that I hated the rules, but I could follow them. I could change everything about my life if it meant that I got to keep it.

So I changed everything, Kyle. I thought you'd notice. I thought you'd ask me about it, and when you did, I planned to tell you. I was like a pop bottle that was all shaken up and the pressure in me was about to explode and all you had to do was notice and ask me, but you didn't.

You just kept going.

Kept working.

Kept living, while I went crazy inside myself.

I went crazy and you never even noticed a thing.

CHAPTER 63

THE LEADING LADY

As the late-morning sun streamed through the long stretch of windows, Nora walked down the suspended staircase and forced a smile at the maid, the one who had told the detectives that Nora could be stuffy. *Bitchy* was what she had meant, and they all knew it. But bitchy was better than being a whore, and they had all managed to keep their mouths shut about that.

One day, if it all came out, that's what the public would brand her. A whore. A slut. A woman who had America's favorite man and then slept with his brother. They wouldn't understand, no matter what she said or how their publicist couched it. She would be vilified, and Hugh would be idolized—that was Hollywood for you.

Eventually, they'd move on. Trent was dead, so they couldn't get a quote from him, and Hugh would do what he did best. Smile. Wave. Stay as far from controversy and drama as possible. He would deliver approved lines that they would agree about in advance, and then he would star in another billion-dollar blockbuster, and the whispers of Nora's potential little affair would fade, at least for a while.

The public would never know the truth because she would never admit it. She would marry Hugh Iverson and become the queen of this castle and live a life of security and respectability, complete with a villa in Spain, more money than she could ever spend, and the recognition and adoration of millions.

She would have everything she'd always wanted, but regardless of what her marriage license would say, Trent would always be the true owner of her heart.

Now they both sat at the breakfast table, and awkward, silent meals seemed to be their new MO. Nora stared at a poached egg and side of salmon. She picked up her fork, then set it down, her stomach churning at the thought of food.

"Mr. Hugh?" Bradford from the kitchen paused beside him, his hand extended. "May I take your plate?"

"Yeah." As he pushed the china away, his eyes met Nora's, and she looked away from the coldness there. He had exuded anger all morning, the emotion rippling from him as he had stalked through the house and then eaten his breakfast without a word of acknowledgment to her.

Bradford left the room, plate in hand, and she leaned forward, trying for conversation. "The filming starts soon for *Equidom*. I was thinking that I could go with you to New Zealand. I have a hiatus then, so the timing works out."

For a moment, his air of anger weakened as he sorted through the statement. She wasn't sure if he had thought through, in the wake of everything else, the filming obligations ahead of him.

"I can't," he said tightly. "I'll talk to Roger. He can figure it out."

She'd already cleared her schedule for the next year, wanting to make sure that her pregnancy would be stress-free and her belly wouldn't cause any role complications. Going off with him, getting out of this house and into a new environment . . .

"It'd be good for you," she said quietly. *For us.* "Dive into a role. Do what you do best. What you love. That's what he would have wanted. And that role . . . it's such a good one. You'd be amazing in it. Award-winning."

"Nora," he snapped. "Stop it. Just—" He rose to his feet. "Just give me a fucking week, okay? A week before you start piling on shit."

"Okay," she said quietly, glancing toward the kitchen. "Okay. Just . . . sit back down. Please. I'm sorry." Maybe it *was* too soon for her to bring up work. But it was hard enough not to mention the media coverage of Trent's death, which was now in every corner of the internet and really required a statement from him.

He sat back down and let out a hard breath. "You think the kid's okay?"

The question both surprised and pleased her, and maybe that's where his stress and hostility were coming from. "Yes, I do. It's Pete, after all." Pete, who had handled private security for all their events, and who had cleaned up Trent's drug and alcohol messes, again and again, over the years. Pete hadn't hesitated at the prospect of an easy babysitting job that would give him serious cash. All he had to do was drive the kid to San Diego, watch him until morning, then release him. "We've always trusted him with our lives, so why not this? Plus, I gave him a bit of a lecture."

He lifted his gaze, and finally, reluctantly, the hint of a smile appeared on his lips. "Yeah. I've been on the receiving end of that lecture before."

Her heart pulled at the sight of the man before her, one who was both Trent and Hugh, constantly and continually. Was it any wonder that she had fallen in love with them both? A woman's heart should never have to defend itself against twins, especially not when they came in such irresistible packaging.

"Mr. Iverson?" Brenda appeared in the doorway, interrupting her response. "The detectives are back. They asked to speak with you. Both of you."

CHAPTER 64
THE DETECTIVE

Farah had hoped for food and wasn't disappointed. A woman in a hunter-green maid's uniform brought out a platter of prosciutto-wrapped melons, mini crab cake balls on top of puff pastries, and a selection of coffee, hot tea, mimosas, and bottled water. Farah requested a coffee with milk and two sugars, then filled up the blue china plate with three of each item before sitting down in the middle of a very plush white sofa.

Kevin waved off the food, probably saving room for a stick of stale beef jerky to top off the two croissants he'd had on the way to the charity. "Just a water, please."

Nora stood by the window in light-blue jeans and a white button-up men's-style blouse, the sleeves loosely rolled to the elbows, her feet bare, hair down. She wasn't wearing any makeup and looked impossibly young and innocent. She was chewing on her thumb with one bare foot perched on top of the other, like a flamingo. "Have you found out anything?"

"We have. Lots of stuff." Kevin relaxed against the cushion and rested his arm on the back of the couch. *Lots of stuff* was a bit of an exaggeration, but Farah let him peacock. "For example, we found out about your affair with Trent."

They had coordinated this stab in the dark, and Farah kept her eyes on Hugh when the line was delivered, needing to see his reaction, though she was dying to see how Nora took the accusation.

Hugh was seated in a leather club chair and smiled, a reaction that caught Farah off guard, as much for its unpredictability as its devastating impact. Full lips, white teeth, a playful light in his eyes . . . and so familiar. A smile she had seen on so many screens in the last twenty years.

A smile. What the hell did that mean? He'd known about the affair? He hadn't? Farah sneaked a look at Nora, who looked unimpressed.

"You didn't *ask* me if I was sleeping with Trent," she pointed out.

"It's an interesting fact that you should have shared." Kevin smiled to take the edge off his tone. "Anything else you've left out?"

"It might be juicy gossip, but it wasn't pertinent. Let's chat about who you two are sleeping with. That's as relevant to this investigation as me occasionally fucking the wrong twin."

Hot damn. Farah's attention flew back to Hugh, but it was too late. Whatever reaction he'd had to Nora's statement was already hidden. He raised his eyebrows in a gesture that seemed to say, *Well? You asked, she answered.*

"*Did* you know about the affair, Mr. Iverson?" Farah clarified, and this was some Jerry Springer–level drama. Talk about a potential paparazzi payday. If she ever went to the dark side, she could retire to Tahiti on whatever Hugh said next.

"*Affair* isn't really the right word for it. Trent likes to fuck. He used Nora at times to do it. That was about it, wouldn't you say?" He raised his eyebrows at his fiancée, and the room felt like a tennis match that she and Kevin didn't know the rules to.

"I don't know about that. It could be argued that I was using him." Nora glared at him. "You are a little cold at times, Hugh."

Farah's gaze darted between the two of them, and she couldn't decipher if the conversation was venomous or playful. "Did you love Trent?" she asked Nora.

The question was one that the actress wasn't prepared for, and she crossed her arms tightly over her chest, as if to protect herself from the thought. "I did." She paused. "I still do. Deeply."

Hugh carefully brushed a piece of lint off the knee of his dress pants, his expression muted but the smile gone. "I don't see how Nora's affections for Trent really matter, at this juncture."

"Would you have thought that he was capable of murder?" Farah asked Nora.

Nora looked at Hugh, and a long moment of eye contact held between the two of them. When she swung her gaze back to Farah, there was an emotion there, hidden but brewing. "I think that Trent had demons. Ones he tried to drown in alcohol and drugs. I know the version of Trent that I fell in love with. I also know the person he became when he was high. Trent would have killed to protect me. To protect him." She pointed to Hugh. "Outside of that, no. I wouldn't think he was capable of murder."

Kevin shifted in his seat, taking a glass bottle of water off a tray the maid presented. "Let's switch horses for a minute and talk about Protect the Children."

Nora took the closest seat to Hugh, crossing her impossibly long legs at the ankles. "Go for it."

"How involved was Trent in the charity operations?" Kevin asked.

Hugh frowned. "Involved? It's an organization that holds a lot of sentimentality for both of us. We've tried to carry on our mother's work through it."

"Which means what? How would you and Trent interact with the organization, and what did you do for them?" Farah pushed.

He gave her a pained look. "I don't mean to be difficult, but why do you care? I fail to see what PTC has to do with any of this. We give them a lot of money and help out however we can. So?"

"So the dead woman in your guesthouse was in Los Angeles on a Protect the Children–sponsored trip," Farah replied, as ready as Hugh to move this conversation forward.

Nora let out an incredulous laugh. "Whaaat?"

Hugh also seemed to find this surprising and leaned forward, resting his elbows on his knees as he stared at Farah. "What kind of trip? Battered woman? Relocation? A scholarship?"

"Make-A-Wish," Farah said flatly. "Her son came with her. He's six. Dying of cancer."

The room fell completely silent as Nora and Hugh absorbed the information, and the silence was a convincing indicator that they knew less about the murder than she did.

"So . . ." Hugh seemed as if he were struggling to understand. "You think Trent met her through PTC and then brought her here and killed her? That's not . . . we don't interact with the recipients, not unless it's a fundraiser or PR event, and we don't even really do much of that."

"What about Nolan Price?" Farah asked. "Do you have any interaction with him?"

"He's a friend of ours, obviously. There's history there. We got him a job at PTC, when he needed one. But again . . ." Hugh shook his head. "I don't see the connection."

"Nolan is the one who set up Kerry Pepper's trip to come here," Farah said.

There was another stretch of blank silence where Hugh and Nora processed the statement.

"So you think Nolan had something to do with my brother bringing her here?" Hugh asked.

"Nolan wouldn't have done that," Nora interjected. "He's a sweetheart."

"Maybe he didn't know what he was doing," Hugh provided.

"I still don't know why he had to bring her *here*," Nora said flatly. "There's a whole city out there. Rent a hotel, or use his own place. Hell, take her to the cabin."

"The what?" Kevin looked up.

"The cabin." Nora paused, her blue eyes darting from Farah to Kevin and registering the blank looks on both. "It's out in the desert, almost to Mojave."

"It's a weekend property of Trent's," Hugh said, stepping in. "He goes up there to get high, stare up at the stars, screw around."

A cabin. This was good. If there was going to be evidence hidden anywhere, a cabin in the middle of nowhere was as good a place as any.

"It's not under his name on the tax rolls," Kevin said.

"It's probably in one of the family entities," Hugh said. "There'll be a key for it on his key chain. We probably have one in the key locker also. I don't know the address, but I can get it from our lawyer."

"Get it." Kevin nodded, and Farah glanced at her watch, then rose.

They had their own cameras to get in front of.

CHAPTER 65
THE HIGH SCHOOLER

Dario French was thirty seconds away from a blow job when Natalie Windreimer paused, her platinum-blonde head turning in the direction of the thin San Diego motel room door. "Wait, I hear something."

He'd heard the same thing, a banging and a yell from the next room, but wasn't interested, especially when his pants were unzipped and her mouth was so close to his dick. He pressed his hand gently on the back of her blonde head, and she twisted away with a frown. "Dario, stop."

She rose to her feet and he swore. Nine months spent flirting with this girl, washing her car on the weekend, kissing her father's ass, and now this. He'd paid fifty bucks for two hours in this room, and they'd already wasted thirty minutes of it.

He went to grab her arm, but she was already at the window, parting the curtains and looking out. "Guy next door is leaving," she said. "Oh shit, he's got a kid with him."

"Natalie . . . please." He came up behind her and wrapped his hands around her waist. When she didn't react, he nudged the hair off her shoulder with his nose and pressed a kiss on her neck.

"Dario, look," she said. "Look how he's running. I think something's wrong."

He gently bit her neck, and she giggled a little and squirmed against him. He pressed forward with his pelvis, reminding her of his erection. He glanced out the window just long enough to appease her, and saw a guy holding a kid in his arms and jogging around the back of a car, over to the passenger side.

"Holy shit, Dario. I think that's that missing kid. The Amber Alert one, from Los Angeles."

His brain had clicked into the same thought, and the blow job was forgotten for a moment at the awareness of the $50,000 reward. He pushed her to one side and cupped his hands against the glass, looking hard as the guy put the kid in the car and then ran around to the driver's side and got in.

Silver Toyota Camry. Four door.

The car had been parked nose out and now jerked forward, turning left, and Dario realized he wouldn't be able to see the tag number from his vantage point. Jerking up his zipper, he worked his belt through the buckle and yanked at the door. The slide bolt was on and he cursed, flipping it open and trying again.

By the time he made it to the middle of the parking lot, the Toyota was gone.

Dario let out a yell of frustration and looked back to their room in exasperation.

Natalie was now topless, with nothing but a thong on, her hands on the window, her mouth fogging the glass as she leaned forward and pressed her big round tits against the clear window. The curtains were wide open, and he glanced around for witnesses, then sprinted for the door.

He was back in seconds and flipped the lock and yanked the curtains closed, then turned to find her stretched out on the bed, beckoning him with her finger. "Should we call the cops?" he panted, his hands fumbling with his belt.

"That was hot, you running out there, all heroic."

"There's a reward. We could—"

She pulled her baby-blue thong down over her thighs, and he forgot what he was talking about.

"I—holy shit."

"You can call the cops in a minute." She patted the bed beside her. "First, I have a better reward for you."

CHAPTER 66
THE DETECTIVE

"I don't get this epiphany that you think you've had," Kevin said as they took the steps down from the Iverson porch and headed toward their SUV.

"It's not an epiphany—it's just clicked in my head that they're both masters of their craft. Their lives, for decades, have been to play a role other than their own. Which means that questioning them is useless because we can't trust a single thing that we see or hear from them. The staff interviews, sure. But Hugh's and Nora's testimonies? Forget it. Doesn't matter how good our Spidey-senses are."

"Yet you still asked them a dozen questions," he pointed out.

"Well, yeah," Farah retorted. "I mean, we did drive all the way over here."

"Plus, you had two of those ham-skewer things left on your plate."

"Prosciutto, K. Prosciutto." She said the word in an Italian accent. "And they were . . . perfetto." She pinched her fingers together and kissed them. "So thank you for waiting as they lied a little longer." She opened the car door and stepped in.

"I don't think they were lying." He got into the driver's seat and shut the door, then started the engine. "The affair . . . that was just weird, their whole exchange. But with the charity, I think they were genuinely surprised to hear about a connection there."

"Yeah, me too." Farah opened her phone and checked her messages. Nothing from Anaïca yet, but she knew that her daughter was heads down and digging. "You ready for this press conference?"

"No, but I never am. Feel up for a drive to this cabin in Mojave after the clown show?"

Farah grinned as she scrolled through her phone. "Thought you'd never ask." She clicked on the activity report on the LAPD's internal database, then cursed. "Nolan Price showed up."

"Yeah?" Kevin leaned over and peered at the screen. "Oh damn."

Farah scrolled through the information, which wasn't much. Car-on-pedestrian fatality. Pomona Freeway. His car was parked on the shoulder, while he was on foot. "That was why traffic was backed up," she remarked. "Shit. I'll call the responding officer on the way, see what I can find out."

"Hey, at least we won't need a warrant now to dig through his life," Kevin said.

It was true, and the fact that they could find any upside in someone's death was a sign of how overworked they were. "I'll have Anaïca jump on his financials and phone records. See if anything stands out," Farah said.

"Damn, this keeps getting worse," Kevin remarked.

He was right. Three dead bodies so far and the lines between them were one big tangled knot.

CHAPTER 67
THE HUSBAND

Kyle was beginning to feel guilt on top of the grief and fear. Meeko was looking at him as if he were a horrible husband, and each question seemed more and more designed to put that all on paper.

What did Kerry spend her days doing? Did she have any hobbies?

He didn't know. All he knew was that dinner was ready by the time he came home, and Miles always seemed happy, and doctors' appointments and chores and errands all were handled while he was at work.

Who were her close friends? Who did she talk to on a regular basis?

He didn't think Kerry had any close friends. She used to, a year or two ago, but once Miles got sick, she hadn't really mentioned going out or seeing anyone.

Was she happy in the marriage? How often did they have sex? When was the last time they went on a date? Had he ever cheated on her?

He had assumed she was happy. He didn't know the last time they'd had sex, but it had been a while. They didn't go on dates, because Kerry wouldn't leave Miles with a sitter. And uh—yeah. He had cheated on her, but she'd never found out about it, so that wasn't part of any of this.

Meeko also seemed to think that he was a shitty dad, and maybe Meeko was a fucking encyclopedia of facts about his kid, but Kyle wasn't. Kyle had been busy making sure that they had money in their account to pay the doctors, not find out what the doctor's name was and how often Miles had seen him.

When Kyle mentioned what he did know—the drawer full of medicine that Kerry had been hoarding—Meeko had brushed that off and referred back to Kyle's comment that Miles had been getting better, before this most recent diagnosis.

And Meeko had already requested a copy of Miles's medical file, so Kyle didn't know why it mattered if he knew the names of every medication he took or the dates of his seizures and surgeries.

All that was what Kerry was for. If she were here, she would tell them. She would tell them what she always told Kyle—he was the best dad and husband and man in the world and she was so lucky and happy as his wife.

He tried to remember if he'd ever said anything like that to her.

He couldn't think of a time, but he must have.

He had to have.

CHAPTER 68
THE DETECTIVE

The press conference was a joke. The chief took center stage, and Farah and Kevin stood like puppets on either side of him, silent and useless. It was probably for the best. Every reporter was a vulture in a suit, and the chief danced between their questions with a grace that Farah would never possess.

As they left out the back, Anaïca fell in step with them and handed her mother a folder. "It's a good thing Nora mentioned the cabin, because it would have taken us a month to find it on our own, if ever."

"Really?" Farah flipped open the folder. "Was it buried?"

"Suspiciously deep," Anaïca confirmed. "We're talking three layers of entities and subentities, and at first glance, it looks like a vacant piece of land."

Farah's steps slowed as she scanned the paperwork. "It was part of their parents' estate," she said for Kevin's benefit. "A hundred and six acres in . . . where is this?"

"Middle of nowhere," Anaïca supplied. "Seven miles outside of the Mojave National Preserve. GPS puts it at an hour and twenty-two minutes away from here. I sent the address to both of your phones."

Farah and Kevin exchanged a glance. He looked at his watch. "It's one thirty. We could be there by three and be back in time for dinner, assuming it doesn't take long to search."

"The cabin's smaller than my apartment," Anaïca said. "Should be a quick event."

"Feel like a drive?" Farah asked Kevin.

"I'm up for it."

"Then let's hit the road." Farah snapped the folder shut and kissed Anaïca on the cheek. "Thanks. Please run tech forensics on Nolan. We need to find a recent link between him and Trent, preferably communication or a money trail."

"I'll hunt one down. Let me know what you find at the cabin. Hey, old-timer?" She lifted her chin to Kevin. "Drive safe."

He flashed her a thumbs-up and opened the driver's door. Farah got in the other side and sighed as she shut the door. "Gonna be another long day," she remarked.

"But not boring."

Her phone chimed with a text from Ty, and she swiped to open it.

Ty: Need me to bring you dinner tonight? I'm making lasagna and can bring plates for you and Anaïca to the station when it's ready.

Her stomach groaned in appreciation, and she quickly texted back.

Farah: Yes. 100x yes. I don't deserve you. Got enough for Kevin?

Ty: You know it.

She closed the text exchange and sent a silent thank-you up to heaven for blessing her with a husband who understood the job. Last night, when she had crawled in bed beside him, he had gathered her against his body and fallen right back asleep. When her alarm had gone off at six, he had already had coffee in the pot and eggs sizzling in the pan.

Granted, both of their incomes were barely enough to cover their expenses, but his job as a copywriter was one he could do from home, and that had allowed them to raise Ana with a steady homelife despite Farah's crazy hours.

As the SUV accelerated past traffic, she looked at Kevin. "Did you read over the statement from Kerry Pepper's husband?"

"Yeah." He lifted a hand in passing to the lot security guard, who waved them through the parking lot exit. "Poor guy. A dead wife and a missing kid."

"A sick missing kid," she amended. "I listened to the audio of the interview on my drive in. He sounds like he's coming apart at the seams."

"Can't say I'd be doing much better, in his shoes. Especially being out of town and all."

"Here's the kicker. They found a tumor in the kid's brain when he was three. They found out it was benign, but it still had to be removed. The kid gets better—then they find another brain tumor and the kid gets worse. He starts improving, the dad thinks they might be in the clear, and then—six months later, another one is found, and it is cancerous."

Kevin whistled. "Talk about a roller coaster."

"That itself was a roller coaster, and now this." She shook her head, thinking of Ty and everything he had done to help raise Ana. He had stepped up to the plate, but Kyle Pepper didn't have to juggle just being a single father—he also had to handle the medical care, something that he said Kerry had always done, and he was clueless about.

Farah chewed on a hangnail that was starting to bleed. "Kyle was the one who made the Make-A-Wish application for Miles."

Kevin stayed silent.

"So the application goes to Make-A-Wish, and Protect the Children reviews the queue and selects ones that they can fulfill. Nolan selects Miles's application, reaches out to Kerry and Kyle, and organizes for Kerry and Miles to come to California." She tapped his arm. "Cut across on Balboa."

"So Kerry and Miles come to California . . . ," Kevin prompted.

"Under protest," Farah reminded him. "Kyle says she didn't want to come, and her Facebook friend was telling her to get out of it."

"And somehow Trent finds out that this woman is here—"

"Presumably from Nolan," Kevin interjects.

"—and gets her in his trunk, we're assuming using drugs . . . and then drives her to Hugh's house, where he ties her up, stabs her a bunch of times, and then shoots himself."

There was a moment of silence as they both absorbed the scenario.

"It's a mess," Farah said. "Would never pass a jury."

"Potential second scenario," Kevin proposed. "Trent's hanging around the Protect the Children offices or talking to Nolan and somehow hears about Kerry. Becomes obsessed with her, maybe reaches out, and they develop some sort of a flirtation or relationship. He meets up with her while she is here, doesn't want to take her to his place, so they go to Hugh's house to party, get into a bad batch of drugs and Trent goes Ted Bundy on her, then starts to sober up, realizes what he's done, and kills himself."

Farah turned it over and decided that she liked it a lot better than hers.

"Though," Kevin mused, "hard to imagine becoming interested in Kerry Pepper when you got Nora Kemp on your jock."

"Maybe he likes a normal girl," she defended. "Not everyone likes staggering beauty. That's got to be exhausting, to look at that level of perfection all the time. I mean, you wouldn't trade Trish for a night with Nora, would you?"

"I'm gonna plead the fifth on that one, and if you ever tell my wife I said that, I'll piss in your coffee."

CHAPTER 69

THE DETECTIVE

As it turned out, Kerry Pepper was the most boring housewife on the planet. Farah fought a yawn as she scrolled through the photos that TID had uploaded to the file. Yet another photo of Kerry and Miles, cheek to cheek, smiling at the camera. This one was at a fast-food restaurant, with the sick kid holding up a french fry like it was an accomplishment.

They were almost to the cabin's address, and Farah had spent most of the drive catching up on the search team's investigation. The missing kid was another piece of the puzzle that just didn't fit into any normal murder investigation. She'd called Officer Sam Meeko on speakerphone, and the missing-persons cop sounded as tired as she felt.

". . . and so that's what we're trying to figure out." Meeko paused, and Farah jumped in before he started another monologue.

"Where's the husband now? Still at the station?"

"Yep. He's itching in his skin. Wants to go out and search for the kid, like we've got a big field to cover or something. Guy doesn't realize that his son could be out of the country by now."

"And the tip line? Nothing there?" Farah asked.

"We've got hundreds of tips, but none that are matching each other. I've got everything from him in a mall in San Francisco to a motel parking lot in San Diego, and no way to tell the good from the garbage."

Kevin leaned closer to the speaker. "What do you hear on the street? Any rumblings from UCs or CIs? No little sick kids showing up anywhere?"

"Nothing so far, but it's not like there's going to be an auction for him. We've ruled out ransom, given the circumstances. What we're trying to figure out is if the kidnapping is a result of the murder or vice versa. I was hoping you could help me with that."

Farah looked at Kevin, and this line of thinking was one that they had yet to go down. Her frustration grew, along with her embarrassment. It felt like they were constantly a step behind, and she wasn't used to feeling so inept.

"Hello?" Meeko called out. "You guys still there?"

"Okay, let's walk down these paths," Kevin said. "Option one— someone wants the kid, so they take the mom and then torture information out of her and then kill her. Take the kid and disappear."

Farah made a face. "It's messy. There are easier ways to grab a kid. And no offense, but the kid isn't exactly the ideal candidate for a kidnapping. We're talking about a potentially terminally ill child."

"Maybe the mom wanted to get rid of him," Kevin suggested. "Like you said, he's expensive. A lot of work. Maybe the mom was selling him. Maybe sold him to Trent."

Maybe Trent wasn't obsessed with Kerry. Maybe he was obsessed with Miles. The thought was too dark to consider, but she flagged it for discussion with Kevin after they ended the call.

"I don't think so," Meeko interjected. "By all accounts the mom was glued to this kid. I've heard that from the husband, the grandmother, and the sister."

"What about friends?" Farah asked. "You talked to any of her friends?"

"Husband says she doesn't have any, other than this Bonnie lady who blocked him on Facebook. She used to, a few years ago, but got off social media and stopped going out about a year ago."

A year ago. Farah flipped screens, from the photos log to Kerry's social media profile. She scrolled down Kerry's feed, which was active and set to public. "She didn't get off it. It looks like she just stopped posting."

"Yeah, and she unfriended everyone, including her husband. Apparently she's in just one Facebook group. A quilting one. Her husband says that it's weird. Says she used to be really into social media. He's wanting us to look into it, but obviously the kid's search is taking priority."

The husband was right. This was strange. Kerry had been posting two, three times a day for what looked like years—then stopped entirely. There was a reason for that. Why?

"Meeko, can you find one of her friends that she stopped talking to? We need to know why she changed. Something had to have happened. Her husband had an affair or she got sick. Something. The husband doesn't know what it could be?"

"He said he didn't know she got off social media until yesterday, when he went on her page to see pictures from their trip. Honestly, he doesn't seem like the most observant spouse. We're asking him a lot of questions, but he doesn't have a lot of answers."

"Does he seem loyal?" Farah asked. "Think he has another Cornhusker on the side?"

"That's Nebraska," Kevin muttered. "They're in Wisconsin."

"I wouldn't put it past him," Meeko said. "But he's distraught over the kid. He also said she's been hoarding medication. Maybe hasn't been giving the kid his."

"Munchausen potential?" Kevin asked and Farah nodded in agreement. Munchausen by proxy wasn't common, but the mental condition—one where a parent faked a child's health conditions or intentionally caused them—was legitimate, though she couldn't immediately see how that piece cleanly fit into this clusterfuck.

"Well, that was my thought, but Kyle—that's the husband—said that she flipped *out* when the kid's cancer came back. That she handled it okay the first round and second round, but when it came up this time, she had a meltdown. Didn't stop crying for days. Says she's been frantic, taking him to specialists and trying to do whatever she can for him to be healthy. He was adamant that she only wants what's best for Miles. Oh—and circling back to your theory that maybe she was giving up the kid—remember that she didn't want to come to California. Tried to turn down the trip, then tried to get Kyle to go with Miles instead of her."

They took a moment to digest the information.

"Okay," Kevin finally said. "Let's go back to the chicken-and-the-egg thing. Scenario two is that the Miles kidnapping has nothing to do with the murder. Mom is taken and killed for who knows why—Miles was outside with her when she was snatched and bumps into a different bad guy, who has him."

"Or the killer—Trent—snatches the kid too and then disposes of him somewhere."

"The kid gets cancer multiple times, then gets kidnapped or worse." Farah shakes her head in disbelief. "Talk about an unlucky kid."

"And a tough one," Kevin said.

Yeah, Farah thought morosely. She hoped that, right now, the kid was sticking it out like a champ.

CHAPTER 70

THE KID

His head hurt, like *really* hurt. His seizure had stopped right before they got to the hospital, which Mustache Man said was really good, like Miles had any control over it. Now it was hurting and normally Mommy had medicine for him but Mustache Man said that he didn't have anything and that Miles would get some at the park.

It didn't make sense that Mustache Man didn't have any. Adults always had medicine. Mommy kept extras everywhere, and if he was a kidnapper, he was not good at it. Mommy said you should always plan ahead for emergencies, but Mustache Man didn't even have a Band-Aid for the cut on Miles's head. The cut also hurt really bad, and Miles didn't think that he had ever been in this much pain, except for maybe the day of his surgery.

Now Miles was in the back seat again and trying to follow the three rules, but he'd started crying two times because of the pain and Mustache Man didn't seem to care at all, other than that he kept cursing and hitting the steering wheel.

Suddenly the whole car jerked and they were wobbling all over the place. Miles tried to grab ahold of something, but the seat was slippery. He grabbed the seat belt, but that didn't work because it stretched. It felt like his head was cracking open, and it was so sharp, the pain right above his ear, and Miles screamed as loud as the pain was and the car suddenly slammed to a stop so hard that he fell in between the back seat and the front seat and hurt his elbow.

He hiccuped and held it with his hand, and the seat creaked as Mustache Man leaned over Miles and breathed on his face. He looked very serious and very scary.

"Listen to me," he hissed, just like a snake, and Miles really wanted to remind him of how happy he had been about his seizure stopping but decided to stay quiet just to be safe. "I'm going to give you very important directions, and you have to follow them exactly. Do you understand?"

Miles sniffed and nodded and tried not to cry, but the tears felt like they were going to burst out of his eyeballs.

"Do you know what happens when you don't follow directions that you're given?"

"Yes." He let out a teeny sob that he couldn't hold in. *Mommy goes away and I get put in dark places and kidnapped and starved to death.* "I'm going to follow—to do what you say."

"It's very easy, okay?" He pointed out the car's window. "All you have to do is walk that way until you see someone with a kid. You're going to see a lot of them, because it's a park. And just go up to that mom or dad and tell them who you are. Who are you?"

"Miles Pepper." That one he knew. That, and his home address, and Mommy's phone number.

"Tell me what you're going to do."

"Walk that way." Miles pointed toward the window, even though he couldn't see out of it, and didn't know if it had a big scary lagoon, or a lava pit, or an obstacle course he would have to go through. "And keep going until I see a mommy or daddy and then go up to them and tell them my name."

"Yep." Mustache Man looked at him the same way that Miles looked at caterpillars, really close and carefully. There were lots of poisonous caterpillars, so you better be careful about which ones you touched. "You feel okay? Feel better?"

He sniffed. "I need my medicine."

"They'll get it for you. Okay. My name is Steve. It's been nice knowing you, Miles."

Miles held out his fist for a bump, and the Mustache Man tapped fists with him, but he didn't blow it up like Daddy did.

That was okay. Miles rolled over on his stomach. "Can I go now?"

"Yep. Run when you go. As fast as you can so you can get away from the cars. Okay?" The man handed him his backpack and helped him put one arm and then the other through the straps.

Miles was good at running fast. Even with a hurt head.

CHAPTER 71
THE DETECTIVE

"Well, this looks promising." Kevin raised his phone and took a photo of the red metal gate with a big chain and padlock securing it to a wooden fence. A NO TRESPASSING sign was zip-tied to the gate.

The wind was howling across the open field and waved the overgrown grass toward them, like the blades were alive. "It's creepy out here," Farah said. "Ominous."

"That's the city girl in you talking." Kevin inhaled deeply. "I love it out here. No smog. Just the sounds of nature." He nodded to the horizon. "Stay here long enough, we'll catch one hell of a sunset."

"I'm sure the women love that as they're being tortured and cut into teeny pieces," Farah said dryly. "You see peace and quiet, I see someone screaming for help and no one around to hear. I'll take my city life over that, any day."

He pulled on a set of gloves, then opened up the evidence bag and withdrew Trent's key ring. "Let's see if Hugh was right and one of these opens the gate. If not, we'll use the bolt cutters."

Farah looked around as Kevin worked at the padlock, uneasy in the wide open field. "Maybe we should have backup," she suggested.

"Backup to help with what? The dead guy?" Kevin scoffed, then yanked the lock open. "Open sesame." He pushed on the gate and it slowly swung inward, then banged against a post.

Down the long drive, so far away that it looked like the size of an outhouse, sat a cabin. Its windows were dark, its structure tired and sagging a little to one side. Farah thought of Kerry Pepper, her hands tied behind her back, the stab wounds to her shoulder, her kidney, her stomach, and her breast.

"Coming?" Kevin called as he stepped into the SUV.

Yeah, she was coming. But she didn't like this at all.

CHAPTER 72
THE MOM

It was Bella who found the news article and the obituary for Andi. I know I mentioned it already, but Andi died the morning before her post of the rules went up.

The news article said Andi was tortured and dumped on the side of the expressway.

After Bella put the links to the articles in the group, we all started to really pay attention. And Andi's account kept making posts. Kept making demands. Kept forcing us to jump, like robots, through hoops that were put before us.

Post proof of clean bills of health, positive doctors' reports.

Post photos of our kids, weekly check-ins that proved all was well.

Social-media audits and scrubs—do this, then do that.

I stopped everything. Stopped giving Miles bad meds. Stopped rubbing in the hair-loss cream. Stopped *inventing incidents. I got off social media except for the group and poured all my time and energy into making Miles healthy and proving that improvement to the psychopath who was now spearheading our group.*

It wasn't just me, making a change. We all tried our best, but it didn't stop more members from dying.

CHAPTER 73

THE DETECTIVE

When Farah opened the door to the cabin, she thought of *Rainchaser*. In the movie, Trent had played a white boy who had been raised by the Sioux and ended up kidnapping and killing a white girl to become chief. In the two hours and fifteen minutes of the movie, Farah had fallen in love with Trent Iverson. He had been both strength and vulnerability up on that screen—his beauty framed in the majestic settings and breathtaking cinematography. He had learned the ancient Sioux language for the role and spoke only four words of English the entire film ("You need to die"), a feat that had won her respect.

While most of America loved Hugh's clean-cut perfection, Farah had always loved damaged men, and Trent had fit that mold to a T. Now, as she stepped over the transom and into the one-room cabin, she felt the lingering buzz of her Hollywood crush dissipate in the single open room.

At first glance, it looked simple enough. A bed, made with hard corners and a neat stack of white pillows. A stackable washer/dryer in the corner, by the open sink, toilet, and tub. A long table along one end with a few bankers boxes, a computer, and a chair. A television—the old box style, with a VCR attached and a folding chair set up in front for viewing.

Kevin stepped in beside her and surveyed the space, then handed her a pair of latex gloves. "Want booties?"

"I think we're fine without them." She blew into the pair, then pulled them on. Kevin went immediately to the table and flipped open the lid to the first box. "Jackpot." He pulled out a small videocassette tape and studied it, then held it up to her. "Says *Andi* on it. Know any Andis?"

"Nope. You betting sex or murder tape?"

"We didn't see a camera at the Pepper scene, so I'm voting sex tape." He shuffled through the box. "And more female names. Yeah. Sex tape."

"I'll take murder for two hundred." Farah took the tape from him and crouched in front of the VCR. "Oh wait, there's one in here." She ejected the VHS tape, then popped open the lid to reveal the mini cartridge. "God, haven't seen one of these in years. Old school." She turned her head to read the block writing on the label. "Says *Tonya*."

Kevin replaced the box's lid and turned to the television, crossing his arms over his wide chest. "Pop it in."

She pressed the power button on the television and then sat back on her heels as the VCR whirred into action. The video had been left midscene, and her chest tightened at the sight of a blonde, who lay on her back on the ground, duct tape over her mouth. There were no stab wounds here. Instead, it was like her brown shirt was moving, and Farah inhaled sharply when she realized what she was seeing.

Ants, thousands of them. The small red insects swarmed over her pale, bare skin, and the woman was twitching and jerking like she was being electrocuted. Farah covered her face, then forced herself to watch. After a few seconds, the woman stilled.

"Is she dead?" Farah asked.

"I think she's passed out from the pain. Pause that for a second?"

She tapped the button, and the video froze on a close-up of her cheek, a lone ant just under her eye and heading toward the strip of silver tape over her mouth.

"I think that's a . . . shit, what's it called?" Kevin looked down at the floor, thinking. "I saw these on one of those *Fear Factor*–type shows. They sting and it's, like, nine times more painful than a wasp. One starts and the rest of them get into, like, a frenzy."

Farah winced. "Not a good way to go. Can they kill her?"

"Maybe death from shock. A better question . . . where's the body? Was it found? When did this happen?"

"No time stamp on the video." She ejected the tape and checked the label. "Or on it. What's the deal with old video like this? There's no metadata, right?"

"Nope."

"It's unique. It should be easy to track down, assuming her body was found." She rose and walked over to the box that Kevin had looked in. Lifting the lid, she scanned the contents. "Damn, K. Twelve tapes, all with different names." She looked at him. "Twelve women."

Kevin rubbed his forehead with the tips of his fingers. "You realize this just blew up into something we won't be able to control, right?"

He was right.

Hollywood—and all of America—was going to lose their minds over this.

CHAPTER 74

THE HUSBAND

They say if a child isn't recovered in the first forty-eight hours, the chances are that they're lost forever. Now Kyle couldn't stop staring at the clock.

This town, this horrible, ugly, greedy town, seemed to have swallowed up his son without a trace. They had hundreds of leads, almost a thousand, between the tip line and the website, and no correlations between any of them. He was as far away as Mexico, then Seattle. In an airport in San Francisco, then a hospital in Santa Barbara. He was in a mall, then another mall, then a playground, then a truck stop. With each possibility, Kyle's heart rose and fell until he was emotionally nauseous with grief.

Three times, Gertie had tried to get him to go to a hotel or to lie down in the break room. He'd refused. He wouldn't be able to sleep while Miles was dealing with who knew what, who knew where.

A volunteer on the left bank of phones stood up and called for Kyle. He sighed and stepped forward, not emotionally ready for another let-down, another false hope. As he approached, he dragged his gaze up to meet the volunteer's face, and he tripped, one foot faltering at the look there. It was a smile—no, a beam. She held out the phone toward him. "Someone wants to talk to you."

Someone. There was only one someone he wanted to talk to.

He took the receiver and stared at it, terrified. If she was wrong, if this was a prank, he couldn't . . . he wasn't sure his heart could take another stab wound. He carefully lifted the receiver to his ear. "Hello?"

"Hi, Daddy." The voice was so strong, so pure, so confident. His chest broke with emotion, and he cracked forward, his breath gasping out of him as he grasped for the table and lowered himself into the seat.

"Miles?" He sobbed out the name, and his chest was shaking with exertion as loud, rasping breaths trembled through his entire core. "Miles? Are you okay?"

"I'm good, Daddy. I was in the dark and Mr. Frog ran out of batteries, and I wasn't even scared. Not even a little bit."

"I'm so proud of you, buddy," Kyle whispered.

"And I'm eating an orange." Miles giggled, and it was the most beautiful sound in the world.

Kyle lowered his head to his hand, curled forward around the phone, and openly sobbed. The cries racked out of him, the effort tearing his lungs in two, and he tried to say something to Miles, tried to tell him that he loved him, but he couldn't stop gasping for air.

"Is Mommy there?" Miles asked, and Kyle tried to pin his mouth closed, tried to force his emotion down, tried to pull himself together for his little boy. God, the smell of him. He would smell like Cheerios and dirt, and his small hands would tug at Kyle's hair and he would press his lips to his cheek and all the memories, all the feelings, were rushing back, like a dam that was broken because he hadn't allowed himself to remember, had walled off everything during the search because he had been too terrified that he would never experience it again.

"Are you safe, buddy? Where are you? I'll come right now to get you."

"I'm safe, Dad. I'm with a family. They said you can come and get me. Is Mommy there?"

He hitched in a trembling breath. "Not right now, bud, but I'll come. I'm leaving right away. I'll—I'll—" He couldn't finish the sentence. "I love you, Miles." And then he was crying again, his shoulders curling forward as if to protect his heart, and then Gertie was there, and she was taking the phone and writing down an address, and he couldn't even formulate the words to thank her.

CHAPTER 75

THE DETECTIVE

There was no cell service in the cabin, a fact that made Farah nervous. Locking the door behind them, they drove four miles to the closest signal, then called the chief and relayed what they had found.

On one hand, the information took some pressure off the gas pedal. They had identified a serial killer. Now they just needed to count bodies, collect evidence, and properly document the crimes. It would give the families closure, exonerate some suspects, and close some cold-case files. It would also devastate Trent Iverson's legion of fans and his legacy of films.

On the other hand, they still had a missing child and a death-by-suicide to understand. If Protect the Children was involved, they would have to launch an investigation to make sure that the threat was eliminated and any accomplices were uncovered and apprehended.

The chief, after a moment of incredulity and a lot of four-letter words, decided that a task force was needed and set an all-hands meeting for first thing in the morning. The decision was expected, and Farah covered a silent yawn with her hand as the chief's instructions poured through the SUV's speakers. Once this was over, she needed a weekend off. Hell, maybe even three days. They could go up to her sister's and relax. She could sleep for longer than four hours at a time. Eat some home cooking. Breathe in air that wasn't laced in smog. Chase her nieces around and catch up on their stories.

"You can take a nap if you want," Kevin offered. "We've got a bit of a drive back."

"I might take you up on that." She stretched her legs out and glanced into the back seat, where the box full of tapes sat. "God, I don't want to watch all of those."

"You didn't see a video camera anywhere at the Pepper scene, did you?"

"No. And none was found in evidence. Does it feel off to you?"

"If it was a murder-suicide, and he knew that going in . . . maybe it makes sense not to film it. I mean, who would the video be for, right? But when's the last time a serial killer was in a murder-suicide? What, it's his thirteenth murder and he suddenly gets remorse?" Kevin shook his head. "I don't like it."

"Maybe he had finished a list of names and killed himself once he completed the task," Farah said. "I don't think these were random crimes of opportunity. There's something deeply personal in all of these. And the Protect the Children connection supports the idea that she was brought here. Not random. Hand selected."

"Okay, so what ties these women together?"

"Maybe they're all married," Farah said, thinking of the woman's wedding ring. "Or mothers."

"She came here on a Make-A-Wish trip for her son. Maybe they all have sick kids," Kevin offered.

A horrible thought, followed by a worse one. "Could they all have Munchausen by proxy?"

"There's a thought," Kevin allowed. "But how would he find them? It's a logistical nightmare. And remember, the kid is still missing. What if they all have missing kids? What if he's doing something with their kid every time?"

Farah recoiled at the thought. Miles Pepper was a six-year-old boy. Had Kerry known, as Trent was stabbing her, that her child was in danger? Farah thought of the wounds on her wrists, the evidence of how hard the woman had fought against the restraints. "God, I still stress over Anaïca. Thought it'd be better when she was grown."

"It never goes away, that fear," Kevin said. "Imagine once you get grandbabies."

That was the problem with being a parent in this business. The love was like a weight around your mind, dragging you down into the depths of what could happen to them.

And in this town, that was a big depth with no bottom in sight.

CHAPTER 76
THE SIDEKICK

Around midnight, Anaïca spun away from the computer screen and twisted her back to the left, then to the right, hearing a satisfying crack of her spine. Standing, she left her cubicle and wove through the research room and out into the wide hall. Taking a right, she headed toward the bank of vending machines that sat before the stairs. The floor was quiet, which was just the way she liked it. Plenty of white mental space for her to think.

Stopping in front of the Pepsi machine, she fished out a crumpled dollar and coaxed the teeth into accepting the bill. Pressing the button for a Mountain Dew, she crouched and waited for it to fall, then moved down to the snack dispenser and got a bag of chips.

She sat cross-legged on the top step of the stairs and stared blankly ahead as she cracked the lid on the soda and mentally sifted through the forensic research she had done on Nolan Price. Most of it was garbage, but all she needed was one fact, one loose string, one out-of-place flag that would lead to another, and then to another, and then to the answer, whatever that might be.

Anaïca had been pushed into the tech side of things by her mom, who wanted to protect her from patrol, but she'd immediately fallen in love with the work. It was like a jigsaw puzzle of lies and secrets and money and crimes. Despite her mock complaints to Farah, she had no desire to be out on the street, driving around with a partner, talking to people and deciphering their lies. The truth was so much more fun, and it was always findable, once you knew what you were hunting for.

"Thought I'd find you here."

She turned at Farah's voice, then scooted over on the step to make room for her mother, who was out of her suit and in a pair of jeans and a T-shirt, her face tired. "You should be in bed, old lady. I thought you went home hours ago."

"I couldn't sleep. Thought I'd check in on you and bring you something better than junk food." Farah eased her way onto the step and produced an orange, then a bottle of water from her purse.

Anaïca rolled her eyes. "The junk food is my brain fuel, and I need something to wake me up after Dad delivered a freaking brain coma via lasagna. Here, try it. Come to the dark side." She held out the soda and wiggled it before Farah.

Farah waved it off. "You heard that Miles was found, right?"

"Yeah, Marcus from the Whiz Kids told me. One good piece of news from today, though it's so freaking random that he was in San Diego." Anaïca took a sip, then eyed her. "You know, I do have a phone. It's one of these high-tech things so people don't have to drive twenty minutes in order to see each other."

"Oh, shush and tell me what you've found so far."

It hadn't taken much digging for Anaïca to find Nolan's secrets. The money was always where she started. Money talks, and it always had a lot to say about a person's mental and financial health.

"In the last two years, Nolan's spending habits have changed. He's flashing cash now—not that he's rich, but he's getting coffee, going out to eat, getting spa treatments—you know." She rubbed her fingers together. "Spending."

"What was he like before?"

"Cheap," she emphasized. "Like, broke as me. He kept himself to a tight budget and had around eight grand in credit card debt. The credit cards were all paid off thirteen months ago . . . which was when things started to get interesting." She paused to take a sip of the soda, then continued.

"Somehow, this bad boy gets a hundred thousand dollars in cash. He was smart with the deposits, and put in less than ten grand at a time, so he didn't trigger any IRS reporting thresholds, but I tracked the deposits and added them up. Ninety-seven thousand. Then, almost a year later, a second surge of cash. Same amount." She rose to her feet and scooped the chip bag off the floor. "Come on, I'll show you the dates."

Back at her desk, she showed Farah the calendar where she'd recorded when each cash deposit had occurred. In a red pen, she'd circled Kerry Pepper's death, which was six weeks after the second deposit.

"Okay," Farah said slowly. "So Nolan gets a hundred thousand dollars. A year passes. Another hundred thousand arrives. I can look up when Kerry Pepper gets contacted by Nolan, but the gist of it is . . . six weeks later she dies. Do we think the first hundred thousand was tied to Pepper, or was it for someone else?"

"Or for something else," Anaïca amended.

"Let's switch horses for a moment." Farah grabbed a rolling chair from an adjacent desk and dragged it over to Anaïca's. "Can you link the cash to Trent?"

Anaïca winced. "Not really." She spun slightly in her chair as she bit into a spicy barbecue potato chip. "No withdrawals of that amount for Trent. To be blunt, he couldn't really afford it."

Farah perked up. "He was broke?"

"I wouldn't say broke, but he's not dropping a hundred grand without feeling it." She reached forward and clicked a few buttons, then gestured to the screen. "Here. This is a rough balance sheet I put together by month and by quarter. You can see how his cash moves. Pretty much all of his savings is here." She pointed to a money market account with $286,322 listed beside it.

"That's it?"

"Well, that's what he has that's liquid, plus about a hundred grand between some of his other accounts. Think about the last time you saw a Trent Iverson movie in a theater. I mean, he's a huge celebrity—but not really a huge moneymaker. And he spends it like he has nothing to save for. Paid eighty grand in cash for that Bronco that was in front of his house."

"Well, if you're planning to kill yourself, why save for retirement?" Farah mused, and sat back in the chair. "Have you looked into anyone else's financials for comparison?"

"Like Hugh's?" Anaïca shot her mother a look. "No. I've behaved. So far."

"Keep doing so. The spotlight on this case is going to be hot, so we have to dot every *i* and cross every *t*, okay?"

Anaïca didn't respond, and her mother kicked her chair. "Yeah, fine. Whatever," she grumbled.

"So what are you looking at now?"

"Almost done with Nolan's phone records." Anaïca sighed. "Which I hate sifting through, by the way."

"Find anything?"

"Nada. Unless Trent and Nolan communicated by carrier pigeon, the history isn't there, and as a wise woman once told me . . ." She paused, waiting for Farah to complete the sentence.

"The history is always there," Farah finished.

"Bingo." Anaïca yawned and took another sip of the soda. "Once I wrap with those, I'll start in on corporate and partnership assets."

"Well, don't work too late." Farah rose to her feet and set the orange on the desk. "The first task force meeting is in less than eight hours. Get at least a few hours of sleep."

Anaïca already had her fingers on the keyboard, the digits a flurry of motion. She dismissed the advice with an impatient nod.

On the other end of the floor, the observation room was quiet, the whir of VCRs the only sound as three uniforms, powered by coffee and years of experience, watched in unaffected silence as they played the kill tapes and listened through headphones. Their attention alternated between the video monitor and their computer screens as they inputted details about background, sounds, victims, and the killer.

By the time the sun rose over the Los Angeles skyline, there were twelve new files in the LAPD database and the FBI had been contacted and briefed on the victim profiles that the team had created, based on the clues found on each video.

CHAPTER 77
THE LEADING LADY

Nora couldn't stop watching the news. It was becoming an obsession, the need to know what was happening. The detectives weren't telling them anything, and she was afraid to call them and ask questions, worried that it would make them look guilty.

At least the little boy had been found. She watched a replay of a tearful reunion video with the kid beaming, his father covering him with kisses. They hadn't heard anything from Pete, but that was what they had agreed to. No phone calls, no texts, no ties that could be tracked, if his involvement was ever discovered. Hopefully, between the big fake mustache that Pete had worn and the giant mole Nora had added to her cheek, any descriptions that Miles gave police would be useless in terms of identifying them. Witnesses, especially young ones, often fixated on specific characteristics, and only remembered those. To be safe, Nora had also pulled her trademark hair into a low ponytail and added a hat and a pair of reading glasses.

"Excuse me, Miss Kemp, but Mr. Iverson is requesting you in the studio." A maid hovered in the doorway, her hands clasped in front of her.

Nora sighed and lifted the remote, turning off the television. "Thanks. Do you know if the guesthouse has been cleared by the police yet?"

"It still has the tape up. I can call the detective if you'd like."

"No, I'll do it." She rose. "You said that Hugh's in the studio?"

"Yes, ma'am." The woman backed through the doorway, then fled at Nora's dismissive wave.

Nora took the long route to the studio, wanting to walk past Trent's guesthouse on the way. The maid was right, the tape was still up, and she walked to the door and looked through the thin strips of glass, curious at what was there.

No chalk outline or Post-it notes, strings with bullet trajectories, or any of the items Hollywood had taught her to expect. She closed her eyes, thinking of the woman in the chair. Him, on his back, his eyes open and still.

This had been their oasis. She rested her head against the door, closing her eyes and thinking of Trent, his eyes heavy with lust, his lips nuzzling her neck, his kiss on her shoulder, his hands sliding up her dress . . .

He had first told her that he loved her in that kitchen, her body pinned against the counter, the taste of whiskey on his tongue, his voice gruff with emotion.

While Hugh had worked tirelessly at fame, Trent had wanted only her heart and her commitment, and had fought for it with his body and soul, and failed over and over again, against the shining star that was his twin.

She stepped back from the door and wondered why, of all places, he had chosen to kill that woman here.

Was it intentional? Was it a spit in the face to their love?

Turning away, she moved down the path, her steps quickening until she was almost running, her heart beginning to pound as she took the stairs up to the studio. It was above the garages, and she and Trent had met here also, a half dozen times, because they couldn't seem to occupy the same space without needing to deprave it.

She stepped inside the soundproof room and pulled the door shut behind her. He was seated at the desk by the window, a script in hand, and she approached quietly, not wanting to interrupt him.

When she was a few feet away, he turned and she smiled. "Hey."

"The detectives called." He set the script down and stood.

Her steps faltered, and she held on to the window's ledge for support. "What did they say?"

"They found something in the cabin. They wouldn't say what. They're going to come by here and talk to us, either tonight or in the morning."

His voice was eerily calm, but she could hear the anger in it. He stepped toward her, and she stayed in place, reminded herself of who he was, of how much he loved her. "Nora," he said carefully. "Why did you mention the cabin to them?"

"I don't know," she said blankly. "I mentioned a lot of things. I was just frustrated. I knew you guys had other land, other properties. It's not like it's a secret."

But it had been. She'd known that. She hadn't known that there would be something there for the police to find, but there had always been tension between the two brothers over the cabin, which Momma Beth had always used as a personal spiritual retreat.

He stopped in front of her, and when he lifted his hand, she stiffened, inhaling sharply as he closed his grip around her neck and pushed her until she was pinned against the window. He lowered his face until his breath tickled her lips. "I don't trust you," he whispered.

She stared back at him, her mouth opening as she sucked in as much air as she could past his tight grip. His hips pushed into hers, and he may not have trusted her, but he did want her.

She reached for him, gripped him through his pants, and when his gaze darkened, she licked her lips. His hand softened on her neck, and his mouth pressed hard to hers.

He didn't trust her, but that was fine because she didn't trust him either.

CHAPTER 78

THE MOM

The Facebook group became a dictator of our lives, with Andi's account holding the megaphone and grading all of our performances.

I thought about just calling the police, you know, but what would I say? I'd have to confess to everything. I'd have to implicate everyone. Our kids would get taken away from us. Our husbands would divorce us. And would they even be able to catch the person doing this? He was smart and tech savvy, and he was ahead of us with every single step.

In that first post, he—or maybe she—told us that he had already captured our IP addresses through a link that had been posted in the group. He'd been prepping for months, maybe even a year. He said he'd been collecting information on all of us, and that if we tried to run or hide, he would kill us.

And that was my new normal, for a while.

Then Miles had another seizure. A real one, this time.

When it happened, I thought that it was God punishing me, and maybe it was. I held Miles in my arms and prayed for it to end, prayed for it to be a fluke, prayed until I ran out of words and found myself in the hospital parking lot, leading him through the halls and back to the wing, back to Dr. Sortensen's office, where I demanded a brain scan and wouldn't leave his office until I had an appointment set.

It was a week out and I spent that time terrified, not of Miles actually being sick, but of what would happen to me if he was.

That's what a horrible mother I am, Kyle. I was worried that there was another tumor because if there was, then I wouldn't be able to report into the group with a healthy report. I wouldn't be able to hide Miles's side effects. He wouldn't believe that it was real. He would think it was me regressing. He would think it was me faking.

That's why I had the meltdown when the doctor called us and told us about Miles's second tumor. It's why I tried to push back against chemo and why I cried when Miles's hair started to fall out.

The Make-A-Wish trip is just another nail in my coffin. I've faked two check-ins so far, but he'll figure it out soon.

And when that happens, I'll die.

CHAPTER 79

THE LEADING LADY

Back in her suite, Nora stepped out of her jeans and pulled her shirt over her head. Standing in front of the full-length mirror in the closet, she examined her naked body. Hugh had never been so rough, so angry—-but she had also never been so desperate, so greedy. She had needed to wipe away the grief, the stress, the worry, the fear, and she had needed validation that—despite everything that had happened in the last forty-eight hours—they still had something, a connection and history that would pull them through this and take them into the next chapter of their lives. The final chapter.

She opened the tall door on the leftmost cubby of the closet and stared at the wedding dress that hung there, waiting for the date that was still three months out. She ran a gentle hand down the front of it, being careful not to damage the custom beadwork. The gown had been designed for maximum impact at the wedding, which would be the new gold standard for decadence and glamour. The dress design hadn't taken into account a pregnant belly, and she considered her options as she looked over the lines with a critical eye.

A wedding was a fitting end to a courtship that had been planned and executed from the first date to the proposal. As her and Hugh's relationship had evolved, so had Nora's status and stardom. Americans had fallen hard for their love story, which had shown a softer side to a man whose long bachelorhood had started to raise eyebrows.

The romantic journey had been coordinated to perfection and layered with staged photo shoots, leaked details, interviews, and exclusives. When paparazzi at the neighborhood gate had doubled, they'd had his-and-her Rolexes delivered to each home in the neighborhood, a generous apologetic gesture that was leaked to *People* magazine and made the cover.

As their supernova had shone brighter and brighter, it had been harder and harder to stop the Hugh and Nora production, to take her foot off the gas, to back away from the relationship that was bringing her so much attention and success. Her followers grew, her wealth multiplied, and Trent understood, at least in the beginning, why she needed to take this path, to prioritize Hugh over him, and to hide their relationship while broadcasting his.

And then, when Hugh's proposal came, when the risk of being outed overcame the reward of being with Trent, she had needed to end it. She had chosen the fame, the success, the security over him.

Trent hadn't taken it well.

Neither had she.

CHAPTER 80
THE SIDEKICK

"And . . . there you are." Anaïca jiggled in her seat at the discovery of Trent's second money-market account, which was in a business name that had become inactive three years earlier. The account had almost $400,000 in it and little to no activity. "I knew you had some money socked away," she whispered, hitting a series of keys and sending the page of transactions to the printer.

"Time to dig deeper," she mused, and clicked the button on the side of her purple Bose headphones, turning up the volume on the Janis Joplin playlist that she was listening to. As "Piece of My Heart" pulsed, she dug deeper, examining the open date, signers on the account (only Trent), corporation filings, and tax returns. The money to fund the account had come via bank wire from Production Plus, a studio.

She pulled up IMDB and matched the studio and the date to a film—*Breakaway Boy*. The total budget of the movie had been $4 million, and Trent had been the lead. The deposit made sense, and she returned to the bank records.

With the account holder deceased, she had full access to the account history, including any amendments made to the initial paperwork. It was there that she struck pay dirt. When the money-market account was opened, there were three beneficiaries listed. Over time, Trent had sent in form after form, until the beneficiary count was at twelve.

Anaïca wrote down the beneficiary names in a neat list. The oldest was Caleb Brown, and she spun to her second computer and searched the news database for the name. There was one result, an obituary mention from 2019.

She clicked on the item, which was for the obituary of Dana Celeste Brown. No cause of death given . . . wonderful mother . . . active in her tennis league . . . Caleb Brown was listed as a surviving child. The date of the obituary was February 19, 2019.

Anaïca glanced back at the beneficiary form. Completed and submitted on February 27, 2019.

"Hot blueberry on a biscuit," she murmured, clapping her hands at the connection. Scrolling up, she found the city—Visalia, California, then linked the county—Tulare—then accessed their police database.

Dana Celeste Brown. The file was right there, and she clicked her tongue with approval at the flags beside it: *Deceased / Murder / Unsolved.*

Clicking on the link, she waited for the file to load. Spinning in her chair, she made eye contact and smiled a hello at Maeve, a data cruncher who loved traffic reports like they were Chris Hemsworth in a thong.

The file opened and she scrolled through the list of police reports inside. Considering that the Trent Iverson death had seventy-two reports and growing, the scant amount here—only three—spoke both to a lack of department resources and the unimportance of the victim. This murder had not warranted advanced forensics or expensive and extensive testing, which was probably why it was still unsolved. Pulling her rolling chair closer to the desk, she clicked on the first document— the initial crime scene report.

Local Realtor found suffocated at an open house she was holding. Was found by her husband, who went looking for her a few hours after she should have been home. House was locked, lights out, but her car was in the drive, and he broke a window, got in, and found her in an upstairs bedroom. She had a plastic bag over her head that was zip-tied around her neck. Autopsy revealed she was four months pregnant.

Interesting.

She scrolled down to the suspects section of the report. They had interviewed the husband, the gardener, and Dana's broker at her real estate firm. All had alibis or lack of motive.

Anaïca closed the file, then opened the autopsy report to see if a paternity test had been performed on the fetus. It had not, and she groaned at the oversight.

The body disposal method was at the bottom. Cremation.

Ugh.

She leaned back in the chair and stared up at the dingy gray ceiling tiles, focusing on a kidney-shaped water mark.

Woman dies and a week later, Trent Iverson adds her son to his bank account's beneficiary list. Yeah, not suspicious at all.

She minimized the file, then glanced at her watch and returned to the beneficiary list and highlighted the next two names. Jessyca and Mario Thomas. Leaning to the right, she entered the names into the news database and immediately got a hit.

CHAPTER 81

THE DETECTIVE

There comes a point when you just run out of patience. With less than three hours of sleep and twelve new murder files on their desk, Farah had hit that point.

"Ian, we're going to need you to just cut the bullshit and tell us what you know." Kevin sat at the long metal table across from Ian McGomery and stared at the Protect the Children director. "What's the deal? You feeding victims to Trent to kill? Selling sick kids to sex traffickers? Talk fast, because I need a suspect and you're starting to smell good to me."

They'd called Ian down to the station, put him in one of the dirtiest interview rooms, and made him wait for an hour. The intimidation tactic had worked, potentially too well. Ian's mouth opened and closed like a hooked fish gasping for breath, and his head swiveled between Farah and Kevin. "I don't—I don't know—" he stammered.

"Screw that," Farah interrupted. "We found boxes of Protect the Children documents at Trent's cabin of torture and links between four victims—so far—that had applications with STC." That was all complete bullshit but allowed in the context of questioning, and the reaction on Ian's face was worth the price of admission.

"I didn't—I don't—Nolan. Nolan was the one who knew everything. He was the one with the history with the twins."

Of course. The dead always were the ones who knew everything.

"Did he ever talk to you about the twins? Ever say anything about them?" Farah asked.

"We had lots of logistical conversations about them. They were our spokesmodels, so there was always some sort of coordination—"

"No," Kevin interrupted. "We're talking about personal conversations about Trent. Or Hugh. Nolan's opinions of them? Maybe stories from their past?"

"No, not really." Ian shook his head, but Farah could sense something there, something poised on the tip of his tongue and wanting to jump off.

She moved closer and held out her hand, stopping Kevin from speaking. "Ian, what might seem unimportant to you might be important to us. So we need you to tell us everything. Right now."

"Well, I mean . . ." He scratched his neck, then tucked his palms in between his thighs. "One time he made a comment about Nora and how much she had changed. That he didn't recognize her."

"Recognize her since when?"

"Well, *Story Farm*."

God, they couldn't get away from this stupid show. Farah stared blankly at him, trying to understand the connection he was referring to. "Nolan knew Nora back when they were kids?"

"Well, yeah. She was on the show."

The air in the room paused, like molecules freezing in a tube. "Nora *Kemp*?" Farah asked, though he couldn't possibly be talking about anyone else.

Ian's eyes darted between the two of them and he paled, as if he'd said something wrong. "Yes?" He delivered the answer as a question. "I—uh, didn't watch the show, but Nolan said that she had changed a lot." He let out a breath and raised his hands in surrender. "So, uh.

That was it. That was, like, the only personal thing that Nolan ever said about them."

Farah withdrew her phone and typed "story farm nora kemp" in the browser. No meaningful results. She removed Nora's name and tried again, then flipped to image results and stared at the cast photo—a foursome of Hugh, Trent, Nolan, and the girl. The chubby girl with curly brown hair who had been really funny and fast-talking and whose character's name she couldn't even remember.

She turned the screen to Ian and pointed to the group shot. "You're talking about this girl?"

He shrugged. "I don't know? Nolan said she had some plastic surgery."

"No shit," Farah drawled. "Like, a face implant? And a stapled stomach?"

There was no way that Nora Kemp—arguably one of the most beautiful women in the world—was the same doughy and plain teenager who had been the punch line of most *Story Farm* episodes. She studied the photo, and the connections just weren't there. Different facial structure, different body shape—she glanced at Kevin, whose brow was furrowed in thought.

"Didn't that girl have an accent?" he asked.

"Yeah, a hick one," Farah said. "Really thick." She thought of Ana's research into Nora. The suspicious backstory. A name change, she had thought.

This potential tidbit felt huge on one hand and inconsequential on the other. Did it matter if Nora was an ugly duckling turned swan? Did that redirect any line of their investigation or theories? If anything, it just clarified a little more about the dynamic in that household. Maybe Nora's nonchalance about the affair was because it wasn't really an affair. Maybe they were all just really close friends. Friends with occasional benefits.

"Anyway," Ian continued, "I swear to God that I don't know why Nolan killed himself or why those woman are on our computers. And I don't know anything about the Iversons. All I've ever done is coordinate with the twins when they stop by the rescue centers to visit the children. I normally try to be there for that, just as a witness to make sure that there isn't a PR or liability issue with one of the kids or parents claiming that they were inappropriate."

"Has that ever happened?" Farah asked, thinking of their earlier theory that Trent may have been obsessed with Miles and killed Kerry to get to him. That theory had been nixed when Miles had shown up, untouched and happy, but maybe . . .

"No." Ian shook his head emphatically. "They were both . . ." He paused. "I always wanted to video or take photos of the twins with PTC kids because they were *great* with them. But press wasn't why they were there, and both of them were adamant that that experience not be exploited for media coverage. I would have trusted either of the Iversons with a child's life. With *my* child's life. They were amazing with them, which is why I just can't . . ." He faltered. "I can't believe Trent would kill those women. It just doesn't make sense."

Farah thought of the woman on the video. Her eyes, widening in pain and fear and then pinching shut as the ants crawled, like an incoming tide, over her face.

It might not have made sense, but that didn't make it any less true.

CHAPTER 82
THE LEADING LADY

Maybe if Nora had been born pretty, things would have turned out differently. Maybe she would have felt more secure, made less-risky decisions. Maybe she would have married a lawyer, popped out some kids. Maybe she'd be addicted to Xanax or banging her pool boy.

Maybe she'd be happy. Maybe she'd be miserable.

Maybe she'd be famous. Maybe she'd be a loser.

Maybe, maybe, maybe. Stack enough of the scenarios on top of each other, and you had a garbage pail of shit.

It didn't really matter where that alternative life would have ended. She didn't have that life; she had hers. And hers—with the exception of four years with *Story Farm*—had been a handful of short straws that God had tied together and labeled as Annie Bayors. She'd had four years in California, and then she'd been flown back to Kansas and back to her ugly life, where phone calls to the twins hit disconnected numbers and she wasn't famous anymore. She was just fat, lazy Annie, who was no longer bringing in any bacon and, instead, just stuffed her face with it.

On her twenty-first birthday, she was living in a youth hostel in San Francisco, checking in visitors and cleaning the rooms in exchange for lodging, when a man walked in, flashed a private investigator's badge, and asked if she was Annie Bayors.

She got in his car, was taken to a bank, and signed papers that assumed ownership of a trust that *Story Farm* had set up and deposited half of her earnings into, every year, for the four years that *Story Farm* had aired, plus thirteen years of syndicated replays. One secret gift from Momma Beth, who hadn't been all bad, not to Nora.

It was over $500,000, and it was hers. Unencumbered cash, just waiting to be spent.

She moved to Florida, rented a small apartment near the beach, and created a plan. A way to change her life, to build a better one, a way to get everything that she'd ever wanted.

The first step of that plan took three years, a legal name change, sixty-eight pounds of weight loss, seventeen facial and body-contouring surgeries, and voice lessons that removed every hint of Kansas hick. A week after her twenty-fourth birthday, Nora Kemp arrived in Hollywood with professional headshots and a curated past. Her first goal was to find her twins. The next goal was to make herself into the biggest name in Hollywood.

It had taken six more years, but she had done it. Captured the perfect life, with the perfect fiancé, the perfect career, the perfect reputation.

At times, it felt secure and untouchable.

Other times, it felt like one single event, one wrong move, could crash it to the ground.

One single event—like a death. Like two.

Nora stared into the mirror and carefully applied makeup over her scars and could feel her meticulously constructed world beginning to pulse and rip at the seams.

Nora's history with *Story Farm* was a secret that she had successfully hidden from the public for a decade. Now, with a microscope pointed at their lives, the story was bound to leak. This was just as juicy—if not more so—than her sleeping with Hugh's twin. The public loved a teardown, and side-by-side photos of her next to fat, ugly Annie would make every housewife grin and every horny husband look away.

It wasn't fair. She'd worked too hard for her ugly beginning to be exposed. To be called a whore. To be labeled the stupid woman who fell in love with a killer.

It wasn't fair, but maybe it was what she deserved. Maybe this was her penance.

CHAPTER 83
THE ACCOMPLICE

You think you know someone; then they sneak out of the house on a Sunday morning and step in front of a semi.

Josie Blank sat in the living room of the home that he shared with Nolan Price and ran a trembling hand over the back of their long-haired calico. As the cat purred, he tried to move, to get up and eat something, to return the detective's call, to put together a funeral. Instead, he sat there, staring at Nolan's chair, and tried to come to terms with the idea that he would never again sit in it. He would never again make fun of Josie's outfits, or complain about his mother, or laugh so hard that he snorted, or kiss him just to shut him up.

It was an impossible task. Three years together. That's all they'd had. And here Josie had been expecting a proposal. A proposal and the excitement of wedding planning. Instead, he got the task of funeral arrangements.

Somewhere, Nolan would have written down his wishes. Probably in the office—the small, cramped room that held Pumpkin's litter box and their much-neglected elliptical machine. Josie forced himself to nudge the chubby cat off his lap and rise to his feet. God, he'd have to call Nolan's mother. She couldn't find out from the internet or the police.

He made it to the office and sat down at the leather chair in front of the rolltop desk. Pulling open the built-in file drawer, he easily found the one labeled *Last Will and Testament*. Sending a silent thank-you to heaven, he placed the file on the desktop and flipped it open.

Nolan's wishes were simple and clear. While the Iversons' team had booked the Getty Observatory for Trent's funeral and would arrange press, crowd control, and a speaking lineup that would rival an award show, Nolan simply wanted cremation and a family-only service at St. Thomas the Apostle.

The will was also short and to the point. Nolan had left all assets and his home to Josie, who would need to rent out a bedroom to cover the mortgage payment. Josie smiled through his tears at the longest page in the folder—a long list of instructions and demands for the care of Pumpkin.

Paper-clipped to the will was a cryptic handwritten note, and Josie read the message several times, trying to understand what it meant.

Mrs. Jenkins was right about the pie the entire time. I'm guilty of providing the ingredients, nothing else. God forgive me for my sins.

Josie didn't know anyone by the name of Jenkins and had never seen Nolan bake or even eat a piece of pie. It must be a code, but he couldn't see through his grief enough to understand what Nolan was trying to communicate.

With the note in hand, he moved into the kitchen and found the pad where he had written down the name and cell phone number of the detective who had called him after Nolan's death. *Kevin Mathis.*

He texted him a photo of the paper, along with a short message:

Found this with Nolan Price's will. I have no idea what it means.
This is Josie Blank, his partner.

He pressed "Send" on the text and then sat down on one of the kitchen's barstools, lost as to what to do next.

CHAPTER 84

THE LEADING MAN

"Hugh," Nora called from the living room, but he ignored her. She raised her voice and repeated the name, but he tucked his hands into his pockets and continued to stare out on the view.

Nora could wait. Better yet, she could go away. She had fucked up by mentioning the cabin and brought the cavalry to this investigation.

With what was in the cabin, the legacy of Trent Iverson would be cemented, dead woman by dead woman, into that of the worst serial killer in Hollywood history. Fuck his body of work. Any positive accomplishment would be ignored as press would focus on the drug use, the fights with paparazzi, and the pile of dead bodies. He'd be a trivia answer, a regular tool on stand-up routines, a *True Hollywood Story*, and the inspiration of a dozen Lifetime movies.

Trent would be vilified while Hugh's name would remain pristine and perfect. The good twin versus the bad. The one who got the girl versus the one who didn't. The public would eat the bullshit, like they always had, and never see the truth. They'd never see the monster behind the mask, the killer behind the charisma.

Now Nora was pulling on his arm, twisting him toward her, and in the setting sun, she was breathtaking. There was a reason her star had taken off so brightly, and it wasn't just Hugh's association with her, though he had certainly tried to make her believe that he was responsible for it. The real reason was that she had become a once-in-a-lifetime beauty, and one who could actually act—a rare combination in this town. "Are you okay?"

"I'm fine." He tried to turn away, but she moved with him, staring in his eyes. For a moment, their gaze connected, and he was almost relieved to see the fear in her eyes, to know that he wasn't alone in his worry. She wrapped her arms around his waist, and he stiffened, then relaxed into her touch.

Her mistake wasn't intentional, and maybe it was good that she'd mentioned the cabin. As mad as he was at the betrayal of Trent, at least it pulled the focus off them. A neat, clean package, delivered straight to their doorstep. Even the LAPD couldn't screw that up.

Maybe they would just accept the gift, close the files, and move on.

Or maybe they wouldn't. Maybe this hell was just beginning.

CHAPTER 85
THE SIDEKICK

Anaïca's fingers were a blur as she swiped screens, typed in names, short-cut actions, and recorded her findings in a master spreadsheet.

Of the twelve beneficiaries listed on Trent's account, all were children under the age of eighteen. Each had a murdered mother—eight moms between the twelve of them—and each had been added as a beneficiary just after the murder. Trent was a killer with a conscience, though an average of $33,000 per beneficiary wasn't exactly replace-your-momma money.

Anaïca printed the spreadsheet and glanced around the room. Only half of the cubicles were in use, and the familiar and relaxing soundtrack of clicking keys was in the air. She'd managed to keep her findings a secret while she dug, but it was time to share her cookies with the other kids on the playground. Out of this room and at the end of the hall was the task force, where at least half of the team was in search of the information that was printing out of her ink-jet. Identifying eight victims out of twelve wasn't bad, and she'd bet all the money in her savings account that she'd find another stash somewhere that was earmarked for the other four victims' kids.

This list confirmed a connection and pattern—the victims were women with kids. There was a motive somewhere, and someone on that force should be able to connect other dots to determine what it was.

She texted the update to Farah, then released a big yawn as the list finished printing. Pulling it off the tray, she stood and bounced slightly on her toes to wake herself up, then headed down the hall.

Unlike the quiet research room, the task force area was as loud as a police bullpen as groups hunkered together over computer screens, in front of whiteboards, and by the coffee station. Anaïca looked around for her mother and spotted her and Kevin in a conversation with one of the suits. Rob Belkiss, the captain of the task force, was by the projector, and she beelined for him.

Before she could reach him, he whistled loudly and the room quieted down. She slunk to the left side of the room and edged toward him, curious what he was about to announce.

"We just got a note that was left by Nolan Price, Trent's contact at Protect the Children."

Not his contact, Anaïca thought dismissively. *Not until you prove the paper trail.* She moved around a stack of boxes and stopped in the space beside him.

Belkiss fumbled with the projector and put a piece of paper on the screen, upside down. Anaïca watched, pained, as he craned his head toward the display, realized his mistake, then flipped it over, still upside down. He corrected the position, and she lifted her gaze to the screen.

There was a photo in the middle of the page, one of a handwritten note that read like a clue to a scavenger hunt.

Mrs. Jenkins was right about the pie the entire time. I'm guilty of providing the ingredients, nothing else. God forgive me for my sins.

"Does anyone have any idea what this means?" He tapped the note on the projector.

Everyone in the room fell silent as they read and absorbed the note.

"Think carefully. We're assuming this had something to do with the Kerry Pepper murder, but it could be about anything."

Anaïca glanced around the room, but everyone's faces were blank. Her mother had her head down, her eyes on her phone, and Anaïca wondered what, right now, was more important than this.

"Okay," the captain said. "Let's create a file and keep it in mind. If—"

"Wait." Farah raised a hand. "I think it's a *Story Farm* reference. Captain, let's sidebar on this."

Belkiss hit the switch on the projector and killed the display. "Everyone else, you know what we're doing. Double down on ID'ing the victims—we need that as soon as possible and before we lose all of this to the Feds. As soon as someone has a potential match, I want to know immediately."

"Oh." Anaïca straightened and cleared her throat. "I have a list of potential victims." She waved the list in the air to catch the room's attention. "Eight of them. Trent set up beneficiary accounts for all of their children, and the causes of death look to line up."

The captain turned and studied her name tag for a moment. "Anderson. You any relation to that pain in my ass in the corner?"

"She would be my mother." Anaïca grinned at him. "And don't worry, the affection between you two goes both ways."

He ignored the comment and took the list from her, then grunted in admiration. "Excellent work." Turning the projector back on, he replaced the photo of the note with her page. "Everyone, listen up. Thanks to the excellent legwork of Mini Anderson, we have a potential list of eight victims. Check these against our dead ladies, and let's match the files to the names. Chop-chop."

Someone in the back of the room began to clap. The action caught on, and there was a whistle of approval. Anaïca blushed and ducked her head, glancing at Belkiss and straightening to attention when she realized the captain was waiting for her to follow him, Farah, and Kevin into his office. "You coming, Anderson?"

"Coming," she murmured, and when she passed by her mother, she accepted the discreet high five and tried to swallow the smile stretching over her cherry Chapstick–covered lips.

CHAPTER 86
THE DETECTIVE

"Okay, what's the note mean?" Rob Belkiss closed the door to his office and sat on the edge of his desk, crossing his arms and giving them a tired look that Farah didn't appreciate.

"You know," she said tartly, "we've been on this case two days longer than you."

"And it took you that long to find a serial killer under your nose," he fired back.

"All right, Rob. No need to be an asshole. You want the info or not? Because we can just take it to the chief and skip this squirrel-and-rabbit show," Kevin said, lazily scratching the edge of his ear as if he were considering the action.

For the first time in hours, Farah grinned, because they were in the unique position of having something Rob wanted, even if she was the only one in the room who knew what it was.

"Just say it already," Rob growled. "I really hope this is worth the jerk-off session I'm going through to get it."

Sure, Farah thought. *A jerk-off with sandpaper.* Still, she stepped up to the plate. "Okay, so I haven't seen the episode, but I just searched for the character name Mrs. Jenkins in the IMDB database for *Story Farm,* and she appears in four episodes. I pulled up each episode summary, and only one could apply. Season 3, episode 9." She glanced up from her phone to make sure that everyone was listening. They were, and Anaïca's eyes were sharp with interest.

"Old lady Mrs. Jenkins sees Luke stealing her pie out of the window and tells his parents. Paul tries to take the blame, but Mrs. Jenkins refuses to believe that it was Paul who did it and the twins must make amends together."

Anaïca closed her eyes in concentration. "Okay, so if the note says that she was right, then it's saying that Paul took the blame for Luke's crime. And Luke's character is Hugh and Paul is Trent, so the note is saying . . ."

Kevin jumped in. "That we're looking at the wrong twin. Trent isn't the killer."

"Bingo." Farah smiled. "It's Hugh."

CHAPTER 87
THE HUSBAND

Kyle sat in the pediatric wing of Cedars-Sinai and watched as Miles slept. His son was dehydrated but otherwise unharmed and happy. His biggest concern was when he would get to go to Disneyland, but that trip would have to wait, at least for a little while.

In the meantime, he was the star of the floor and had been spoiled by every nurse and doctor in the division. Now, in a moment of peace and quiet, Kyle tried to turn off his thoughts.

It will be okay. He stared at Miles and knew that tomorrow he would need to tell him about his mom. How did any parent do that? How, when Kyle still broke into tears at the thought?

It will be okay. He studied the tube that ran from Miles's nose to the oxygen—just an extra precaution, they had told him—and wondered how, with his job and his complete ineptitude at life, Kyle would manage Miles's doctors' appointments, insurance forms, and medicine all by himself.

He took a deep breath and reminded himself that Miles was alive. He wasn't harmed. He was here, and that was what really mattered. All the rest, Kyle would figure out.

His gaze fell to the backpack, which Miles had come back with. The police had already checked it for fingerprints or DNA but came up blank, all the contents wiped down with bleach. Now Kyle pulled each item out, grateful for a distraction from what tomorrow would bring.

There was Mr. Frog, who had already had his batteries replaced and whose green stomach lit red when you squeezed him. The water bottle, which Kyle would need to refill before they left the hospital. Miles's crayons, half of which appeared to be missing. A notebook, the edges bent and worn.

He pulled out the notebook and flipped through the first few pages, smiling at the drawings that Miles had done. Kerry's handwriting was on the opposite side of the pages, and he flipped back to the front, glancing briefly at the words, then studied them closer when he saw his name.

Dear Kyle, the first page read. *If you're reading this letter, I'm probably already dead.*

Mr. Frog fell from his hand and to the floor. Reaching out, Kyle found the switch for the lamp and clicked it on, illuminating the page. Slowly sitting back in the recliner, he started to read and didn't stop until he reached the very last page.

CHAPTER 88
THE MOM

We got the invitation to Disneyland at the beginning of August, and you presented it to me like it was a gift. It was a monogrammed card, thick stock, dark blue with the words in a silver ink. The message was short, simple, and caused dread to piston through my veins.

We would like to extend a formal invitation for Miles Pepper to visit Disneyland in Anaheim, California, as a guest of:

Protect the Children Charities, Los Angeles

Miles will be given VIP access to the park, plus a variety of special activities. One parent may attend as his companion. First-class flights and hotel accommodations are included. This award is a result of the Make-A-Wish application that was submitted for Miles.

"What's wrong?" When you saw my face, you moved around until your sweater brushed against my arm.

You didn't understand why I was freaked out, but I couldn't tell you the truth. A year back, I would have instantly taken a pic of the invite and posted it, then tango-line danced my way into the bedroom and started to pick out outfits for the event. Instead, I almost collapsed. I had to sit on the closest stool. You know, the one that wobbles.

You were bobbing your head and grinning like a little kid who just got a letter from Santa. I remember you being all jazzed up about the first-class ticket, and you did this stupid fist pump that made me want to grab the diet pop out of your hand and smash it into your head.

I told you I wasn't going. I said you could go, but you said you'd have to work, which made sense. I suggested your mom, but you didn't like that either.

I know you'll remember the fight because I didn't have a good excuse for why I didn't want to go, but now you'll know the truth.

Going to Los Angeles would be against the rules. It would be seen as me benefiting from and exploiting Miles's sickness. The sickness that HE thought I was faking. If I go—and if this psychopath finds out—he'll kill me.

He'll kill me, and he'll never believe—or care—that Miles is really actually sick, you know?

I'm on the plane right now, and our son is beside me, his head on my lap, his little fingers twisted in my hand.

I love him so much. He loves me too. You believe that, don't you?

Please remember all the good memories. All the good things that I did. There were some good parts, mixed in with the bad. You remember those, right?

I hope this isn't the last entry in this journal that I make, but if it is, know that I love you. I'm not a monster, but can understand if you think I am.

With love, forever,

Kerry

CHAPTER 89
THE NEWS

Lights, camera, kill?

Word on the street is that's what Hollywood bad boy Trent Iverson has been up to for the past decade. Yesterday, LAPD detectives discovered a remote cabin that belonged to Trent, containing explicit death tapes—homemade videos of the movie star torturing and killing young women.

Trent Iverson, who is the brother of Academy Award–winning actor Hugh Iverson, was recently found dead of an apparent self-inflicted gunshot wound, alongside the body of a tortured mother—Kerry Pepper—who is now believed to be Iverson's latest victim.

Sources close to the investigation say that the video-tapes are extremely graphic and appear to be the solo work of Iverson, who has suffered for decades from drug and alcohol addictions. Once a popular child actor from his role as Paul on the faith-based show

Story Farm, Iverson saw a brief career spike in the early 2000s but has been on a slow decline ever since, as he has become more known for his off-camera antics.

The videotape victims have not yet been identified but could number as many as twelve.

A funeral and memorial for Trent Iverson was planned for this Saturday at Getty Observatory, but the event is no longer listed online. A representative for the Iverson family could not be reached for comment.

Blake Jersnith, *Entertainment Press*

CHAPTER 90
THE DETECTIVE

The four of them left Rob's office and moved down the third-floor hall, toward the chief's.

"It's just a note," Farah said to Kevin. "It could be a lie or a red herring."

"Or it could be true, and the most famous movie star in the world is a serial killer."

Yeah, there was the rub right there. And not just that but . . . "But Trent was in the guesthouse with the woman. So did Hugh kill him too? Or was Trent somehow involved as well?" It wasn't a question that anyone could answer but was one they would need to figure out.

They reached the chief's office, and Farah steeled herself for the bomb that they were about to drop on his desk. Rob pushed open the door, and at their entrance, the chief raised his brows and then let out a curse at their faces.

"Okay," he rasped. "Sit down and give it to me."

"It's not a lot," Farah admitted after they had laid out the case and the potential references in the note. "Ignoring Nolan's letter, the evidence does point to Trent, not Hugh. And the—"

"Actually," Anaïca cut in, "I bent over backward looking for a connection between Trent and Nolan and couldn't find one. There were two large cash deposits to Nolan in the last three years, and they didn't seem to come from Trent. One was six weeks before Kerry Pepper's murder, so that could have been the payment for setting that up. This line . . . 'I'm guilty of providing the ingredients, nothing else.' I mean, that fits, right?"

"Yes . . . ," Farah said. "But we have to remember the fact that these victims were identified because Trent named their children as beneficiaries. Which points the guilty finger back to him."

"Any obvious connection between the victims?" Rob asked.

"They're all mothers. Other than that, they're kind of a hodgepodge. Some stay-at-home, some working. Most with just one or two kids," Anaïca said.

Mothers . . . Farah looked at Kevin. "Miles Pepper," she said. "Maybe he *was* important."

At the chief's confused look, Kevin stepped in. "Early on, we were trying to figure out if Miles was kidnapped as a crime of opportunity, after Kerry was taken—or if he was the main victim in this. We decided Kerry was the primary target."

"And she had to be," Farah stated. "I mean, the woman's dead—and no other kids were kidnapped, right? They're all alive and well?"

"Yeah, best I can tell," Anaïca said. "I can dig deeper."

"So Miles's disappearance was an anomaly. But maybe he was why Kerry was chosen and killed," Farah said. "We've discussed Munchausen's a few times. What do you know about the kids on Trent's beneficiary list?" she asked Ana. "Any of them sick?"

Anaïca shook her head. "I don't know. I was concentrating on ID'ing the victims and finding a paper trail. I could look at the twelve children and have an answer within an hour or two."

"Do that," the chief grunted. "But to clarify, you didn't find a financial or communication link between Hugh and Nolan? Or Hugh and Kerry?"

"Well, I haven't looked." Anaïca shifted in a way that Farah recognized as annoyance. "I was focused on Trent."

"Well, we can't arrest Hugh Iverson for murder off a cryptic note that could be just as easily referring to a cooking recipe." The chief tented his hands before him. "We have to be very careful about this. Document everything. Keep everything quiet. If the press drops this before we make an arrest, we'll get a steel rod up the ass, so don't say one word of this to *anyone* outside of this room. Anaïca, put the sick-kid research on someone else, and you focus on giving me something—anything—that could connect Hugh to these murders or to Nolan Price."

"Can I color outside of the lines?" she asked. "My hands are going to be pretty tied if I can't look at bank or phone records."

"Absolutely not. I'll talk to the judge, but for now, I need everything as squeaky clean as possible. Pretend IA is looking over your shoulder. We've got full access to Nolan, so look at the records on his end. Same with the dead women and Trent. Work backward." The chief turned to Rob. "Have your team look at these new victims' death dates and check Trent's activities at those times; see if we can eliminate him as the killer. Maybe he was in jail or Antarctica when one of these ladies got it. I'll need probable doubt on Trent to convince the judge for a warrant on Hugh."

"Trent did die on Hugh's property," Kevin remarked. "That doesn't mean anything?"

"Hell, you guys did that investigation," the chief stated. "You didn't find something on him then, I can't go pointing to that as an excuse now."

Farah chewed on the edge of her nail and tried to find something helpful to contribute to a case that had spiraled far outside their jurisdiction. "Where's the FBI with all of this?"

"Breathing down my neck. Them and the CBI." He glanced toward the hall. "They've both got full access to our network, so they can see everything we're doing. So far, they've stayed out of our hair and are focused on comparing the videos to their unsolved cases. We're sending over the names on Anaïca's list, so that'll keep them busy, but in three hours, I'll have another meeting and have to disclose this and whatever else we have."

The frustration rose in Farah's chest. The clock never stopped ticking, and right now, unless she had forensic skills or a computer degree, she seemed to be useless. "So what are Kevin and I doing? Sitting on our asses?"

Kevin squeezed her shoulder in warning. "We'll go back. Look at the evidence and walk through everything again. We'll find a smoking gun, or maybe a couple."

The chief nodded, satisfied. "And remember—no one says Hugh Iverson's name outside of this circle. Your first responsibility is to hide this from the press. Second responsibility—solve the case."

Talk about screwed-up priorities. Farah stood and caught eyes with Kevin, who gave her a pained grin.

Only in Hollywood.

CHAPTER 91

THE DETECTIVE

They had the information and clues—more than they'd ever need—and just had to sort through the madness and tie the pieces together.

Farah and Kevin grabbed all the folders, moved up to the fifth floor, and claimed a private workroom to spread out the files. Farah swapped her soda for a coffee, ordered an extra-large meat lover's pizza, and started a group WhatsApp chat between them, Anaïca, and Rob. She placed her phone on the table and turned up the speaker in case any updates came in from the channel.

Good ole police work. She had to believe that it would solve this. After all, that—tight questioning and cornering—had led to their discovery of the cabin, which had revealed twelve more victims. Tech hadn't done that. They had. And here . . . she looked across the grid of folders. Somewhere here was a clue. They just needed to prove their worth and find it.

———

Farah's eyes were starting to cross when the first ping came across WhatsApp. It was a message from Rob.

two of the twelve women—Trent couldn't have killed. He was in rehab or filming in a different location on those dates

Anaïca immediately responded. I'll check Hugh's schedule for those dates. Send me locations of the two murders

Farah relayed the update to Kevin, who was at the other end of the table, flipping through the autopsy reports.

"Let's make a list of all of the things that don't fit," he suggested.

"With the Iverson/Pepper death or with—"

"With everything." He walked over to the whiteboard and uncapped a marker. He raised his brows at her, and Farah stared at him, her mind a blank.

"Okay, I'll start." He began writing on the board in bright blue.

2 death scenes that Trent couldn't be at

Farah's mind finally clicked into gear. "How did Kerry get to the Iverson house? Dottie says that Trent was alone in the car, so unless she was in the trunk . . ." She glanced down at the files and rummaged through them, looking for the evidence report on Trent's car. "Did they check the trunk for hair and DNA?"

Kevin moved beside her and watched over her shoulder as she flipped open the folder. Scanning the contents, she found her answer. "Okay, there was human hair and DNA found . . . but we're waiting on the results to know whether it was a match to Kerry." She glanced at him. "If it isn't, maybe it's from one of the other victims."

"So you think Trent *is* the killer?"

"Maybe they both are. It'd be the most obvious answer. The two of them work together. If Trent is in rehab or at a movie, Hugh steps in and vice versa."

Kevin returned to the whiteboard and wrote *Both?* as a column on the right, then moved back to the other side and added Farah's question to the list of unknown items.

How did Kerry get into the house?

"She could have come in with Hugh," Farah mused. "If they're both in on this together. He came in at 10:15 p.m., according to the gate report."

"And Kerry left the hotel when?"

Farah shuffled through the folders until she found the one she wanted. "It was 9:47 p.m. I'd say Beverly Hills is about thirty minutes from there, wouldn't you?"

"The timing works out. Maybe that's all a judge would need for a warrant for Hugh's vehicle. It's a big SUV. She could have been in the back seat or the way back."

Farah warmed to the idea. Granted, it was convenient, maybe a little too convenient, to just pair up the twins as double murderers. Anytime that Hugh didn't fit, Trent was certain to, and the ease of the transition felt lazy to her, especially in a case like this, where it had been a Christmas-lights tangle right from the start.

"Okay," Kevin said. "What else is off?"

"It's not that it's off, but there is Nora's involvement with Trent," Farah said. "Anything there we need to root out?"

"Maybe she found out about the murders. She gave Hugh an ultimatum, he pinned all of the blame on Trent, then killed him so that he couldn't dispute the story."

Farah nodded. "Not a bad theory. I like it."

"The problem here is DNA." Kevin rested his fists on the table and looked over the sea of folders. "The twins have identical DNA, not to mention their looks. How are we going to pin anything on Hugh versus

Trent? We could have Hugh on video, slicing a throat, and he'll just say that it's Trent."

"And a jury would believe it." Farah walked around the perimeter of the table, needing to get her blood pumping and her brain working. "You've got a train wreck on one side and a golden boy on the other. It made sense for Trent to be the killer. I didn't blink twice at it."

Kevin took a seat and studied the board for a while, then shrugged. "Maybe he'll confess."

"Well, if he's guilty, the timeline will trip him up," Farah said. "We've got twelve murders, and there are probably more that we don't know about. They're in different states, so there's travel involved. This isn't a blue-collar bachelor in Arkansas. You're talking about the most recognizable celebrity in the country, and one with staff, agents, managers, drivers, publicists, and a famous fiancée. If he left town, someone knew it. When he was in Los Angeles, there'll be records of it."

"We're also talking about a master of disguise," Kevin reminded her. "This is the guy who played Johnny Franks *and* Thomas Jilt. He could be a thirty-year-old skinhead or a crazy senior citizen, all in the same day. We can't assume that someone would have recognized him. If he didn't want to be seen, he wouldn't have been."

Farah stopped in place by the whiteboard. "Yeah, remember what I said when we left their house that day? How we couldn't believe anything an actor said?"

"I remember." Kevin shook his head and smiled. "Hey, that's the problem with Hollywood. We're in a sea of professional liars and seducers."

"And killers."

CHAPTER 92

THE DETECTIVE

8:47 a.m.

This time, when Kevin and Farah pulled up to Dottie's gate, they weren't on the list and were armed with a warrant for Hugh Iverson's vehicle and home. It had taken an early-morning meeting with Judge Coolidge and a lot of him hemming and hawing, but the old man had come through, and now the LAPD just needed to keep mud off their face.

Dottie reviewed the paperwork and raised an eyebrow in skepticism. "They with you?" She nodded at the evidence van behind Kevin's SUV.

"Yep. One car will be staying here with you, just to make sure that the residence isn't alerted," Farah said.

The woman let out a sharp laugh of incredulity and shook her head in disgust. "Good luck," she said as she pressed the button to raise the gate.

"You know, it's like people don't realize that we're trying to save lives," Farah mused as they rounded the first manicured curve.

"Naw, they just don't like being babysat. I don't blame her. I'm betting these owners are pretty generous at Christmastime. They don't wanna bite the hand that feeds them."

He had a point, but still. Catching a serial killer was a pretty worthy reason to nibble away. Not that Dottie realized that they were doing that. She looked over at Kevin. "How are we getting in?" Farah asked. "Think they'll just open them for us?"

"Let's give it a try." He turned into the drive and stopped at the keypad. Pressing the "Call" button, he waited, then turned to Farah with a smile as the gates began to part. "Easy peasy."

They pulled in slowly, their second vehicle following closely, and as the mansion came into view, she was surprised to see Hugh and Nora standing on the front porch.

"And . . . it gets weirder," Farah muttered. "Why does it feel like they were expecting us?"

———

Hugh and Nora looked as if they'd been through a war zone. They took the warrants without reading them and didn't flinch at the group of officers who filed in behind Farah and Kevin and started to systematically go through the home.

"We have some questions for you, Mr. Iverson," Kevin stated.

Hugh nodded. "We can use my study."

Study, Farah thought as they left Nora behind and followed Hugh up the stairs and down a hall. *Not an office, but a study.* Such precise word choices. Where did rich people learn it from? She'd read up on Nora after finding out about her *Story Farm* connection. Annie Bayors had been full-bred white trash yet now spoke like she was the product of an Ivy League orgy. No wonder no one had ever connected her with the chubby hick from the show. It wasn't just the looks; it was the entire act, and Nora had it down to a science.

Once they were alone in the study, Farah started her voice recorder, and Kevin read out the Miranda warning. Hugh seemed resigned to the process and sat in a rolled leather chair, his hands linked together and resting on one crossed knee. Farah waited for him to call his attorney, but he didn't mention it, and she wasn't going to do the work for him.

"Nolan Price left a note behind, one that implicated you in the Kerry Pepper murder." Kevin started out swinging.

"That's ludicrous." Hugh snorted.

"It's ludicrous that he would leave a note, or ludicrous that you're involved in the Kerry Pepper murder?" Farah pressed.

"I don't know anything about the former and didn't have anything to do with the latter."

"Are you familiar with any of these women?" Kevin unfolded a page of the confirmed victims' names and pushed them across the desk.

Hugh studied the list briefly, then shook his head and returned it to Kevin. "I don't think so."

Well, that was helpful. Farah tried another tactic. "Mr. Iverson, at the cabin, we found videotapes of twelve women who were tortured and killed. Were you aware of those tapes?"

He considered her carefully before answering. "I've seen tapes at the cabin. I've never played them."

"Did you film them?" Kevin asked.

"No." His voice was calm and resolute. With a normal person, Farah would have been convinced that he was telling the truth. With Hugh, she didn't know what to believe.

"Were you on the videos?"

"No." He paused. "Well, since I haven't seen them, it's hard to say. But if they're videos of any violent behavior, then no, I'm not on them, and I haven't had any part of their filming."

Again, Farah's bullshit meter was silent. From the glass cabinet behind him, Hugh's Academy Award glinted at them, as if reminding them of his abilities.

"So you're saying it's your brother on the videos? He tortured and killed twelve women?"

Hugh's features tightened. "If that's what you're seeing on the videos, then yes."

"Why would he do that?" she asked.

"You asked me that question a few days ago, in regards to the woman in the guesthouse. I quoted Isaiah then, and I'll refer to it now. My brother wouldn't have killed someone without a reason. I'm not saying it was valid or right, but that's the only answer I have for you."

"The problem is that Trent couldn't have committed these crimes, at least not on his own." Kevin laid down the first trap.

Hugh rested his elbow on the chair's armrest and regarded Kevin thoughtfully but stayed silent.

"Two of the deaths happened on dates that Trent was in rehab or filming," Farah elaborated.

"Okay. Did you have a question?"

"If Trent didn't kill those women, and you aren't on the videos, then who is this?" Kevin pushed forward a screenshot taken from a video, one that showed a slightly blurred photo of Hugh, looking down at a woman.

He studied the photo, then looked from Kevin to Farah. Sitting back, he crossed his arms at the wrists and rested them behind his head. "Trent didn't kill any of those women, and the man on this video isn't him."

"We know it isn't him," Farah said impatiently. "It's you."

"No, it's not." The edges of his mouth curved in an almost playful smile, like he knew a secret that they didn't. "It's Hugh."

"What?" Farah said stupidly. "What do you mean?"

"This is Hugh. All of the tapes are of Hugh."

"Is this a third-person reference, or are you saying that you're not Hugh?" Kevin asked.

"I'm saying that Hugh killed all of those women and that I'm not Hugh. I'm Trent."

CHAPTER 93

THE DETECTIVE

"You're Trent?" Farah repeated.

This was ridiculous and, at the same time, feasible. They were, after all, identical twins. But there was medical evidence proving that the dead body was Trent. So, no. *No.* No hot potatoing the blame here.

"I'm Trent." He nodded, and that smirk—Trent's smirk that she had drooled over as a teenage girl—suddenly bloomed across his face, as sexy and cocky as ever. Farah stared at him, unsure of what to trust because the Hugh facade—only two minutes earlier—had been just as convincing.

"So you're saying that Hugh is dead?" Kevin clarified.

"I'm not saying it—it's true. Hugh's dead. Guess he finally felt bad about what he was doing."

Red flags were firing like automatic weapons in Farah's brain. She looked at Kevin, and any line of questioning that they had planned was thrown in the trash.

Farah spoke tersely, her anger mounting as she went. "If this is true, you realize that you've obstructed a police investigation by not sharing this until now, right? You've wasted dozens—if not hundreds—of hours of police work and—"

"Send me the bill." The man shrugged, and now his legs were uncrossed, splayed open, his seat in the chair more of a sprawl. He was changing right before their eyes, and how could she have ever thought he was Hugh before?

"It's more than money, Mr. Iverson," Kevin snapped. "It's an obstruction of justice. A young boy's life was at stake, and you were toying with us."

Farah wondered if Nora knew. Had both of them been laughing at their investigation this entire time? What about the staff?

His grin dropped and he leaned forward, sobering. "Look, I'm sorry. I was processing what had happened and what to do. I have a deep loyalty to my brother. The desire to protect his legacy was warring with my civil duty. I'm sorry if I chose the wrong side."

"Don't act like you're choosing the right path now," Farah said tartly. "You're backed into a corner and flipping over to show your underbelly. The only reason you're saying this—and I'm not saying that we believe you—is because we're getting ready to arrest you for these crimes, and this is your easiest way out."

"Detective Anderson makes a good point," Kevin said. "Can you prove that you're Trent and not Hugh?"

The actor—whoever he was—paused and seemed to consider the question. "Not really," he said. "I mean . . . our genetic blueprint is identical." He shrugged. "I don't believe that either of us have ever been fingerprinted. But line up ten people in this room, and someone would be able to find a question that only I, and not Hugh, would know."

"Trent has a savings account," Farah said, testing him, "with a beneficiary that recently changed."

"Not that recently." He squinted and looked toward the ceiling. "About six months ago. Added Kaitlyn Mercer."

Farah didn't have the beneficiary list in front of her, wasn't prepped for this line of questioning, but he seemed to know what he was talking about, so she plowed forward. "Why did you add Kaitlyn?"

"My brother killed her mother. It was a penance of sorts."

"A penance she won't get now," she pointed out. "Given that Trent is, apparently, still alive."

He grinned, and despite everything, her knees grew a little woozy at the sight. "You don't believe me. That's funny."

"Our job is to not believe you," Kevin cut in. "Don't take it personally."

For a moment, his grin dropped and his tone sobered. "I'm sure you think of me as a monster, for knowing what Hugh was doing and not stopping him. I get that. Trust me, no one thinks worse of me than myself. As I told you before—Hugh dealt with his guilt and demons one way; I took a different path. I don't drink and do drugs for the high. I do it for the lows. I do it for the punishment and destruction that it brings to my life." He rubbed a hand roughly over his cheek, then looked at them. "He was my brother. That probably doesn't mean anything to you, but it meant something to us. There was good there, even in the bad."

Kevin spoke up first. "Look, the truth is—"

"The truth is that you don't know your asses from your elbows, and it's going to take months to try and piece everything together." He sat back. "I'll fully cooperate and solve your whole case for you right now." He slung one arm over the back of the chair. "Sound good?"

"Sure," Farah said. "Hit us with it."

"In exchange for immunity."

Kevin was already shaking his head, but Farah was interested in at least riding this pony to the opening gates. "Immunity for what?"

"A few counts of assisting with remains. Failure to report a crime to the authorities. Whatever"—he waved his hand in the air to encompass their past—"obstruction I did by not clarifying which one of us was in the guesthouse."

"So you're saying you were an accessory to murder?" Kevin asked.

"Accessory after the fact, and only in a few cases." He shrugged. "I'm not asking for a lot. Without immunity, my crimes would plead down to a misdemeanor and a year or two of jail time, tops."

"It's a little more serious than that," Farah said—though would it be? He was right. With the best legal representation money could buy, he could probably avoid jail time altogether, though he'd pay a hefty fine and be on house arrest and parole. Where his punishment would really lie would be the court of public opinion, though Hollywood had already branded Trent as trouble. Hell, this might even make him more of a legend.

"I could make this case a legal nightmare and clam up, or I could open the vaults." He made direct eye contact with Farah, and no wonder Nora had hopped into bed with the man. Same looks as Hugh, but Trent was a flip of the switch, one that turned the sexual attraction to level gazillion.

"We can't make a deal on our end," Kevin objected, and at least he was immune to his charm. "We need to get the DA involved."

"Sure." He nudged the phone on the desk. "Take your time. I'll take a walk."

Farah watched as he strolled toward the hall and tried to understand what in Cinderella's castle was happening. Were they actually going to call the DA and try to get a plea deal for a man who had lied about his identity for the past four days?

He shut the door behind him and Kevin sighed, then pulled his cell phone from the front pocket of his shirt. "I'm going to call the chief."

For once, Farah was grateful for their gruff figurehead. There wasn't a better strategy player in town, and he was a golf buddy and confidant of the DA. The chief would know how to handle this.

The book would have said to tell this guy to pound sand, slap the cuffs on him, and figure out his identity back at the station, under a twenty-four-hour hold. In a different town, with a different suspect, that might have worked—but this was an environment where the public was their employer, and every move would be scrutinized in the courts, in the press, on social media, and in the history books.

They needed to tie a bow on this and make it look good. This Iverson—whichever one he was—could either help knot that bow or potentially lead them on a wild-goose chase.

"What's your gut?" she asked Kevin. "Think he's Trent or Hugh?"

He shook his head with an irritated scowl. "Not a damn clue." He moved the cell in front of his mouth. "Hey, chief, it's Mathis. We have an issue at the Iverson house."

As Kevin recapped their conversation, Farah took the liberties granted by their warrant and wandered the office, opening up drawers and cabinets and looking through the contents. It was very organized, each drawer in precise order. She thought of the cabin and the perfect fold and make of the bed, then thought of Trent's bedroom and the pile of sheets. The cabin had definitely been a Hugh locale, which would make this the office of a serial killer.

The question remained, though—which twin was the dead one? She looked toward the door that Hugh had left through and knew, without hesitation, who he had gone to find.

The one woman who would be able to tell them apart.

CHAPTER 94
THE LEADING LADY

Nora was in the rose garden, trying to control her emotions at the thought of strangers going through everything in their house.

There is no reason to panic. She willed the thought to pass through her body and out through her fingertips and toes.

They won't find anything. She had already tossed Hugh's video camera in a dumpster downtown, waited and watched as a trash compactor lifted and crushed the contents, then drove away.

No one will ever know. Trent was the best actor in the world. He had swapped places with Hugh countless times, more than anyone would ever know. That famous scene in *Continuum*, the one that had brought the audience to tears? That hadn't been Hugh on the screen; it had been Trent. The Golden Globes acceptance speech, which Hugh had missed for some secret trip that he didn't include her on—also Trent. There was no reason why Trent couldn't, for the next few decades, fool everyone into thinking that he was Hugh. All he had to do was stay clean, and Nora could help him with that. Now that she knew what had been triggering him—and there weren't dead bodies piling up anymore—he wouldn't have the guilt and agony. They could forget the horror of his past and build a happy new future.

"Nora."

She turned, and there he was. Trent stepped forward and cupped her face in his hands and kissed her lips, then her forehead and cheeks, then pulled back and stared down at her. "I told them."

"Told them what?" Oh *no*. Her mind screamed silently while she searched his eyes and hoped that he hadn't stepped down *that* path.

"Who I am." He smiled at her as if he didn't realize what that admission would mean. Surely he had thought through this, had realized why he needed to play this role—the role he was born for. "You knew, didn't you?"

She stared at him wordlessly, not sure what to say or how many moves this game had left.

He didn't wait for a response; he pressed his mouth to hers, and it was like it used to be—raw desperation and need. Only now it wasn't forbidden and hot; it was just the two of them, standing in Hugh's rose garden, waiting for their new world to collapse.

She went limp in his arms and tried to figure out what she would tell the police when they came for her.

CHAPTER 95
THE DETECTIVE

In a normal world, it would have taken twenty-four hours to get the chief to coordinate with the district attorney on a potential deal. In the world of A-list celebrities, it happened in fifteen minutes.

Before Farah had a chance to track down Nora, the DA and chief had agreed on a deal for transactional immunity. In layman's terms—it would give Trent protection against any charges in the future based on matters linked to the information he shared but didn't block the DA's office from charging him for something that wasn't related to his testimony.

Farah wasn't happy about it, but she also wanted to see what bullshit Trent was about to unveil. He was promising to solve their entire case in a few minutes? That sounded good to her, but she would believe that when she heard it.

Just a few minutes after the deal was struck, the front door swung open, and Hugh's attorney walked in. He was wearing a Grateful Dead T-shirt, faded jeans, and black cowboy boots. Flashing everyone a smile, he shook hands around the group, then wrapped Trent in a bear hug that lasted uncomfortably long.

"I got the deal paperwork on the ride over. I've reviewed it. It looks good, but I reserve the right to step in and advise my client as we go."

Of course he did. Farah kept her features mild and nodded her agreement. The warrant team's search of the house had so far turned up nothing. She was getting itchy for a win, even if it had red tape hanging off it.

The search team still needed to sweep the office, so they moved to the dining room and got the district attorney on the phone as everyone took seats around the table. Kevin put his cell on speaker and nodded for Farah to start the voice recorder.

"For purposes of the recorder, this is State District Attorney Mildra Parks, and we've just agreed to the terms on contract number CA24419. Okay, Detectives Mathis and Anderson. Just continue with wherever you'd like with the questioning. Mr. Iverson, you have the legal freedom to answer the questions as best you can, with the understanding that this immunity does not cover murder, just potential accessory items. Also, you are still under the Miranda rights that were read to you earlier, and this is an official interrogation. Do you understand?"

He nodded. "Yeah."

Finally, it was showtime, and the actor began.

"Look, Hugh and I had a shitty childhood. I dealt with it by getting drunk and high. Hugh dealt with it by tracking down parents who make their kids sick and killing them."

Farah was in the midst of processing his assertion that he—son of Momma Beth—had had a shitty childhood when the second part of his statement hit.

Kevin was ahead of her. "You're talking about Munchausen by proxy?" And there it was. They'd circled it so many times and still hadn't quite confirmed the mark. It was annoying, having their suspect be the one to fill in the blank.

"Yeah, if that's what it's called. It was an obsession of his, finding these parents and then punishing them."

"Is that why Kerry was killed? She was hurting her child?"

He frowned. "To be honest, I don't know. I didn't want any part of Hugh's vigilante efforts. I knew why he was doing it, but I didn't know any details."

"But you were here at the house when he died," Farah pointed out. "Why?"

"You don't have to answer that," Jeff Bourdin interjected.

He waved the attorney off. "I'll answer any questions you have. I came over that night because Hugh said he needed help with something. He didn't say what it was, but I didn't think it had anything to do with hurting someone. I didn't think he'd take that risk, especially with Nora being here."

"What happened when you got here?"

"We talked by the pool. He said he was busy in the guesthouse, so I told him to text me when he needed me. He wanted me to distract Nora, so I hung out with her some—I took a shower. Went to the roof deck and did some lines of coke. Nora and I ended up in the theater, where we got drunk. I passed out at some point and was woken up in the morning by Nora, who told me Trent was dead."

Talk about a screwed-up dynamic. Hugh's twin brother hooking up with his fiancée while he was busy stabbing a mom to death. *Keep Nora busy, Trent—and later, help me deal with this body.*

"Okay, just a minute." Farah held up her hand. "So you never saw Kerry Pepper—not until you went downstairs the following morning and saw her and your brother dead in the guesthouse?"

"Correct."

"And you and Nora were alone in the theater when you fell asleep?"

His mouth twisted. "I'm not sure if she had already gone to bed by the time I fell asleep. To be honest, I was drunk and high. The evening is a bit fuzzy."

"So you *could* have seen Kerry Pepper?" Kevin asked.

He shook his head. "I wasn't *that* drunk. Hugh never let me see him hurt anyone. He knew I wasn't okay with that. Even if it was an abusive parent, I wouldn't have been able to just stand by and not step in to stop him."

"But you were fine with hiding their dead bodies?" Farah asked.

"I wasn't fine with it. I hated it. Hated every part of it. Look at my worst drug binges and you'll be able to line them up with when I helped him with cleanup. I saw three dead women, ever. The rest he handled on his own. Look, except for those three situations, all I did was cover his absences so he could travel without anyone knowing. I stepped in with some of his filming or with Nora—whatever he needed to cover his ass."

There was a piece that wasn't connecting, and Farah struggled to fit it together with the rest. "You said that Nora woke you up and told you that Trent was dead?"

He nodded.

"But you said that you're Trent. So . . ."

He lifted his shoulders in a shrug. "She was confused, and I didn't correct her."

"Oh, come on," Farah protested. "She tells you that you're dead in the guesthouse with a murdered woman and you just play along with it? Why?"

He shifted in the chair, and for the first time since they had all sat down, she sensed trepidation in him. "I . . ." He blew out a breath, and the mental debate was visible on his face. "Shit, this is embarrassing." He looked to the side and rubbed his cheek with his fingers. "Sometimes I come here and pretend to be Hugh. It's something I've done for decades. I'm sure he'd pretend to be me if there was any benefit in being a washed-up loser, but it's pretty much a one-way street. When I get tired of being a D-list celebrity, I have one of his drivers pick me up at the studio, and I spend a few hours at his house. I've stayed overnight if he's on location. I use his club memberships and shit."

It was shame he was hiding, Farah realized. Not guilt. And for a fairly good reason. He had been playing dress-up with his brother's life and his brother's future wife. She tried to keep her features bland and not react to the admission. "And that morning?"

"Well, I was still pretty loopy when I woke up. I was trying to remember what had happened the night before and if I had been posing as Hugh when I fell asleep. By the time I sobered up and had a better idea of what was going on, I'd also had a chance to think through things." His gaze flicked to Farah and then Kevin, and he made eye contact with both of them before he continued. "You ever been in love, Detective Mathis?"

"Sure. Married twenty-eight years."

"And you, Detective Anderson?" He looked at Farah.

"Close to him. Married twenty-four."

"I've been in love with Nora ever since she walked back into our lives. I've accepted that I'll never get her as Trent. What she wants—respectability and security and fame—I can't give her that. Hugh can and has.

"If I started now and worked every day of my life, trying to convince the public to see me in that way—and that's what she needs, the public's approval—I couldn't make it happen. But here . . ." He cupped his hands around an invisible basketball. "Here was a life, one with the woman I loved, one with everything that I would never have, just sitting there, waiting for me to take it. All I needed to do was keep smiling and keep letting everyone think what they already wanted to think—that Trent was a monster and Hugh was still alive and squeaky clean."

He dropped his hands to the table. "So that's what I did. I played the role until the cat caught its tail, and here we are, in reshoots." He smiled, but there wasn't any happiness in the gesture.

"What does Nora know about Hugh's activities?" Farah asked.

Jeff cut in. "You don't have to answer that. Hearsay."

Trent ignored his attorney. "I know that we both did everything we could to keep it from her. It would take a lot, a *lot*, to get Nora to leave Hugh, but if she had found out about this, she would have taken off.

And not to me. I can't . . . I'm a liability to her. And the public percep-
tion of her leaving Hugh for me would never fly. So while I can't know
everything going on in that head of hers, I'm confident that she might
have suspected that we were up to something, but she didn't know what
it was. No way. She would have run and never looked back."

CHAPTER 96
THE DETECTIVE

Trent was cuffed and put in a squad car. Farah watched as he ducked into the back seat and didn't know what to believe. Was the man guilty or innocent? Trent or Hugh? Lying or being honest?

Farah turned back to the house and paused, seeing Nora Kemp in the front doorway, her beautiful face tight, gaze glued to the squad car as it pulled away. Farah climbed up the steps and stopped before her. "We have some questions we need to ask you."

"I didn't know about the murders," she said immediately, her attention straying to Kevin, who joined Farah on the porch. "I read about them this morning. About the videos, in the cabin. I . . ." She swallowed and her eyes glistened with tears. "I didn't know," she whispered.

It was a convincing monologue, one Farah took in with skepticism. This woman had been sketchy from the start, and given the fact that she'd been sleeping with both twins, she was guaranteed to have been close to the killer, maybe even involved in his crimes.

"Let's go inside so we can ask you a few questions," Farah said, as nicely as she could.

Nora cast a worried glance over her shoulder, and Jeff Bourdin immediately materialized, approaching with a bounce in his step that didn't match the fact that his client was just put in handcuffs.

"What'cha got crackling?" he asked with a shit-eating smile.

"We need to question Miss Kemp," Farah informed him.

"Oh, come on. Don't you think you got enough stuff for today?" He nodded at the direction Trent had left in. "Hell, Trent gave you buckets of stuff to use. Not much left to solve now, is there?"

"Oh, we're just getting started." Farah scraped her soles against the mat and maneuvered past them and into the house. "Miss Kemp? Where do you want to do this?"

"It's been a stressful day," Jeff Bourdin interjected. "Let's have her call you tomorrow, okay?"

Farah sighed. "Jeff, the more you try to keep me from asking Nora our teensy-tiny list of questions, the more suspicious we'll get and the more we're going to focus all of our gee-willikers energy on Nora and how the heck she plays into this big ole stack of dead bodies. Mmkay?"

"Stop," Nora snapped, holding up her hand. "You can ask me the questions in the sitting room. But please, make it fast. This has all brought on a migraine that's about to make me vomit."

"We'll be faster than a mouse's fart in a tornado." Farah mimicked Jeff's drawl, and he narrowed his eyes at her.

"You know," the attorney said under his breath as they moved into the front room, "it's only cute when I do it."

"It's actually not."

Kevin took a stuffed chair by the window, and Nora perched on one arm of the couch, her arms crossed impatiently over her chest. She raised her brows as soon as Farah's butt hit the cushion beside her. "Well?"

"We'll try and be quick, Miss Kemp," Kevin said easily, and his grace with assholes was really admirable. "What we really need your help on is understanding who we just took to the station. Now, we understand that you had an intimate knowledge of both brothers." He paused. "Would you say that you knew them better than anyone?"

She huffed in annoyance. "Yes, I would say that. But it doesn't help with what you're asking. You want to know if that's Hugh or Trent, and I don't know the answer to that. I know what I want to be the answer, but that doesn't really matter, now does it?"

"No, but I do have to say that I'm curious." Kevin smiled, and it was hard not to be charmed by his smile when he put energy behind it.

Nora didn't react, and Farah deflated a little in her spot.

"I want Hugh to be alive," she said, "and I want Trent to be guilty of the murders." She looked down at the engagement ring on her finger, then back at them. "So, see? Wishing and wanting is useless."

"So you're saying that Hugh *is* guilty of the murders?"

"I'm not saying anything because I didn't *know* anything. I didn't even suspect anything. And isn't my opinion"—she looked at the attorney—"isn't it hearsay?"

"Detective, please ask a specific question that Miss Kemp would be qualified to answer," Jeff said.

"Fine." Farah met Nora's eyes. "To the best of your ability, and understand that we are strictly asking your honest opinion, who do you think the man we just arrested is?"

She sighed. "I think it's Trent, but I don't know for sure."

"Okay." Finally, they were getting somewhere, though Farah wasn't sure where. She believed and recognized Nora's frustration, and it was nice to know she wasn't the only one confused. "Has he told you who he is?"

"Oh my God." She threw up her hands. "We're professional liars. What part of that is confusing to you guys? We stand in front of the camera and lie. We play pretend. Trent is the best in the world at it, and Hugh is a close second. I don't have a magic ability to see through that. It doesn't matter what that man said to me, but if you're asking—he acted like Hugh for four days, then alluded to being Trent just now. And I believed him both times, so . . ." She bit her bottom lip, and Farah recognized the crack in the veneer and suddenly realized that Nora Kemp was on the edge of falling apart.

This bite in her voice wasn't bitchiness—it was helplessness. And Nora wasn't angry at them—she was angry at herself. She didn't know the difference between the man she loved and the man she was going to marry, and Farah didn't believe for a second that she wanted Hugh to be alive. She'd bet her job that Nora was hopelessly in love with Trent and in a mental pretzel between mourning him and potentially celebrating his sudden return to life.

Nora swallowed. "You never saw them together, did you?" There was a rasp in her voice, and she coughed to clear the emotion.

"No. Not in person," Farah said. Kevin grunted his agreement.

She stood up and walked to the window by Kevin, looking out onto the front entrance and hugging her arms tightly around herself, as if to keep her emotions in. "It's not just their looks. When they speak, it's identical. The way they kiss. Their . . . anatomy." She swallowed. "I know that you must think terrible things of me, but my life was like a house of mirrors where my heart didn't know what to trust and what to fall in love with. And they were okay with that. It wasn't this horrible, forbidden thing where I was cheating on Hugh. They have shared everything, their whole life. The good and the bad. I was just another . . ." As Farah watched, she pinched her lips together and fisted her hands and straightened to her full height, and it was like a physical buttoning down of emotions. "Another thing."

It sounded both horrible and wonderful, to be shared between the two men. Wonderful when you thought of their public personas. Terrible when you realized that one of them—or maybe still both of them—was a serial killer. Could a man who had killed a dozen women have the capacity to love? Could he be loved? Farah couldn't imagine falling for a man like that and not realizing that something was inherently broken in him.

Nora turned back to them and sighed. "Honestly, my head is killing me." She pulled a tube of pale-pink gloss from the front pocket of her jeans and swiped it quickly across her lips. "Is there anything else I can answer for you?"

It was funny, that she thought this was over. Though they did have to wrap this up now, to get Trent to the station and processed . . . this was just the beginning for Nora. She would be a major witness to help unwrap the last six years' worth of events. She would have to be cleared as an accomplice and would have to convince the world, again and again, that she had no knowledge of the crimes. Their immunity deal was with Trent, not her, and Farah wasn't about to trust the woman until she proved her innocence.

"Is there any way that you can tell the men apart? Anything at all?" Kevin asked.

"Why don't you just look at their medical records? Hugh's got to be a freak show under his skin."

Kevin's and Farah's gazes met. "Meaning what?" Farah asked.

"His mother, Momma Beth?" She said the name like it was poison. "She liked to break his bones like they were commandments. Half of the *Story Farm* scenes had Trent playing both parts because Hugh was always in the infirmary. Hell, they had a hospital room built at the mansion, to keep up with his constant medical needs."

Another link, connected. A burned-out room. Medical supplies.

"The body in the morgue has broken bones," Kevin said, "but they match Trent's medical records, not Hugh's."

A smile played across her lips. "You aren't thinking like Momma Beth. When the injuries were too bad, when she needed a doctor for drugs or X-rays, she couldn't sell a doctor on a child who was that accident prone or that constantly sick. Didn't make sense. It would have raised a red flag. So she'd trade their names in and out. Take 'Trent'"— she put air quotes around his name—"to the doctor for a shattered collarbone and take Hugh the next month for a fractured wrist." She rubbed the back of her neck. "Did you request Hugh's records? Put the two of them together, and it will probably equal the body you have. And if it does, it's Hugh. Definitely."

"Momma Beth didn't hurt Trent?"

"No." She shook her head. "She ignored Trent. Wouldn't so much as touch him. She burned one child with the heat of her affection and froze the other one out. She was horrible." Her voice dropped in sadness. "Honestly. At least to them."

"Trent said he often pretends to be Hugh. Have you ever caught him at it?" Kevin asked, switching gears, though Farah could have listened to Momma Beth stories all day long.

"Um, not caught him exactly, but there are times when I know he stood in for him. On press events or for certain scenes. Trent is a stronger actor, between the two of them. Some of Hugh's most famous scenes—Academy Award–winning scenes—were actually Trent. So I wouldn't be shocked if he continued the charade at times. This house, this lifestyle, the admiration—it's what Trent deserves; he just couldn't get past his demons long enough to achieve it."

"And you, right? You're what he deserves?" Kevin prodded.

Nora gave a small and almost genuine smile. "I'm a lot like him—like both of them. A pretty exterior that distracts and hides a whole mess of crazy."

On that note, Farah fully agreed with her.

CHAPTER 97

THE DETECTIVE

While the remaining Iverson sat in a private holding cell in the Beverly Hills substation, Farah and Kevin started back at the beginning and tried to reassemble all the puzzle pieces, taking into account what Trent and Nora had said.

Surprisingly, everything suddenly fit.

Farah stood in front of the whiteboard and stared at their notes. "So . . . Hugh was the mastermind and the killer. Trent just came in for cleanup at times—"

"And covered for Hugh if he needed to be out of town for a kill."

"Do we believe that?" Kevin asked. "It seems convenient for Trent to help him after the fact but not actually be involved in snatches or kills. And Hugh isn't here to dispute his claims."

"Actually, I do believe him," Farah said. "I mean, why admit to it at all? He didn't need to. We didn't have any evidence or clues that suggested an accomplice might have helped, and it would have been hard to pin anything on him if we did."

"Good point." Kevin came up beside her and rested his hands on his hips. "I guess I believe him too—at least on that."

"That being said, we can have the task force investigate every murder, especially now that they have the full list." That was another nugget that Trent—after seeing Hugh's medical records, Farah was finally ready to concede that the remaining twin was Trent—had shared: the list of women killed. As it turned out, Trent wasn't the only one who had planned on providing for the victims' families in the afterlife. Trent had gotten the idea from Hugh, who was doing it on a much larger scale—a million dollars had been set up for each child, each in an anonymous trust that would unlock when the child turned twenty-five. Unlike Trent's money-market account changes, which happened after the deaths, Hugh had set up Miles Pepper's trust prior to Kerry Pepper's death, which lent some credence to his suicide after the murder.

The suicide was still sticking in Farah's mind. She didn't like it—never liked it when a crime was pinned on a victim who wasn't around to defend themselves. In this case, it was a mountain of crimes, all hung around Hugh's dead neck.

"How'd Hugh get the victims?" she asked. "Munchausen by proxy isn't exactly a condition that people are advertising." She turned to the map, which had a wide scattering of dots where each victim's body had been found. "I mean, these women are all over. And not all are murders. This one—" She pointed to a dot in Seattle. "I mean, she jumped off her balcony. Both Trent and Hugh were in Los Angeles at the time. Why's he giving money to her kid? Why's she on this list?"

"And we've only linked four of them to Make-A-Wish or Protect the Children," Kevin agreed. He picked up his clipboard and nodded toward the direction of Trent's cell. "Let's go ask the man."

In the narrow holding cell, Trent was sound asleep, one arm hanging off the metal twin bed. Kevin and Farah stopped at the gate to his cell and looked at each other in amusement. "Nice to see that he's making himself comfortable," Farah mused.

"That's either innocence or psychosis." Kevin rattled his clipboard against the bars. "Trent. Wake up."

Trent's eyes opened and he stared at them, then slowly sat up, swinging his long legs to the side of the bed. "What's up?"

Kevin held up the list of victims. "How did Hugh identify them? How'd he know they were hurting their kids?"

Trent let out a huge yawn, then shook his head slightly to wake himself up. "Umm." He stared at the white brick wall in front of him. "Just a minute, let me think if I ever asked him this."

So much for the clear-cut puzzle-solving key Farah had hoped for.

"I know early on he had a guy. A private investigator who he was having check on the wellness of some of the kids that were passing through Protect the Children. Anyone Nolan found suspicious, this guy would look into."

"The guy's name?"

"Oh, I don't know." He grimaced. "He worked on *Lethal Badge* as a consultant. You should be able to find him through that. I don't think the guy had any idea what Hugh was doing with the information, though, so I don't want to get him in any trouble—"

"We'll just talk to him," Farah said. "See if he can fill in some of our holes."

"But then he had something with the internet he was doing. Like an MBP support group he had dialed in on or joined—something like that. I haven't heard him mention the PI in a while. Like, for years." He shrugged. "That help?"

Farah thought of Kerry's husband and his insistent mentions of her Facebook activity and the woman who had blocked him. She left Kevin and Trent and returned to the room, flipping through the stacks until she found the notes. Kerry had been a member of one Facebook group. A quilting one. She picked up the phone and called Anaïca and relayed the information.

Hanging up the phone, she turned back to the board and looked at the lines of names. So many dead women. So many affected families and individuals.

As she stared at them, another note appeared on the screen.

> Brittany Morrens confirmed as "MBP-likely" by doctors
> and a school nurse.

Shit. She uncapped the dry-erase marker and put a star next to the name. So far, eight of the twelve women had stars. One of them, Pauline Webb, they had underlined in red. Her child hadn't been sick—he was deceased, the cause now suspicious.

As a mother, she didn't know how to feel about the list. It was like a twist of sadness and relief. She had been in the hall when Kyle Pepper had told his son about his mother's death. She had heard the child's cries, the genuine pain and sorrow in his voice. Kerry Pepper had been in a bad situation, a woman who had seemed to be trying, had started to help and not hurt, yet she still ended up a victim.

Kyle Pepper had turned over a journal, one that he'd found in Miles's backpack. Rob's team was going through the contents of it now, and would be sending the scanned pages over shortly.

As if on cue, another message appeared.

> Kerry's journal is now in the bucket. You're going to
> want to read it asap.

Farah showed the message to Kevin, and they both sat in front of the monitors and pulled up the new attachment.

It took Farah twenty minutes to read, and Kevin a few minutes more. Twenty minutes that tied so many loose ends together but also sparked so many new questions. Kevin sat back and looked at her, then picked up the phone. "I'll call the FBI and update them."

This would mean one more investigation added to the pile—one in the federal jurisdiction—and Farah wondered how many group members there were, and how many lives were about to be changed with the follow-up investigations that would occur.

The FBI would handle that. That and Miles's kidnapping would be ongoing investigations, and were officially off Farah and Kevin's workload. She didn't envy their tasks. The kid's descriptions of his captors were comic book villains at best, and he almost seemed cheerful about his adventure, at least in his retelling to them. And this Facebook group . . . that was a dark evil that Farah was happy to be clear of. Tomorrow would bring new cases and, in this city, new deaths and investigations.

Kevin opened the door and looked into the room. "Chico's tonight? We should be done with the paperwork in, what, three hours? I could have Trish get us a table for four—or five, if Anaïca can make it."

Farah turned away from the board and smiled at him. "Kevin Mathis, sometimes I forget how brilliant you are." She took a seat at the desk and picked up her cell. "I'll text Ty and Anaïca."

She opened up her texts and paused, seeing a new string of messages that had come in an hour ago, from an unrecognized number.

Farah, this is Nora.

I just wanted to say thank you for your diligent work and attention to this case. I'm sorry it has been such a mess and hope that Trent is helping to sort through the pieces.

It's hard for me to wrap my head around how blind I must have been these last six years. I feel like a fool and it hurts my heart to think that women's lives could have been spared, if I had only been less blinded by love and my continual pursuit of fame.

I'm ashamed at myself and can't imagine how you see me.

I promise, somewhere inside, I do have common sense and intelligence. I'm going to work on finding that, and rediscovering myself, away from Hollywood and the cameras.

I'm at your disposal, day or night, if you have any questions or need me to shed any light on Hugh's activities, mindset, or demeanor in the context that I knew him.

This is my cell, use it anytime. Thank you again for your service.

Farah read the message through once, then again. All in all, it wasn't a bad final act.

CHAPTER 98

THE LEADING LADY

On the upper deck, the sky was a sea of stars above Nora and Trent. They lay on the double chaise lounge, their naked bodies covered in a thin sheen of sweat, and she wondered, staring up into the dark clouds, if it was really over.

"You know why he did it." Trent lay beside her, his arm under her head, his eyes closed to the view. "You know what he dealt with. He just didn't want another kid to go through that."

Nora rolled toward him and wrapped her leg around his and burrowed into his chest. "I know." She ran her fingers across the light layer of chest hair and across his abs. "You know I do." Only four people in the world knew how the twins had suffered, and now two of them were dead. Half the cast of *Story Farm*—and the show's dark secret—gone.

It was amazing, with so many people working on the production, that no one had ever found it odd that, for the entire fourth season, Hugh and Trent were never in scenes together. Their mother blamed it on an alternate school schedule, but the core cast knew the real reason. While Hugh was kept in the medical bay in the Iverson mansion, Trent carried the show, playing both roles and switching skillfully between the two characters' personalities and mannerisms. That was when Nora really fell in love with him—when she saw his raw talent, the ability for him to change into the skin of the role he was playing. That, and the care and love he exhibited for his brother.

"I never understood why she only targeted him." He ran his fingers gently through her hair. "It wasn't until I was older that I realized it was because she needed me to be healthy so I could cover for both of us. The healthier I was, the more she could do to him. Plus, he was always her favorite."

"Why didn't you just tell someone?" Nora slid over until she was on top of him and looking down on that famous face. His hair was rough from sex, a shadow of unshaven growth framing those kissably soft lips.

"We did. We told Julie."

"Oh no." Understanding dawned as she realized why their talent manager—the woman who had been a mother to all of them—had been fired unexpectedly, without explanation. "Is that what happened to her?"

"Mom made sure that she was well compensated for her time in exchange for a strict nondisclosure agreement."

"So she sold your safety away for a payoff?" Rage burned deep in Nora's chest. "I can't believe I ever loved her. And I did. I remember wishing that she was my mom. Talk about stupid of me." And she truly *had* loved Julie. When Julie discovered her camping out on set, she started bringing Nora home with her in the evenings. Nora could still picture the woman's big fluffy golden retriever and her plaid couch that she made up into a bed. Sleeping on that couch, Nora had dreamed of Julie inviting her to stay for a summer, maybe a year, maybe even adopting her.

It was unthinkable that that woman, who was supposed to champion the four of them, had found out what Momma Beth was doing to Hugh and taken a payoff to abandon them. When she left, they had gotten that bitch from New York, the one with the pierced eyebrow who hadn't yielded or cared about anything other than production timelines and state requirements.

Trent's hands journeyed up her thighs and gripped her waist, tightening her connection with him. His fingers splayed over her stomach, and she thought of the baby that was growing there. It was, at least in her mind, Trent's. She had always considered it his and—with what she now knew about Hugh—needed it to be that way. A DNA test would never give her a straight answer, but maybe that was for the best. "Stop," she protested as he tilted his hips and pressed himself hard against her sensitive pelvis. She grabbed his hands and pulled them away, then shrieked as he flipped her over and pinned her wrists to the lounge on either side of her head. "We need to talk."

Dropping his head, he kissed her as he lowered his body atop hers, from torso to feet, and she let out a happy sigh.

"You wanted to talk?" he asked gruffly.

Yes, she did. Not about the baby—that could wait. Right now, they had to figure out a game plan and how to implement it. Trent's arrest and Hugh's reveal as a serial killer had deposited a steaming pile of dog shit into their laps, and they needed to engineer how and when to spin it into a chapter in their public love story.

But maybe that could wait. She let out a laugh as his facial scruff tickled her neck. "I love you so much," she said softly and wrapped her arms around his neck.

And she did. She wouldn't have killed Hugh for them if she didn't.

One day, Trent would appreciate it enough for her to tell him the truth. He'd understand the mental release that it gave him—that it gave them both. The future tragedies and agony that it saved them from. There had been no possibility of a successful future for Trent, as things had been. The guilt from Hugh's actions had been an anchor that had kept dragging him into drinking and drugs. Without it, he would succeed.

She knew it, just like she'd known what she had to do when she had passed by the guesthouse and almost walked into that unexpected situation. Hugh hadn't seen her on the porch, and she had cracked the front door, then ducked into the guesthouse and listened. He'd never noticed. He'd been too focused on the woman in front of him, too absorbed in his gloating monologue detailing how and why she had ended up here and what he had done to so many women in her position.

As she had watched, he'd stabbed the woman a third time, then a fourth. The man she loved. The man she lived with, whose ring was on her finger. Stabbing a woman without hesitation, despite the muffled screams, the bulge of her eyes.

His tools had been laid out on the kitchen counter. Knives. A gun. A hammer. Bolt cutters. She had silently eased her way behind him and picked up the gun. A .38 special, a revolver that she'd handled dozens, if not hundreds, of times during filming and weapons training. She walked up beside him and pressed the muzzle to the side of that beautiful head.

It had been hard to pull the trigger. The man had been so damn smart. So savvy. He hadn't had Trent's passion, but he'd had precision and calculation and planning, and she had loved that. She would miss Sunday crossword puzzles on the balcony and strategy sessions and contract negotiations and script analyses.

She'd fired before he had a chance to react, and he'd fallen to his knees, then pitched backward. She had pulled off his glove, put it on her own hand, then turned in a slow circle, looking for somewhere to pull the trigger without the chance of the bullet being found.

She decided on the guest room bed and pulled back the sheets and mattress cover, fired the second bullet into the soft mattress, then reassembled the bed. Returning to the room, she worked the glove back onto his hand and put the gun near it. She turned to face the woman.

She was dead, her eyes wide and still, her face wrenched in pain. Nora looked away quickly, then closed her eyes and ticked through all the possible trip points.

The details, Hugh had always taught her, were what cinched an act. Minor details that sold the big picture.

Like the gunshot residue that would now be on his glove.

The bed that would never be looked at twice by the police.

The Xanax that she would put in Trent's drink when she returned upstairs to him.

The scene that she checked a second and third time, making sure that no evidence went unconsidered.

Nora had spent hours in bed that night, analyzing the options and potential paths of action. She formulated one that would give Trent the life he wanted and keep her fairy-tale love story in place.

It hadn't worked out. Trent hadn't played the game, not to its finale. But that was okay because she could make this new scenario work. She could write a new script. A new love story, one he would star in, the beautiful and heartbroken couple who found solace and comfort in each other when mourning a terrible loss.

It could work. It could play.

She would build the role, and all he would need to do was act the part and smile for the cameras.

SIX MONTHS LATER

The wedding of the century is happening in a few short months, but the groom has done a switcheroo. In a plot twist worthy of any Hollywood blockbuster, Nora Kemp is still wearing her six-carat diamond ring, will still be clad in bridal couture, but will now walk down the aisle to Trent Iverson, her dead fiancé's twin brother—and the future stepfather/uncle of her child.

Social media is divided over their opinions on the subject, with half swooning over the unconventional love story while Hugh loyalists scream their outrage over the supposed betrayal. In Nora's defense, her original relationship did seem to have a few cracks—mainly, the dead bodies stacking up in Hugh's spare time. His serial kills made Trent Iverson (*Story Farm*, *Galaxy's Own*) look stable, despite his history of drug and alcohol abuse.

A. R. Torre

Anticipated by cheerers and jeerers alike, the wedding will be one of the most-watched events of the century and will cement Nora Kemp—soon to be Iverson—on the throne as the reigning queen of Hollywood.

Juliann Frank, *The Hollywood Gossip*

ACKNOWLEDGMENTS

It takes a village to raise a child, and almost as many people to get a book into a reader's hands. This book was nearly a year in the making, and I must first start by thanking Megha Parekh, for never giving up on me, no matter how many crazy plot ideas I send her way for consideration. Additional kudos to my agent, Maura Kye-Casella, who has been by my side for a decade now and never fails to champion me and my stories.

The first draft of this book . . . I laugh when I think back on it, because only my trusty alpha reader Tricia Crouch saw that one. After finishing it, reading it a few times, and giving myself a generous (and completely undeserved) pat on the back, I realized the awful truth—it needed to be trashed. All of it. The entire novel, pitched toward the can.

I reached out to the lovely Megha, who was kind enough to grant me a generous extension (I'm still beaming with gratitude for that!), and I started back at the beginning—with the same story but told in a different way. A much better way. A way that you, dear reader, will never see. One with black market organ sales (yes, really!) and a completely different story line for Miles. You were saved from the fate of that draft by Charlotte Herscher, who is brilliant at locksmithing a plot and steered me to a more satisfying (and believable) plotline, one that came together really nicely in the end.

Additional thanks to Tamara Arellano and her team of wordsmiths, including Kellie and Tara W. I'm so happy that this book has a home with the Thomas & Mercer team and Amazon Publishing, and would like to send verbal cookies and chocolates to the marketing, design, formatting, and executive teams. You are all so talented, kind, and wonderful to work with. Thank you for making every experience a pleasure.

And to the team behind me—thank you to my fabulous husband, who never runs out of patience, support, or Dr Peppers. You and the rest of the family keep me sane and happy and let me keep the drama and the killings in the book. Thank you.

Lastly, the readers. Thank you for picking up this book when there are so many incredible options to choose from. I hope you enjoyed it. It was so much fun to write (and edit and edit again), and even though I spent twice as much time in this world as I did in some of my others, I still wasn't (and am not) quite ready to leave it. Thank you for your support, which allows me to create stories for a living. If you'd like to get updates on what I'm working on next, please visit www.alessandratorre.com/newsletter and sign up for my free email updates.

Until the next novel . . .

Alessandra (A. R.) Torre

ABOUT THE AUTHOR

Photo © 2022 Jane Ashley Converse

A. R. Torre is a pseudonym for *New York Times* bestselling author Alessandra Torre. She has been featured in such publications as *ELLE* and *ELLE UK* and has guest-blogged for *Cosmopolitan* and the *Huffington Post*. In addition, Torre is the creator of Alessandra Torre Ink, a website, community, and online school for aspiring authors. Learn more at www.alessandratorre.com.